ie;

;5713

.com/librar'

RUDDY GORE

Running late to the Hinkler gala performance of Gilbert and Sullivan's *Ruddigore,* Phryne Fisher confronts a gang of thugs and rescues a gorgeous Chinese man, Lin Chung, and his grandmother who mistakes her for a deity. Denying divinity but accepting cognac, she later continues safely to the theatre. But her night is again interrupted by a most bizarre death onstage. What links can Phryne find between the entertaining plot of *Ruddigore,* the city's Chinese community, and the actors at His Majesty's Theatre? Phryne must solve an old murder and find a new murderer, and, of course, banish the theatre's ghost, who seems likely to kill again.

RUDDY GORE

Republika

RUDDY GORE

by

Kerry Greenwood

Magna Large Print Books
Long Preston, North Yorkshire,
BD23 4ND, England.

British Library Cataloguing in Publication Data.

A catalogue record of this book is
available from the British Library

ISBN   978-0-7505-4478-8

First published in Great Britain in 2015 by Constable

Copyright © Kerry Greenwood, 1995, 2004, 2012, 2015

Cover illustration © Beth Norling
Cover design © www.simonlevyassociates.co.uk

The moral right of the author has been asserted

Published in Large Print 2017 by arrangement with
Little, Brown Book Group Limited

Magna Large Print is an imprint of Library Magna Books Ltd.

Printed and bound in Great Britain by
T.J. (International) Ltd., Cornwall, PL28 8RW

Please note that all Chinese names in this book are derived from the sixteenth-century classic *Outlaws of the Marsh*. The 1928 cast of *Ruddigore* did not include any murderers. No identification with any persons alive or dead is intended or should be inferred.

To my sister Janet Greenwood,
for her courage and her delightful spirit.

With thanks to Jean Greenwood of the tireless feet, Foong Ling Kong, Jenny Pausacker, Richard Revill, David Greagg, Themmy Gardner (ol' pal, ol' buddy), Laurie (cariad) Horner, Matthew Gordon-Clark, Tim Daly, Dr Andrea Walker, Brian Di Caffa, Sarah Jane Reeh, Stuart Reeh, Arnold Pears, the memory of my great-uncle Gwilym Davies, the Chinese Museum, the Performing Arts Museum, the management of Her Majesty's Theatre and the archives of the Victoria Police.

'They do it with mirrors, my boy.'

Arthur Horner, *Colonel Pewter in Ironicus*

CHAPTER ONE

'How's Bloodygore?'
'It's Ruddigore.'
'Same thing, isn't it?'
'Does that mean when I say I admire your ruddy
countenance, it means I like your bloody cheek?'

Conversation with
W. S. Gilbert (attrib.)

The hatchet flicked past, end over end, and
struck a wooden shutter with a hollow thud.
Light gleamed along the polished blade.

Phryne Fisher closed a leather-gloved hand on
the handle and extracted it with one strong pull.
She hefted it. An admirable weapon, well-
balanced, not too heavy, wickedly sharp.

'Were you trying to attract my attention?' she
asked politely.

An Asian face turned to her out of the mass of
struggling bodies. He saw the black hair and pale
face, the body shining silver like a Taoist goddess,
and screamed at her, *'Jau!'*

This meant nothing to Phryne, who had seen
an old woman go down without a cry under three
attackers clad in dark blue. Little Bourke Street
was chill, empty and dark. Sodium glare from the
widely spaced street lights turned every puddle
on the slick cobbles into a mirror and left black

15

velvet pools of night in between.

In one of these some sort of street fight was occurring. Phryne was on her way to a gala performance of *Ruddigore* at His Majesty's in celebration of Bert Hinkler's triumphant flight. She was beginning to wonder whether taking a short cut had been such a good idea as it had seemed ten minutes before.

Bunji Ross gasped, 'There's an old lady in that crowd of Chink blighters!' She ran towards the fight and vanished into it like a fly in a frog's mouth. Something would have to be done.

Phryne stepped lightly to a corner, yelled, 'The cops!' and watched as two blue-clad toughs scrambled up and ran away. The other one stopped to kick the recumbent old woman again, and Phryne could not allow that. He had had his chance. She walked quickly up behind him, waited until his head was in the right position, and clipped him neatly with the hatchet, considerately using the back. She was clad in an outrageously expensive dress and did not want to get blood on it.

He collapsed with a satisfactory moan. A returning blue-clad person grabbed him and dragged him off. The soft scrabbling footsteps died away and Phryne hauled Bunji up by the arm. She was much disarrayed but seemed uninjured.

Phryne brushed Bunji down, found her hat, and said, 'I wish you weren't so hasty, Bunji dear. This looks like a private fight, you know. And that is – it was – a rather nice new dress.'

'Yes, yes, and I'm sorry about the dress old thing, but we can't allow old ladies to be

16

attacked. It might start a fashion,' panted Bunji, rubbing her midsection. 'Ooh, drat, that hurts! One of those thugs punched me in the stomach. Don't they know you aren't supposed to hit a woman? I got him a good one, though. He'll know how I feel about this sort of thing.'

'Unchivalrous in the extreme,' agreed Phryne, sighing. Bunji Ross, who was good friend and a brave and determined flyer, was very hard on clothes. Since everything that Phryne had ever lent her had come back ruined, Phryne had paid for a new dress for her short plump companion. It had been a flowing but restrained dark plum velvet sacque with matching hat and shoes, but a roll in the gutters of Little Bourke Street had not improved it. Bunji was wet and muddy and had holed both her stockings.

The young man got to his feet, supporting the old woman. She straightened slowly, wiping a shaking hand over her bruised face, then fastened her eyes on Phryne.

She saw a small woman dressed in silver; a brocade dress which fitted close to her slim body, a cap of the same material with wings at each side, and on her small feet silver kid boots with wings at the ankle. Over the dress, she was draped in a flowing velvet coat with a yoke of brocade. She had a pale face and startling green eyes, and black hair barely longer than the cap. The hatchet swung loosely in her gloved hand. The old woman, creaking in all her joints, bowed. It was possible, she considered, that she had been rescued by a spirit, doubtless sent by the ancestors.

The young man, who knew that there were no

spirits, saw through his one functioning eye a woman of surpassing otherness, immensely attractive, supremely alive and shining from head to heel.

Phryne abandoned the attempt to make Bunji elegant and decided that she would be acceptable if most of the mud was removed. Someone spoke to her and she turned.

'Ngo zhang lei koh yan cheng,' said the old woman, speaking to Phryne's knees in a soft, cultured voice.

'My grandmother thanks you,' said the young man. 'She says that we are deeply in your debt, Madame.'

'Not at all,' said Phryne. 'Is your grandmother hurt?'

'She says it is nothing to signify,' the young man bowed in turn. 'I am Lin Chung; it is the Lin family you have rescued in so timely a fashion.'

His accent, to her astonishment, was pure Eton and Oxford. Phryne took the offered hand and looked appreciatively at him. She could not tell if he was handsome, as the recent altercation had split his lip and blackened his eye. However, he was not much taller than herself, beautifully compact and sleek, the hand in her own strong but gentle. She was intrigued.

'Mr Lin, I have an engagement at the theatre. I really must restore my friend to respectability — can you provide us with a wash and brush up?' He nodded and walked to a nearby door. It opened to his tap and the old woman hobbled inside.

'I say, Phryne, is this safe?' whispered Bunji. 'They aren't white slavers or something, are they?'

18

It was too dark for Phryne's withering glare to have any effect, so she settled for saying, 'Don't be so silly, Bunji. Besides, I've still got this hatchet.'

They were in an anteroom to a warehouse, piled with bundles which oozed such pungent and alien scents that Phryne sniffed with delight. Saffron, she was sure; but what was that strange antiseptic reek, and what on earth could anyone use those evil-looking dried eels for?

'In here, if you please, Madame,' said Lin Chung. 'I will send someone to attend you.'

He conducted Phryne and Bunji into a small room of such elegance that Bunji exclaimed, 'By Jove!' and Phryne gasped.

The walls were hung with red silk – bolts of it must have gone into the decoration. It was figured with small medallions of thread which, from the soft gleam, Phryne decided must be pure gold. Bunji stood on a priceless silk carpet carved with phoenixes and did not dare to move.

'I say,' she whispered, 'what have we got ourselves into?'

'I don't know, but it's very pretty.'

A door opened in the silk-clad wall and a young woman as distant and aloof as a porcelain doll entered. With her came a stout elderly woman in a print dress and apron.

Unspeaking, the woman and the girl laid a sheet on the floor, poured hot water into a huge T'ang bowl decorated with horses, and produced fluffy towels and soap. They divested Bunji of her dress, which was taken by an unseen person outside the door, and then dabbed gently at the mud stains and a small graze on Bunji's knuckles.

19

Bunji stood in exquisite embarrassment, not wishing to interrupt what appeared to be a ritual, as she was cleansed, dried, and provided with new stockings and wrapped in a padded silk gown. While the old woman took the washing things away, the girl produced a decanter and poured a stiff brandy for each woman, still mute. She looked about sixteen and had evidently been in bed, for her waist length hair was still in its night-time plait. Phryne accepted the glass and said, 'Hello.'

The girl looked at her for the first time.

'Hello,' she replied sulkily. 'Is this the sort of thing you drink? Only Grandmother said to look after you because you rescued her and I'll get into trouble if it isn't right.'

'It's just what we wanted. Thank you. What's your name?'

'Here they call me Annie. I'll go and get the dress. Po Po's maid is cleaning it.'

'Annie, what did we interfere in?'

'I can't tell you.' The composure broke and Annie's black eyes flashed. 'I'm not going to tell you. Why did you have to come along just then?'

'Fate,' said Phryne, nettled. 'Can you find a safe place for this?' She handed over the hatchet. Annie took it.

'Grandmother wants her address,' she pointed to Bunji.

'Oh, why?' Bunji's thoughts had clearly turned to white slaving again.

'So that she can send you a present. To thank you for rescuing her.'

'Very well,' said Bunji, writing down her name

and address in a silk-covered notebook which the girl held out. 'But it was my pleasure, really,' she said doubtfully. Closing the book, Annie reverted to her doll-like stillness, bowed to an exact degree and left.

Phryne looked at Bunji, who shrugged.

'They're Chinks, they're aliens, what did you expect?'

'Bunji, do stop calling them Chinks, it's not polite.'

'What else can I call them?' asked Bunji reasonably. 'That's what they are. This is a nice robe, though.' She smoothed the decorated material with a hard hand.

The elderly woman returned with the dress, invisibly mended and cleaned of stains, and Bunji pulled it on and shoved her hat back onto her head, hiding her short hair.

'Well, let's go, it has been an exciting evening but I don't want to miss seeing Bert again, though I don't know about this opera, Phryne, I've never been a culture shark like you. Is it all fat ladies bellowing at each other?'

'No, it's very funny and you'll like it,' said Phryne firmly. She finished the cognac and put down the glass, wondering if they should just walk out. Bunji settled this by striding through the ante-chamber and into Little Bourke Street and Phryne followed. She had reached the door when the young man appeared, touched her arm and said, 'Madame, we are in your debt. Can we know who you are?'

'Why do you want to know?' asked Phryne, pausing at the door. 'It was all my friend's idea, I just cleaned up after her. She's the valiant one.' He smiled at her, an action which must have hurt.

'I wish to come and express our family's gratitude in some tangible form.' The sensual suggestion was strong and Phryne was attracted. She found her card and held it up.

'What will you give me, then, Mr Lin, to express your gratitude?'

'I will sit at your feet and sing your praise all night, Silver Lady.' The voice was soft and Phryne felt an answering smile curving the corners of her mouth. 'Most beautiful lady,' said Lin Chung, 'I will do whatever would most please you.'

Phryne felt that this offer was agreeably unconditional. She allowed him to take the card, swept her velvet coat around her, and said, 'Come on Thursday night, Mr Lin. To dinner at eight o'clock. I will think of something that you can do for me by then.'

By then, she reflected as she walked quickly away behind Bunji, his face will have healed. And she calculated that she would at least get a length of that absolutely exquisite silk for the trouble of hitting an assailant over the head with a hatchet.

Lin Chung gazed after the twinkle of her winged heels as the Honourable Phryne Fisher receded into the night.

His Majesty's Theatre was ablaze with light as they walked up to the corner and turned into the main street. Expensive cars were stopping to allow expensive by-invitation-only patrons to alight. There was a scent of French perfume so strong as to be almost a stench, and a flurry of coats and cloaks and glossy top hats.

'There–' Bunji dragged Phryne through the ranks. 'There's Bill, and Captain Larkin – come on, Phryne.'

It was easy to find the flyers. They were gathered into a tight little group in one corner of the foyer, looking uncomfortable among the most shrill and glamorous of Melbourne Society.

'What ho, Cap'n,' Bunji hailed. 'Is Bert here yet?'

'No, he's being smuggled in through the back. I say, Miss Fisher, you look spiffing! Mercury, ain't you, like the Greek god? Remarkable, even down to the winged shoes.' Phryne, who had been keeping her ensemble for just such an occasion, smiled warmly at the captain. Bunji nudged him.

'Well, how's poor Bert bearing up? He must be a nervous wreck by now.'

'Oh, yes, the hero of the hour, poor chap,' observed Captain Larkin, smoothing his moustache complacently. 'Can't bear publicity. I bet he's wishing he was back up in the sky.'

'Oh, why?' asked Phryne, who had preserved her cloak uncrushed in her passage through the multitude by following exactly in the stouter Bunji's wake.

'Simple, it's all predictable up in the air.'

'Predictable?' Phryne could not think of a less predictable pastime than flying.

'Yes, only a certain number of things can go wrong, and only a few of those will kill you. Pity about Chubbie Miller and old Bill Lancaster breaking a wing, though. Otherwise they might have made it in before Hustlin' Hinkler.'

'Why is he called hustling?' Phryne was shoved against Captain Larkin, who smelt delightfully of Floris's stephanotis.

'He leaves on time – every time. He arrives on time though Hell should bar the way. Most amazin' chap. And he made the flight from Croydon to Darwin across all those islands and countries in fifteen and a half days. Remarkable man. But he'll be deeply embarrassed by all this adulation. Not one for the populace, Hinkler.'

'No? Dislikes his fellow man?'

'Hates crowds and doesn't trust enthusiasm any more than a Presbyterian,' rejoined Bunji. 'Unsentimental, perhaps that's it. He really only likes a few people, his co-pilot and some flyers and his Mum. He hasn't even given his plane a name.'

'Now that is interesting,' Phryne said, 'I thought all planes had names.'

Bunji agreed. 'Yes, well, there's *Red Rose,* that's the Miller/Lancaster Avro, and your *Rigel* and my *Tiger Cat* and Bill's *Moonraker* and Lindbergh's *Spirit of St Louis* and Kingsford Smith's *Southern Cross.* Yes. We all give the planes names – but he just calls his GE BOY, the call sign. Either he doesn't want it to develop a personality, or...'

'He just doesn't think like that,' concluded Captain Larkin. 'By the way, Bunji old girl – someone took up a Tiger Moth and did some very pretty stuntin' to welcome Hinkler. You wouldn't happen to know who it was, would you?'

'No,' said Bunji, blushing the colour of her dress. 'No, really? I can't imagine how I missed it.'

'I can't imagine either,' said Captain Larkin drily.

Bunji, desperate for a distraction, asked, 'Phryne, who is that woman in the red dress? She's been staring at us.'

'Oh, that's Diana Ffoulkes,' said Phryne, returning the gaze of bright blue eyes with interest. 'Terribly rich, terribly bored, with a penchant for celebrities. Her last affair was with a flyer, I believe; her lovers never last. I wonder if she's prospecting for a new one?' She caught a glimpse of spun-silk hair and cupid's bow mouth as Miss Ffoulkes bent her regard elsewhere. Phryne caught Captain Larkin smoothing his moustache complacently, a movement just short of preening, and grinned at him. He coughed and said quickly, 'Come along, ladies, let's go inside. There's a surprise in the theatre.'

Phryne, who considered that she had had enough surprises for one night, took his arm and followed him up the steps into the dress circle.

Red plush was the dominant motif in His Majesty's Theatre. That and gilt equal to the output of the Ballarat goldfields for at least three months. Everything glittered and shone which wasn't draped and soft. Phryne sat down and looked at the stage.

Over the proscenium was a large map of Hinkler's epic journey, with the fuel stops picked out in red lamps. There were a lot of them, dotted across Europe and Asia.

'Look up,' invited Captain Larkin.

Phryne leaned back and stared up into the blue dome with gold stars which dominated the

25

theatre and gasped.

There, circling on a hidden line, was a scale model of Hinkler's Avro Avian, its propeller revolving slowly in the hot air.

'I say!' said Phryne. 'That *is* impressive.'

'It's mine,' said the captain modestly, 'made it this winter. Luckily both the contending flyers were in Avros. Brought it into the theatre this morning and spent most of the day riggin' it up, to the groans of the stage hand chappies, by the way. Said it couldn't be done without ruining the sightlines, whatever they are. Said it would cast shadows on the stage – apparently there are banks of lights on the dress circle, can't say I've ever noticed 'em. They insisted on hauling it up that high, don't know why. But it looks good, don't it?'

'It does indeed.' Phryne was impressed. 'Very nice work, Captain. And the map over the stage, that's Hinkler's journey?'

'Yes. Started at Croydon, see, then stopped for fuel all the way across. Through Lyons and Dijon to Rome and Naples, then Catania, Tripoli, Benghazi, Sollum, Cairo, then Baghdad, Ur, Bushire, Bandar Abbas, Char, Karachi, Jodhpur, across India to Kuala Lumpur, Singapore, Muntok – that's where Miller and Lancaster came to grief – then Surabaja, Bima, Atambua and Darwin. Amazin' journey. All on his own. Have to admire him.'

'Yes, I do,' said Phryne. The model plane circled endlessly against the gold stars of the ceiling, and Phryne wondered what it would be like to set out on a cold night with real stars burning like lamps in the sky, nothing at all to mark your passing but

26

the icy slipstream screaming past, and no one at all to notice if you fell out of the sky but a few startled fish as the pitiful wreckage of balsa wood and canvas floated on the uncaring waves...

She shook her head. Night, cold and solitude were too threatening in a plane.

People were leaping to their feet as a diffident figure was shoved to the front of a box.

'There he is,' observed Bunji. 'Poor old Bert.'

He was dark, small, and dreadfully embarrassed, as the captain had predicted. He waved valiantly to the assembled multitude and sat down hurriedly out of sight.

The orchestra came on and the crowd applauded the conductor, as their hero Hinkler was no longer in evidence. The sounds of the pianist's 'A' being repeated on a variety of instruments sent the usual frisson of excitement down Phryne's spine.

'You're sure that this isn't going to be in German,' said Bunji uneasily. 'You promised, Phryne!'

'No, I tell you, it's in English and it's funny. Why do you think it's going to be German? What have you got against Germans? The War's over, you know.'

'I went to a theatre in London when I was there with the Flying Circus,' said Bunji, wounded, 'and there was the most God-awful row going on, all these women in armour shrieking at each other and a bloke who I wouldn't have cared to meet down an alley trying to hack an anvil in half. They wouldn't let me out until interval and it went on for four hours. Four hours!'

'Well, next time you see the word "Wagner" on

a poster, don't go in,' said Phryne unsympathetically. 'Now, hush, Bunji, there's a dear.'

'Tell me what's going to happen,' said Bunji.

Since her companion was showing signs of being
ready to bolt at the flourish of a Valkyrie's spear,
Phryne drew a deep breath, consulted her programme, and said quickly, 'It's a parody of a
bloodtub melodrama plot. Rose Maybud has to
choose between a poor farmer called Robin Oakapple, a dashing Jack Tar called Dick Dauntless
and the local wicked Squire, Sir Despard Murgatroyd. He belongs to a family that has a curse,
they have to commit one bad deed a day or die
horribly. She eventually decides to marry Robin.
Then Dick and the Squire get together and reveal
that Robin is actually Ruthven, Despard's elder
brother and therefore he gets the Lordship and the
curse and Dick gets the girl.'

'Phryne, that's the silliest plot I ever heard.'

Giving silent thanks that she was not attempting
to explain something truly silly, like *Il Trovatore*,
Phryne went doggedly on. 'But Rose still can't
make up her mind. So there is poor Sir Ruthven
Murgatroyd who used to be Robin Oakapple making up his mind to do one bad deed every day. And
Mad Margaret who was spurned by Sir Despard is
back with him and sane once he is relieved of his
curse. Then ... that'll do for the moment. The curtain's going up.'

The huge red curtain rose slowly on a scene of
village life. Various maidens in bodices and print
smocks were watching the entrance of a row of
bridesmaids, who were lamenting their under-

employment. An older woman in widow's garments entered and began to sing of the Ruddigore curse.

'That's Agnes Gault playing Dame Hannah,' observed Phryne, noticing that Bunji was getting interested in the play.

Each Lord of Ruddigore
Despite his best endeavour,
Shall do one crime or more
Once, every day, for ever!
This doom he can't defy,
However he may try,
For should he stay
His hand, that day
In torture he shall die!

sang the respectable Dame Hannah, outlining the dreadful fate of the Ruddigores. The audience were settling down to enjoy the unfolding of the ridiculous plot. Phryne looked across to Hinkler's box but could not see the daring flyer. She hoped that he liked music, or that he could sleep through it.

A slender young woman in a pale green smock and a froth of petticoats, clutching an etiquette book, denied all intention of marrying.

'That's Rose Maybud,' whispered Phryne to Bunji, 'played by Leila Esperance.'

'Nice voice,' commented Bunji. 'Pity about the clothes.'

It was true. Leila's dark slender charm was entirely muffled in the wodge of drapes and gathers, and her celebrated profile was extinguished by the frilled linen sunbonnet. Phryne reflected that Miss Esperance was credited with a truly volcanic temper and felt a pang of pity for the wardrobe mistress who had been required to insert the star into this regrettable costume.

Robin Oakapple sidled onto the stage, a shy young man in farmer's clothes. He and Rose conducted a conversation remarkable for what it did not say. Robin was tall, blond, and moved with a grace that spoke of ballet training. Phryne consulted the programme.

'Walter Copland,' she said. 'You remember him in *Hamlet*.'

'He was the gabby old man who got himself spiked through the tapestry,' agreed Bunji. 'Washes up well, doesn't he?'

'Poor little man!' sang Rose, and, 'Poor little maid!' sang Robin, both managing to avoid mentioning that they were in love with each other.

An old man entered, so convincing an old man that Phryne could practically hear his joints creaking. He revealed that Robin was actually Sir Ruthven Murgatroyd and announced that his foster brother Richard Dauntless was even now approaching.

'The old man's Leslie Franklin – and here comes Dick Dauntless, played by Gwilym Evans – well, well.'

The sailor, escorted by a chorus of adoring bridesmaids, entered stage left and the play was transformed.

Gwilym Evans was not tall, but stocky and strong. He swaggered rakishly across the front, the ribbon on his Jack Tar's hat fluttering behind him.

His every movement was vigorous, robust and sure; and Phryne could just catch the wicked grin which he awarded Robin. He was so attractive that he almost stopped the show, yet he was not conventionally beautiful. He had immense gamecock assurance.

'Well, well,' murmured Phryne, but Bunji, though not immune to his charm, was frowning.

'Looks like a bounder to me,' she commented.

'Absolutely, my dear Bunji, but a very attractive bounder. Bounders usually are; that's why they are successful,' said Phryne as the sailor came down to address the bridesmaids on the subject of maritime glory.

'I shipped, d'ye see, in a revenue sloop,' he began, in a voice full, rich and strong, with precise diction which made every scandalous anti-French word audible.

'He won't do no good for his brother,' observed Bunji, quite caught up in the plot. 'It's not safe to ask him to make love to the girl instead of Robin!'

So it proved. When Dick Dauntless caught sight of Rose Maybud, he fell in love – the audience saw him do it. He stepped back half a pace and stared at the girl, his burning eyes absorbing her every detail, from her beribboned shoes to her lace cap, at such ambient temperature that Phryne half expected her to burst into flame.

Pleading Robin's case was wiped from Dick's mind like chalk off a slate, and Rose Maybud's objections vanished likewise. Robin re-entered and managed to change her mind again – until she left the stage with Robin. Dick Dauntless stood alone. He took off his hat, his whole body expressing desperate hurt; although all he did was to look inside the hat, turn, and walk away, one hand to his face as though he was weeping.

Mad Margaret leapt on stage, alternately screeching and whispering, clad mostly in weeds, her hair tangled around her. 'Violet Wiltshire,' said Phryne. 'An imitation Ophelia.'

'Not a good imitation,' said Bunji. 'Far too sensible.'

'He gave me an Italian glance,' mourned Mad Margaret, 'Thus,' and she bent on Rose a perfect imitation of Dick Dauntless's gaze. The burlesque was instantly recognised and got a laugh. 'And made me his,' continued Mad Margaret, suddenly convincing, and Phryne remembered that Gwilym Evans was followed by scandal wherever he went. She would have hazarded good money on the object of Gwilym's latest *affaire de coeur*.

No crime—
'Tis only
That I'm
Love-lonely
That's all!

sang Mad Margaret, and Phryne detected what critics called 'truth' in her voice.

A group of bucks and blades entered and began to impress the village maidens. Phryne reflected that this was probably roistering – she had always wondered what that meant.

They were followed by a saturnine person. 'Sir Despard Murgatroyd,' murmured Phryne, 'Selwyn Alexander – the patter singer.'

He was the perfect melodrama villain. Moustaches, black hat, dark makeup, a glitter of eyes under the brim and a most professional sneer. He looked personable and a little dangerous as he explained that he was balancing his bad deeds with good ones. Richard Dauntless the sailor, approaching, made an interesting contrast. Beside the sailor's vigour Sir Despard appeared a weary rake; his lustre was dimmed. Dick Dauntless's plan was adopted and the wedding gavotte came to an abrupt end.

'I am that bad baronet,' Robin confessed, and Richard removed Rose Maybud's hand from his. She turned away from the new baronet and smiled on the sailor, and even Bunji was impressed by the intensity of her regard.

'I say,' she whispered, 'there's something between those two.'

Phryne nodded and opened the box of Hillier's chocolates. Bunji prodded them, looking for soft centres.

The bridesmaids went into their chorus as Sir Despard – now reformed – claimed Mad Margaret – now sane – and everyone was dancing and singing except poor Robin Oakapple, now Sir Ruthven Murgatroyd, who put both hands to his head, reeled, staggered, and fell senseless to the stage.

'That was a very convincing fall,' said Bunji, rejecting a truffle and finding a mandarin cream.

'Very convincing,' said Phryne, staring at the fallen actor. Was it her imagination, or was he actually convulsing? The soggy thump with which he had hit the boards had been heard even over the concluding choruses. The bridesmaids danced forward and hid him from the audience in a froth of frilly white skirts.

The curtain came down, the house lights came up, and there was the rustle of patrons finding bags and shifting in their seats.

'Well, Bunji, how do you like it?'

'It's jolly good,' said Bunji, finding a strawberry cream. 'Jolly funny, too. I didn't know that opera was allowed to be funny.'

'It wasn't, until Gilbert got hold of it.'

'But that girl, Phryne, that Rose Maybud – what a silly girl! So far she's changed her mind three times.'

'Yes, I don't think that Gilbert really admired sweet English maidenhood all that much. All of his delicate little maidens are as tough as nails and as fickle as weathercocks – though I admit that Rose Maybud is an extreme example of the species.'

'And that sailor – he's a dashing fellow,' commented Bunji. 'I wonder what he's really like?' Phryne captured the last coconut cream, her favourite, a split second ahead of Bunji's probing forefinger.

'Actors aren't half as interesting as you'd think – they either expend all their emotions on the stage and are as cold as frogs off it or they have egos the size of a small planet and no topic of conversation that doesn't begin with "When I played…" Tedious, really. Though the manager, Bernard Tarrant, used to be an actor, and he's an old sweetie-pie so it doesn't always follow.'

'Tarrant? The brother of Charles?'

'Yes, do you know him?'

'He flies with Bill. Reasonable pilot.' This was high praise for Bunji. Phryne was about to agree to Captain Larkin's suggestion of slipping out for a quiet tot when someone came stumbling over outraged patrons' feet and tugging at her sleeve.

'Miss Fisher, please, Miss Fisher, can you come with me?' begged a white-faced young man in full evening dress. 'Sir Bernard wants to see you. There's been an accident.'

CHAPTER TWO

ADAM: *Richard Dauntless and Pretty Rose Maybud are here to ask your consent to their marriage. Poison their beer.*

Gilbert and Sullivan
Ruddigore

Phryne gave Bunji the chocolates and said, 'Back in a tick, old thing.' She followed the young man down the stairs and round several corners into a dark corridor. It smelt of dust and old oilcloth and paint was peeling off the walls.

Phryne was conducted into an office which contained, reading from right to left, a hysterical older lady, a young woman in evening dress supplying same with smelling salts and handkerchiefs, and Sir Bernard Tarrant and his trademark cigar.

It was rather crowded.

35

'Phryne my dear, sorry to drag you out of the house, but something's happened.'

'Sir Ruthven?'

'Yes. Dammit, that was the best fall he has ever taken – as soon as I saw him fold in that perfect boneless manner, right on cue, I knew something was wrong.'

'Well, what is wrong?'

'He's been poisoned,' said Bernard reluctantly. 'At least, either that or he gave himself a big dose of something.'

'Does that seem likely?'

'Er...' Bernard looked at the women, 'probably not.'

'No!' wailed the old woman, raising a countenance purple with tears. 'Not my Walter! Walter would never leave me! He'd never do such a thing!'

Bernard Tarrant was an old friend of Phryne's. He was tall, stout and always immaculate, from his smooth white hair to the bright red rose in the buttonhole to the toes of his polished patent-leather shoes. Now Bernard, who had always been larger than life, looked smaller than life and Phryne realised that the situation was serious.

'Look, why don't we all sit down. You can dispense some of the good whisky and tell me all about it.'

'So you'll help me,' said Bernard eagerly.

'Don't know. It depends on what you want me to do. If it is to perform in your chorus the answer is "no". I've done enough performing lately. Come now, Bernard dear, this is not like you. You're the manager.'

'Yes, so I am.' Bernard stood up to his full height, smoothed his blameless waistcoat front, and found the decanter. 'It's been an unlucky run,' he commented. 'Mrs Copland, have a glass of this, it will make you feel better. Oh, I'm sorry, I haven't introduced you – Miss Elizabeth Copland, Walter's sister, and his mother Mrs James Copland. This is the Honourable Phryne Fisher, an old friend of mine and a most enterprising young woman. I'm hoping that she might be able to help me.'

'I've heard of you,' said Elizabeth. 'You investigate things.'

'Yes. How is your brother?'

'The doctor's with him now. He says...' She choked, took a sip of neat spirit and choked again, 'He doesn't know what it was, but he thinks...' She began to cry.

Phryne left the two women to comfort one another and said crisply, 'Bernard, you will now tell me what is going on.'

Bernard glanced admiringly at the silver figure perched on his scarred desk. On another woman that outfit would have looked overdone – but on the admirable Miss Fisher it was stunning, a touch outré, and altogether picturesque. So assured. So soignée.

And, he observed, beginning to look so impatient. He pulled himself together.

'He collapsed on stage. Luckily I fished a G and S-loving doctor out of the audience. Copland must have taken something – the doctor thinks he might ... er...' At this both ladies wailed.

'Come for a walk, Phryne dear,' said Bernard,

looking harried. Phryne tucked one hand under his elbow and he led her out into the passage and said rapidly, 'I need your help. This is only the latest thing that has gone awry. Let me take you to supper, Phryne darling, and I'll tell you all about it.'

'If there has been an attempted murder, Bernard, you have to call the police.'

'But, Phryne, the scandal.'

'You really must,' she insisted, and Bernard realised that he really had.

'Oh, very well,' he said pettishly, 'but the scandal will be immense. You see, it's not just poor Walter. There's been a lot of ... well, I'll tell you about it later. Robert Craven can go on as Sir Ruthven, he's a good lad enough, but not up to Walter's skill. Nothing like as good an actor, and G and S requires good acting. I ... yes?'

A panting boy slid to a halt before the manager.

'Mr Craven's asking if he should go on.'

'Tell him yes and to break a leg. See if they can get the costume off...' He noticed Phryne's raised eyebrow. 'Well, no, I suppose not, there's a change anyway for the second act, go and ask Mrs Pomeroy if she can cobble up a baronet's garb, and get a move on, Herbert.'

The functionary ran away along the peeling corridor. Phryne released Sir Bernard's arm. He smelt agreeably of port and cigars and expensive pomade.

'I'm going back to my seat,' she said. 'I'll come to your office after the show. But I still think you should call it off and send for the cops. They won't like it if you just clear the stage and try not to think about a murder, Bernard.'

Bernard drew himself up to his full six foot height and snorted theatrically, regaining his old performer's assurance as he spoke, his voice gaining bass notes and increasing in volume until it rang like a trumpet. He brandished his cigar like a crusader's banner.

'Miss Fisher, you know the old saying,' he said pompously. 'I'm not going to interrupt the Hinkler gala, the high point of the theatrical calendar – I got the hero of the hour over some mighty stiff bidding from the Prinny, you know – just because someone has tried to kill my Sir Ruthven. Consider our glorious history and the traditions of the Craft. We went on with *The Mikado* in New Zealand when there was an earthquake. We carried on with *Hamlet* through the Zeppelin raids in London and when the stage hands went on strike we did not miss one performance of *Pirates* even though we had to work the lights ourselves and Mollie Webb burned her hands on a follow spot. We soldiered on with *The Merry Widow* after old Charles had a heart attack in the wings and when that soprano whatever-her-name-was set her hair on fire by standing too near a candle. The show must go on!' he declaimed.

Phryne kissed him resignedly and threaded the labyrinth back to her seat, contemplating actors, and deciding that the stage really was another world.

The Hero of the Hour was dragged onto the stage at the end of interval to the cheers of the populace. He smiled weakly.

'Poor Bert,' commented Bunji, discarding the

empty chocolate box and applauding with enough vigour to split her gloves. 'This'll take more courage than low flying in fog through them Malay mountains. I hope they aren't going to force the modest old blighter to talk.'

'They certainly are going to demand a speech. Hard cheese if you don't like being a hero. His mother looks pleased, though,' returned Phryne. The small bundle that was Bert Hinkler's mother was radiating pride and delight.

'Who wouldn't, with a son like that?' observed Captain Larkin. 'Yes, he's going to talk. Silence for the hero.'

'This has been a wonderful reception,' said Bert Hinkler with a fair show of firmness, 'and it's nice to be here. And the performance has been really wonderful and I wouldn't think of interrupting it any further,' he added, and almost bolted off stage and out of the public eye. And off-stage he firmly remained, despite three cheers of such deafening force that plaster flaked off the ceiling and snowed down on the audience.

'That's Bert,' sighed Bunji. 'It's no use expecting him to be a lion. He's good at flying, not talking.'

The ladies sat down again and the curtain opened on a gloomy hall, lined with portraits.

Robert Craven entered, as Sir Ruthven, and managed the patter song with Old Adam competently. He had little presence, but the part carried him. The audience did not appear to have noticed the substitution.

Enter Dick Dauntless and his Rose, singing gaily that she was a neat little, sweet little craft. Sir Ruthven's attempts to abduct Rose were foiled by the production of a Union Jack, a piece of burlesque which Dick played with complete, self-absorbed seriousness which was irresistibly comic. Phryne laughed aloud, and Dick Dauntless heard her; there was a heightened alertness in his manner, though he did not deviate from his part by one iota.

Releasing Rose to go off with the sailor, Sir Ruthven confronted his ancestors.

The lights dimmed. 'Painted emblems of a race all accurst in days of yore' stepped down from their frames and railed at him. 'Alas, poor ghost!' said the kneeling descendant, reminding Phryne of Prince Hamlet – could Gilbert have really been burlesqueing *Hamlet?* Well, why not? It was only a play. She chuckled when she considered what a particularly pompous Shakespearan actor of her acquaintance would think of her calling *Hamlet* 'only a play'.

Meanwhile the ghosts had sung a fast, whirling song stating that being a ghost was not all that bad. Robert Craven as Sir Ruthven was managing the dialogue with the ghost of his father fairly well until Sir Roderick said, 'Very well – let the agonies commence.'

The ghosts circled him as he fell and writhed on the floor, but they did not speak. The spectres danced more quickly, and someone bent to whisper to the recumbent actor. Finally he gasped out his line.

'Stop it, will you? I want to speak.'

Sir Roderick dragged him to his feet, holding him strongly around the body, and omitted a whole chunk of the play by signalling the chorus

41

into 'He Yields!'

'Something's wrong,' said Phryne, as the ghosts completed their dance and retreated to their frames. Sir Roderick handed his son over to Old Adam, who announced unilaterally that he was going to kidnap a lady and escorted his master off stage.

Despard and Margaret came in, dressed in sober black, announcing that they were now very respectable, and danced a blameless dance. Margaret requested her new husband to use the word 'Basingstoke' to restore her to sanity and they launched into the patter song with a shaky Sir Ruthven.

Phryne noticed that either one or the other of the black-clad pair kept a hand under his elbow. Something was wrong with this Sir Ruthven Murgatroyd as well.

Did someone dislike *Ruddigore* so much that they had poisoned both Sir Ruthvens?

It seemed unlikely.

Meanwhile, on the stage, Adam brought in Dame Hannah, fighting tooth and nail. Being dragged across difficult country had not improved her temper, and she attacked Sir Ruthven, who was rescued by his father.

It then transpired that Sir Roderick ought not to have been dead – as refusing to commit a dreadful deed exposed the Murgatroyds to death, that was effectively suicide and suicide was certainly a dreadful deed, therefore Sir Roderick ought not to have been dead, and suddenly wasn't. He sang a touching duet with Dame Hannah.

Phryne was staring at Sir Ruthven. In his

embrace with the utterly faithless Rose, he was leaning on her heavily, but she was bearing him up and still contriving to speak.

'When I was a simple farmer, I believe you loved me?'

'Madly, passionately,' answered Rose, staggering under his weight.

'But when I became a bad baronet, you very properly loved Richard instead?'

'Passionately, madly!' replied that blameless flower of British womanhood.

'But if I should turn out not to be a bad baronet after all, how should you love me then?'

'Madly, passionately!'

'As before?'

'Why of course!'

'Darling!' groaned Sir Ruthven, gathered his courage, and sang his finale. Rose, keeping a firm grip on him, answered. The jilted Richard stated that he would take the chief bridesmaid, destined for a life of 'bread and cheese and kisses'. His wicked charm carried over the footlights effortlessly; Phryne smiled, and Bunji blushed.

'He's a rotter,' she muttered. 'But a dashed attractive rotter.'

'Happy the lily when kissed by the bee,' sang the chorus, and the red and gold curtain came down.

Subsequent and repeated curtain calls revealed no sight of either Sir Ruthven Murgatroyd.

'You busy tonight, Miss Fisher? We've got a bit of a "do" on at my place for poor old Bert, he'll need a few restorers after facing this lot,' invited Captain Larkin. 'Bunji's coming.'

'No thanks, Captain, really, have to sup with an

old friend,' said Phryne, suppressing a private predilection for airmen – in any case both her powder and her shot would have been wasted on Hinkler, it was well known.

Phryne gathered her cloak around her and walked quickly through the thinning crowds to the stage door. Something stirred in the gloom under the stair, and a man tacked towards her. He was the doorkeeper, a bowed figure in a greatcoat and scarf. He had evidently been keeping out the cold with one of the cheaper forms of tawny port.

'Yes, Miss?' Phryne recoiled under a pub-cellar exhalation and said, 'Can you tell Sir Bernard that Miss Fisher is here?'

''Erb! Nip up and tell Sir B that Miss Fisher's 'ere!'

A boy wearing carpet slippers and a dark suit evidently made for a younger brother sauntered for the stairs. His slowness evidently displeased the port-swiller.

'Get a move on!' he snarled, and flung a boot. The bare calves flashed upwards and the boy yelped something very derogatory and returned the boot, which bounced and was fielded with a facility that spoke of a cricketing youth.

'Sorry,' said the doorman, putting the boot on a shelf in his little box and settling his greatcoat. 'Cheeky little blighter. Knows I can't chase 'im. Me bronicals are something crook in this weather, ever since the Somme they been bad. I went as a stretcher bearer – wanted to see what glorious conflict was like, see? Weren't like the Bard says and that's a fact.' He coughed experimentally. 'Now, Miss, what's goin' on in the 'ouse? I reckernise you – you're Sir B's friend what's a detective. What's been 'appenin'? No one ever tells me anythin', but I've 'ad to call for a doctor and now 'is Nibs says he wants the cops.'

'Someone has been poisoning your Sir Ruthvens,' said Phryne. 'Who could have done that, do you think?

'Plenty of reason for wantin' Mr Ruddy Copland gone,' said the man, consideringly. 'Rude. Difficult. 'Ard to please. Never a good word to throw to a dog and mean as a tick. Nothin' against Robbie Craven though – nice young lad. But there's been funny things 'appening. Funny even for the Maj, I mean.'

'What sort of things?' Phryne leaned against the doorman's box and drew her cloak closer. It was freezing in the small corridor. 'Shouldn't they get you a heater of some sort? It's cold, no wonder you're wearing a greatcoat.'

'Yair. Perishin'. No one cares about a doorkeeper. I was lucky to get this job, though. You'd never believe that me and Sir B is the same age – somethin' cruel, innit? Known 'im for a long time, I 'ave – I been with G and S since I was a nipper.'

'I thought you had a London accent,' said Phryne, wondering why stage-door entrances were invariably so shabby.

'I was there when they did *Ruddigore* for the first time. I seen Sir Arthur Sullivan conductin' with 'is lighted baton, and Mr Gilbert shoulderin' out into the fog to walk the Embankment and chew 'is cigar until they found out if it was a hit or not. 'E was a toff, Mr Gilbert was. I remember 'im looking for his wife – 'e says to me, "Tom,

45

have you seen Mrs Gilbert?" and I says, "She's round behind, sir," and he says quick as a flash, "I know that, Tom, but where is she?"' The door-keeper laughed heartily, coughed, and took a sip out of a bottle artlessly concealed in a biscuit tin. Phryne laughed.

'When did they do it first? It's my favourite.'

'In 1887, Miss. Ran over 200 performances, but never been really popular – that's why Mr Gilbert wanted to call it *Not as Good as The Mikado*. They had a lot of arguments, them two. Mr Gilbert said they should call it *Robin and Richard Were Two Pretty Men* and Sir Arthur says, "No, my dear chap," and Mr Gilbert growls, "Oh all right, we'll call it *Ruddigore* then!" and outs with 'im into the street. Then they complained that the title was rude, so he says, "Well, what about *Kensington Gore?*" and Sir Arthur wouldn't 'ave that, so he said it had to be *Ruddigore* and that was where they left it. Takes a person of refined musical tastes to appreciate, does *Ruddigore*.' He grinned at Phryne, showing unexpectedly white teeth and a deeply lined face.

Phryne was about to ask about Walter Copland again when Sir Bernard came down the stairs and took her by the hand. 'Phryne darling, I'm so sorry to keep you waiting and I'm afraid that I can't take you out, something else has happened.'

'Yes, I saw it. How is the poor boy?'

'Not good. Come upstairs, at least I can offer you some tea. Until the police come. Oh, Lord, the newspapers are going to have a jolly time with this!'

Aware of the doorkeeper's ears flapping, Phryne

46

laid one finger on Sir Bernard's lips and allowed him to escort her back to his office, which now contained no Coplands but a girl laid out on the couch in a state of hysteria, being scolded by a middle-aged woman.

'Sit up, girl, drink your tea, and pull yourself together,' she snapped. 'This is no time for hysterics, Leila. Sit up or I will slap you.'

There was no doubt that she meant exactly what she said, and the young woman obeyed. Phryne recognised Dame Hannah and Rose Maybud.

'Ah. Miss Phryne Fisher, this is Miss Leila Esperance and Miss Agnes Gault. Is that tea? Good. Miss Fisher is considering helping us. She is a private detective.'

Miss Gault stared hard at Phryne and then smiled a broad relieved smile. 'Yes, please do, Miss Fisher. This company's on the edge of a nervous breakdown, so many odd things have been happening. I've been in the business since I was three and I've never known things to be so ... so strange.'

'We're cursed,' announced Miss Esperance, 'haunted!'

'Haunted? Sorry, I don't deal in ghosts. You want the Society for Psychical Research,' suggested Phryne.

'Ghosts, forsooth,' Sir Bernard poured out stewed tea and loaded his with sugar. 'We don't have a ghost, we have a trickster of some sort – not dangerous.'

'Not dangerous, with poor Robert Craven and Walter laid out?' Miss Esperance's voice rose to a shriek. 'We're doomed!'

Miss Gault delivered a slap to Miss Esperance,

then offered a shoulder onto which the star collapsed.

'Perhaps I'll just take her back to her dressing room,' she murmured. She encouraged Miss Esperance to her feet and led her out.

'That was a reprise of her role of "Black Nell" in *The Shadow of Huntley Hall*,' said Sir Bernard dryly. 'The trouble with actresses is ... well, that they are actresses.'

'You can't fault them for being what you want them to be,' said Phryne briskly. 'Now, what has happened? I'm intrigued.'

'Lots of things. Both Copland and Craven are very ill. The doctor's with them now. Before that ... well, if I believed in ghosts, which I don't, I'd begin to think that we were haunted, Phryne darling.' He put down the cup. 'Do you want this disgusting tea?'

'No,' said Phryne, who had not tasted it.

'Then let's have some whisky.' He found two glasses and poured out a liberal dose. Then he stared, pointing a quivering forefinger.

'Look!'

'I don't think it's supposed to be that colour, you know,' Phryne observed.

The manager's good and expensive Scotch whisky was a brilliant and repulsive green.

'Oh, Lord, that's it, that is the final straw, I have had enough!' Bernard bellowed, swelling and taking on the sun-kissed hue of a ripe tomato. 'This must stop! When I find out who's doing this I shall personally suspend them by the... I shall suspend them from the tower of this theatre for daws to peck at!'

48

'Very good, Bernard, now tell me what has been going on, or those daws are going to go hungry. What are daws, anyway?'

'I presume that they are jackdaws,' said Bernard coldly. 'Very well. There have been several incidents. The first was the disappearance of Rose Maybud's glove, which vanished while she was on stage and turned up in Mr Alexander's room.'

'That is susceptible of a romantic explanation.'

'Yes, but he swears he didn't do it.' Phryne smothered a smile. 'Then, there was a bag stolen from the chorus's dressing room – which turned up in Mr Alexander's room again.'

'And it wasn't him?'

'I really think it wasn't.'

'No, it would seem a touch foolish. Was anything stolen from the bag?'

'A bottle of hyacinth scent.'

'For which Mr Alexander would presumably have no use?'

'No. Then Miss Esperance lost a telegram, one of those "good luck and break a leg" ones, which was found torn up in the chorus room. Any one of the chorus could have done that, I admit. Then Monsieur Dupont the chorus master got a note to go to Leila's dressing room, where he met Mr Evans. They are both attracted to her, and she's not decided which one she wants, but she swears she didn't send the notes and she certainly wasn't there at the time. There was a bit of a fracas. Nothing really hurt but their ... expectations...' Sir Bernard grinned.

'Have you got the notes?' Phryne asked.

'Yes. But they're block printed on brown paper and I don't think even a Sherlock like you can deduce much from them.'

He produced two notes, lettered in some greasy dark substance. 'Come to my room at interval. Leila.' He was right, Phryne thought. Nothing to be deduced from the content or the writing, though the ink seemed familiar. She had seen that dark smudgy line before. Eyebrow pencil.

This did not seem to take her any further. Everyone in the cast used eyebrow pencil.

'All right. What else?'

'I'm now beginning to think that Selwyn's illness might have been induced. He was as sick as a dog last week during rehearsals – but he got better and we thought at the time that it was just a stomach bug. Now someone's taken another one of Leila's gloves and poisoned both my Sir Ruthvens and I don't know what to make of it, Phryne darling, I really don't. Please help me.'

Phryne took the offered hand and said, 'All right. I'll do what I can.' Sir Bernard hauled out a key ring from his fob and detached a large iron key.

'Come and go as you like,' he said heavily. 'See what you can do, Phryne.'

There was a knock at the door, and the call boy bounced in, alight with unholy enthusiasm.

'The police are here, Sir B,' he announced, as though it was something that he had wanted to say all his life.

CHAPTER THREE

Is life a boon? If so, it must befall
That Death, when ere he call
Must call too soon.
Though fourscore years give
Yet one would pray to live
Another moon.

Gilbert and Sullivan
The Yeomen of the Guard

Detective Inspector John 'Call me Jack, everyone does' Robinson did not like theatres. Bit of a night out at the variety or even the Tiv was fair enough, but ever since a high-minded relative had forced him to sit through an Ibsen festival at an impressionable age, theatres had always been synonymous with what he called 'high art', a portmanteau term for everything self-indulgent, terminally tedious and incomprehensible in the world of culture. This naturally did not encompass Shakespeare. He was a playwright for whom the detective inspector thought it would be a real pleasure to buy a few beers, have a nice sit down and a talk about life.

His sergeant, John 'Alias' Smith, was straight out of a long and gruesome inquiry into baby-murder by a nurse in a hospital and was delighted to be anywhere which did not smell of carbolic. This

51

place, he noted, smelt of paint, dust, and perfume in roughly equal proportions.

Accompanying his superior officers was a very large police constable, William Naylor, at least three axe-handles across the shoulders and reputed to be free with his hands. Robinson had been assigned to make the decision about either promoting him or sacking him; Robinson was still undecided as to whether Big Billy would be more dangerous in the force or on the street.

The doorman saw them and drew himself to attention.

''Erb, go tell Sir Bernard that the police is 'ere,' he said, and the boy flew up the stairs. 'Nasty goings-on, sir,' he commented. Robinson grunted. He did not like to talk at the beginning of a case. He wanted to absorb the atmosphere.

Theatres appeared to have more atmosphere than was comfortable. Overhead, feet were running, doors were slamming, and a female was screaming. Then he heard a familiar voice.

'Well, well, Miss Fisher,' he said, as a silvery woman descended like a goddess into his ambit. 'What are you doing here?'

'Chance,' said Phryne, extending her hand. 'How nice to see you, Jack dear. This is Sir Bernard Tarrant, the manager of His Majesty's Theatre.'

Robinson shook Bernard's hand and introduced his officers.

'Can you tell me what is happening, Sir Bernard? All I got from the clerk was a mention of poisoning.'

'Yes, both my Sir Ruthvens – both of them, and

who is to go on tomorrow I do not know – and who would have had a grudge against poor Robert Craven I can't imagine ... boy wouldn't harm a fly...'

'Come up, Jack,' said Phryne. 'You can assemble the whole company on stage if you like. Tom here says that the doctor's wanting to remove both of the victims to hospital.'

Thankfully, Jack Robinson escorted the wittering Sir Bernard up the stairs and blinked as he came out onto the stage.

It was much bigger than it looked from the front. The box sets of the Ruddigore ancestral hall only occupied half of the space available, though the back was festooned with electrical wiring and ropes. The policemen picked their way gingerly over the sandbags which steadied the canvas frames.

'On stage,' Sir Bernard clapped his hands. Magically, out of the wings and clattering down the stairs, came a multitude of people in various states of undress.

'Keep everyone here,' said Robinson. 'Where is the doctor?'

'Men's dressing room,' said the call boy, who was at his elbow. 'I'll take you, sir.'

Phryne, unnoticed, tagged along behind as more yellow corridors were traversed and steps climbed.

The chorus's dressing room was crammed with clothes, littered with props and gear and redolent of sweat and grease-paint. Other odours had been added. A familiar figure climbed wearily to his feet from beside two figures on the floor and looked around.

Curly hair and an unforgettable profile, red mouth and dark unreadable eyes, their brightness somewhat dimmed by strenuous combat with the black angel.

'Open that window, someone,' he ordered. 'Fresh air, that's the ticket. I think they'll ... who are you?'

'Detective Inspector Robinson, who are you?'

'They called me from the house at the end of the show. I'm Dr Fielding. Luckily Miss Webb is a trained nurse, and we borrowed some equipment. Hello, Phryne!'

'Mark, how nice to see you. How are your patients?'

'I've done all I can here – washed out their stomachs. They need observation and rest, and they might pull through. This chap had a lot less of it, whatever it was. The older fellow's really intoxicated.'

'Intoxicated? You mean they're drunk?' asked Robinson.

'No, I mean they're poisoned.' Dr Mark was weary but polite. 'An opiate, I think – see how the eyes are dilated.'

He bent over one of the recumbent figures and peeled back an eyelid. A pupil as dark as a pansy bloomed open, then winced away from the light.

'Good, that's an alert response. I think we may have got to them in time. Thanks, of course, to Miss Webb here, who has been very helpful.' Mark smiled at the actress, who had extinguished her bridesmaid's gown in someone's paint-stained smock. A duster confined her long, ringletted golden hair. She grinned back at him.

'Thanks to you,' she said in a small gruff voice.

'Yes, well, I'm sure that you've done a splendid job, Dr Fielding,' Robinson interrupted. 'Did your patients say anything about where they got this stuff, or who gave it to them?'

'No, they were both comatose when I first saw them.'

'Miss Webb?'

'No, not to me, but I think Leila was talking to poor old Robert. She was actually holding him up on stage, you know. She might have heard something.'

'Good. You can take them away, Doctor, I'll have an ambulance called directly – you go and do that, Naylor – but I'd like to search their clothes first.'

Dr Fielding flicked a glance at Phryne, who nodded. He pointed to a pile of discarded clothes and stepped away from his patients.

Sergeant Smith turned both Sir Ruthvens gently to one side and another, feeling for a box or a pill bottle. They seemed deeply asleep. Their heads lolled like broken dolls. Phryne walked to Mark's side and put a hand on his arm.

'Opiate?' she asked.

'Yes, something derived from opium – morphine, maybe.'

He was watching Sergeant Smith's handling of the patients jealously.

'How much?'

'Hard to tell, too big an initial dose will usually produce vomiting. But I would have thought that the elder man had at least ten grains. I've preserved all the matter. The laboratory can test it.'

'How would it have been delivered?'

55

'In a pill, in a liquid – even in an injection. I didn't search them for injection sites. I was trying rather hard to save their lives.' He sounded nettled. Phryne patted the arm.

'Where are you going from here?'

'Why, to hospital, to see them settled. Then I'm taking Miss Webb to supper. Without her they would certainly have died. I can't handle all that apparatus on my own and speed is of the essence in poisonings. Well, have you finished with my patients?' he asked Sergeant Smith. 'Found anything?'

'No, sir, and I can hear the ambulance coming. Naylor'll help with the stretchers. What hospital, Doctor?'

'Royal Melbourne,' said Dr Fielding shortly. 'I'll be back as soon as I can, Miss Webb.'

'I think it will have to be another night, Doctor,' said Mollie Webb, dragging off her duster and shaking her head. 'I don't think that the police are going to let us out early. Too many odd things have been happening. But leave me a note at the stage door later this week.'

'All right,' Mark Fielding smiled at Miss Webb, then turned to Phryne. 'In the thick of it again, Phryne,' he commented. 'You look absolutely beautiful. Well, I'd better go. Nice to see you again.'

'Yes,' agreed Phryne, her breath as always slightly taken by contemplation of his profile. 'Yes, it is.'

Stretchers were carried out, supervised by Dr Fielding. The police surgeon tutted his way in to certify that various pots of gruesome leavings

56

were indeed parts of a chain of evidence. He was in evening clothes and even worse tempered than usual. This rendered his mood roughly similar to that of a cinnamon bear, expecting a quiet evening with some other bears of equal social status, which suddenly found itself in unpleasant company with one foot caught in a trap.

'Poisoning? You know how it is with theatres. Rogues and vagabonds,' he snorted, making notes in his small black book. 'Yes, Simmonds, take all that stuff away and I'll do the analysis in the morning. Thank you for ruining a fine bridge game,' he snarled as he passed Robinson. His eye caught Phryne shimmering quietly in a corner and he added, 'Outrageous!' as he stumped off towards the stairs, followed by an attendant carrying the evidence. The detective inspector caught him by the arm.

'Take this too, Doctor.' Robinson handed over a small blue box. 'I found it in that smock. I want to know what the remaining pills are. Thank you for your courtesy, Doctor,' said Robinson quietly, and Phryne smothered a laugh. 'Right, back to the stage. You too, Miss Webb, if you please.'

The stage was crowded. Phryne reflected that there were more people in the theatre than the cast. Among the half-dressed people with paint incompletely removed from their faces were three men in overalls, an ancient who was emphasising points in his discourse with a screwdriver, five boys including the over-excited call boy, six persons who appeared to be connected to the principals, a stately woman leaning on a dress basket, a girl waving a pair of curling tongs, a stout gentleman in a high state of excitement making French gestures and a calm, bearded man with a bound book in his hands. The noise of trained voices expressing their opinion of the situation was remarkable.

'Sir Bernard,' said Jack Robinson, 'call your people to order, please.'

'Overture and beginners,' announced Bernard in his big, rich voice, and the noise died down.

'Now, my name is Detective Inspector Robinson,' began Jack in a calm voice. 'I want to know who you all are and where you were during the performance. This is my sergeant. He'll take down your names and then we'll call you all one by one and you can tell me anything you know about tonight.'

'May we know, Detective Inspector,' asked the calm man, 'how Robbie and Mr Copland are?'

'Both still alive and in hospital.' There was a general sigh of relief. 'Who are you, sir?'

'Stage Manager, Thomas Loveland-Hall.'

'And what are your duties, Mr Loveland-Hall?'

Eyes creased as the bearded man made a broad gesture which encompassed the stage and everyone on it.

'Why, all of it,' he said.

'Right. Now, I presume you are responsible for the building and lights and tickets and all that?'

'No, that's between Mr West our electrician and his two assistants, and Mr Brawn, our stage carpenter and his two assistants. Then there are the box office and the front-of-house staff, they belong to Sir Bernard, and of course there is Mrs Pomeroy, the wardrobe mistress, and her three girls. There's the doorkeeper Tom and the call boy Herbert, and the dressers.'

'Dressers?'

'A dresser is responsible for all the costume and makeup changes, hair and appearance, and, well, for delivering the actor onstage in his or her right mind, in possession of all props and still remembering the lines. Theatres could not run without dressers.'

Mr Loveland-Hall had a soothing voice and everyone he had mentioned smiled at him.

'All right. We'll take the people who aren't actors first. Just go over there, would you, ladies and gentlemen, and give your names to Sergeant Smith. We won't keep you long.'

Phryne was standing next to the overflowing dress basket, which was almost as tall as she was, surveying the stage. Through a froth of petticoats, she could see Gwilym Evans whispering into Leila's ear. Her hand was being held by the patter singer Selwyn Alexander, who had retained his villain's black hat. The moustache appeared to be real. Mollie Webb had returned her smock to the stage painter and sat down on the floor, fluffing out her hair with her fingers and leaning on Mad Margaret, who had loosened the buttons on her tight Victorian collar and was fanning both of them with a newspaper.

The chorus were clustered together like sheep around the French gentleman, holding hands for comfort. Phryne suddenly wondered about the Copland ladies.

'Bernard, what did you do with Miss Copland and her mother?'

'Sent 'em to wait in the foyer – they'll have seen the ambulance. Lord, Phryne darling, this is terrible!'

'Yes. How does the company look? Is anyone behaving in an unusual manner?'

Bernard pulled himself together and scanned the crowd.

'Let's see. There's Selwyn's dresser Bradford arguing with Walter's dresser Hansen – they loathe each other. And that's Miss Gault's Jill snubbing Miss Wiltshire's Kitty – that's standard. They're sisters – neither of them could manage on the stage, so they became dressers. They're stage-struck. Kitty thinks that Violet Wiltshire should have got Dame Hannah and that heavenly song, when Violet sings patter like nobody's business but has no top range at all, and Jill thinks that Agnes Gault should have got Mad Margaret when she has a lovely soprano range but can't sing faster than 3/4 without choking. Artistic judgement is not their strong point. No. That's normal.' Phryne laughed and Sir Bernard continued his catalogue, pointing out each cast member as he went. 'Violet fanning Mollie, they're friends. Selwyn wooing Miss Esperance from one side, demonstrating sinister charm, with that Welsh boy whispering sweet Celtic nothings in her other ear? They've been doing that for months. Agnes trying to calm the chorus, leaning on Cameron Armour's arm? They're old ... er ... friends. I gave him Sir Roderick because he's a bit past the more athletic parts but he's got a good presence and can still deafen the back stalls. The chorus palpitating in time around Monsieur Dupont? First time they've been

60

in harmony all night and he has a firm hand, bad temper though, all chorus masters have either a natural or assumed bad temper. No, situation as usual, Phryne darling, except that Walter Copland and poor Robbie are in hospital. That's not normal, even for the Maj.'

'Anyone missing?'

'Let me see. I let the box office and the ushers go home, now have we got all the hands? Yes, I believe so. And the chorus ... Doris, Winnie, Madge, Annie, Mellicent, Patricia, Jessie, Marie-Claire, Betty, Emma – yes, all present. Reggie, Col, Frankie, Roy, Leslie, Norman, Eric, Jimmy, Raymond and Louis – no, where's Louis?'

'Is he the one hiding behind the curtain?' asked Phryne, sighting a pair of shoes and the shadow of a frightened face.

'Yes, that's him – silly boy. I'll just go and get him.'

Sir Bernard bustled away. Phryne beckoned to the call boy.

'Hello, Herbert,' she said. 'You read detective stories, don't you?'

'How could you tell?' asked the boy, impressed.

'I'm a detective,' said Phryne. She judged Herbert to be about eleven, a smidgen overgrown and underfed but alight with enthusiasm.

'I like Sexton Blake best,' he confided. 'Ain't this grouse? I mean, isn't this exciting? Nothing interesting's happened around this place the whole time I been here ... I've been here,' he corrected himself. Someone was evidently trying to teach him grammar.

'Do you want to be an actor?' Brown eyes in the

61

thin mobile face fixed on her with uttermost conviction.

'Yes,' said the boy, flatly. 'I'm going to be a great dramatic actor but Mum's got no money for lessons so I got myself this job. Sir B says he'll give me a part as soon as we do a panto. Christmas. Peter Pan. I'm one of the Lost Boys. Like this, see?' His whole body drooped, his eyes filled with tears, and he reached down to stroke something lying on the floor. 'Poor Wendy,' said Herbert, and Phryne could almost see the curve of the girl's cheek inside the caressing cupped hand.

'What's the rest of your name, Herbert?' she asked, impressed.

'Cowl. Reckon I'll change it, though. Cowl's good enough for a factory-hand but not for an actor. Sir B thinks that it should be a big name, like Savage or Moreland.'

'I'll watch your future progress with great interest, Herbert,' said Phryne. 'Now, what do you think about these attempted murders?'

'You mean you want me to help you, Miss?' the shadowed eyes lit up again.

'I might. You know more about the theatre than anyone else, don't you? You go everywhere and see everything.'

'Can I be your ... irregular?'

Herbert's reading had obviously included the Great Detective. Phryne nodded.

'I think so. A quid a week and expenses?'

'Done,' said the boy, and they shook hands.

The stage had been cleared of the technicians and the sergeant was beginning on the chorus. It was late and cold and the harsh working lights illuminated patches and holes even in the ancestral hall of the Ruddigores. The floor felt odd under Phryne's feet, until she realised that it was painted cloth. The theatre looked battered and faded and Phryne was glad of her cloak.

'I've sent Naylor to search the dressing rooms,' commented Robinson as the last sobbing girl was led away to sit in the body of the theatre and wait until she could be searched by a police-woman. 'Now there's just the principals and then we can get out of here and into somewhere warm. Miss Fisher, are you retained in this matter?'

'Yes, Jack.'

'You know, for once, I think you might do better than me,' he said slowly.

'Oh, why?'

'Well – this is a different world,' he said, shielding his tired eyes against the light. 'All these people are used to being someone else. I've never had so many tears poured all over me, never – and a good three-quarters of 'em were false. I can get a confession out of anyone in their right mind – but I don't reckon actors have a right mind. You'll have to keep me posted, Miss Fisher.'

'All right. Can I sit in when you talk to the principals?'

'Yes,' said Robinson wearily. 'Let's start with the men. I've had enough women for one night. Begging your pardon, Miss Fisher.'

Mr Selwyn Alexander was pried loose from Miss Esperance and strode up to the detective inspector. 'This is outrageous!' he began. 'Is no one safe?'

'Probably not all that safe,' said Robinson quietly. 'What do you mean?'

Mr Alexander took the offered chair, identified himself as forty-seven years old, Australian, unmarried, and an actor. He removed the black hat with a flourish. He was older than he looked on stage; wrinkles grooved the greasepaint.

'I mean, since this run of G and S began we haven't had a moment's peace – it's as though we were cursed. You'd think we were doing the Scottish play.'

'You mean Mac–' began Robinson and Phryne tapped his lips.

'Not in the theatre, Jack dear, it's unlucky to name that play, as it is to wear real jewellery on stage, whistle backstage, and a multitude of other superstitions.'

Robinson paused to digest this, then went on. 'Cursed, Mr Alexander?'

Selwyn leaned back and flicked his hat back over his shoulder without checking whether his dresser was there. He was. A grey, fat, balding little man who held the hat as though it was a crown.

'I mean we have had all sorts of odd things happening with no explanation. Things going missing and turning up in odd places. I was extremely ill for a week during rehearsals – I am now beginning to think that I was poisoned, too. It's been one thing after another.'

'Did you see either of the victims eat or drink anything tonight?'

'No.' Selwyn lost interest. 'I was in my dressing room most of the time – I need to rest. Sir Despard is a demanding part, you know.'

'Well, thank you, Mr Alexander. Mr Evans?'

Selwyn slouched past the young man as he left

Miss Esperance with a backward glance of melting longing which Phryne registered as about 6 on the Richter scale.

Then the actor turned the full force of his personality on her. My, she reflected, he was attractive. Even Bunji had noticed it. He had clearly defined features and brown hair, dark blue eyes with shadows under them and a red mouth which owed little to greasepaint. He was still clad in his sailor's suit but had doffed the hat and cleaned the makeup off. He scanned Phryne, from silver heels to the hood of her black cloak, then smiled a smile so full of sensual appreciation that she grinned in reply.

'Gwilym Llewellyn Evans, born in Wales,' he said in his cut-glass voice. 'Thirty-one years old and an actor by profession. How are Robbie and Walter?'

'Alive.' Jack Robinson repeated his questions and got the same answers – Mr Evans had been occupied with Miss Esperance. Dismissed, he added to Phryne, 'You laughed at that business with the flag – that was you, wasn't it?'

'Yes, how did you know?'

'Celtic intuition. Thank you. I was waiting for someone to notice how funny it was.'

'My pleasure,' said Phryne, taking a small step backwards under the onslaught of his practised charm.

Mr Cameron Armour, questioned, had nothing to add. Neither did Miss Gault. Violet Wiltshire said that she had been terrified that Robbie was going to fall but he had somehow kept his feet. She had seen nothing else. Old Adam, alias

Leslie Franklin, was almost too shocked to speak. He could not have been more than twenty, young bones emerging eerily through the old man's face. He said he had noticed the new Sir Ruthven fading gradually, as though he was falling asleep, whereas Walter Copland had just collapsed without warning.

Miss Mollie Webb sat down and gave her age as twenty-five, her nationality Australian, and her occupation as actress. She rubbed her hands across her eyes.

Robinson warmed to this efficient and un-affected young woman. 'Miss Webb, I know you're very tired, but did you notice anything that might help us?'

'No, neither of them could speak by the time the doctor came. Isn't he a nice doctor, though – terribly good at his job, I mean. Most of them never even notice nurses. Where was I? I'm playing Zorah, the chief bridesmaid, and I'm off stage for the beginning of Act 2, that's the Ruddigore curse bit. Then I come on again for the finale, and it was after that they called for a nurse and that's what I used to be. My mother disapproved of actresses, so she made me get a trade first. I suppose it will be useful when I'm too old to act. Sorry, I'm so tired I'm babbling. Ask me questions.'

'Did you see either of them eat or drink anything during the play?'

'No. Except for Walter and his indigestion pills. He took three just as we came on at the beginning.'

'He always takes them?'

'Yes, they're a chalk and bismuth compound,

quite harmless. He thinks he's got an ulcer – and he might have, too. All that bile rots the stomach.'

'In a little blue box?'

'Yes. Did you find the box?'

'We did.'

'Good,' said Miss Webb. Her glance strayed to Gwilym Evans, who was waiting in the centre of the stage, Miss Esperance having vanished into Selwyn's embrace. Phryne intercepted a come-hither so blatant that had she been in the habit of blushing, she might have blushed. Dismissed, Miss Webb stirred and put back her hair with grimy hands. Gwilym held out his arms and she walked into them, nestling into his embrace with her head buried in his shoulder, while his dark profile was outlined against the backlights like a cameo. It was a very effective picture and Phryne appreciated it.

Jack Robinson beckoned with vast reluctance for the attendance of Rose Maybud, Miss Leila Esperance, the star of the show.

Sir Bernard cut Selwyn Alexander neatly out, seated the lady, then remained standing behind her chair.

'Leila Esperance, aged twenty-five, actress,' she said in a fairly clear voice. 'Oh, it was awful. I had to hold him up and he was collapsing all over me.'

'Robert Craven?'

'Yes.'

'Did he say anything to you which might in-dicate how he was poisoned?'

'No. He just whispered "Hold me up, I can't stand, we have to finish the show," and then at the end he said "I'm dying," and I thought he

67

was, poor Robbie.'

'What about earlier, with Mr Copland?'

'He seemed a little slow,' she said consideringly. 'Not bright, not up-to-tempo like he usually is. And his eyes seemed bigger – I know that sounds silly. But I couldn't smell anything on his breath. He wasn't drunk. No, just slow. Then he managed to stay on his legs until the curtain and then ... oh, Lord, it was the Hinkler gala so we couldn't stop the show, it's terrible being on the stage, no one gives us credit for anything, and there was poor Robbie battling on even though...' she seemed to struggle with tears but Phryne observed that her eyes were dry. 'Can I go home now?'

'In a little while. Did you see either of them eat or drink anything?'

'No, but then, I'm mostly on stage,' she said artlessly. 'Mr Loveland-Hall won't allow any alcohol at all on the stage or the wings. If we need a drink of water, the dresser brings it – they have to be there when we enter and leave to check the costume. I had a cigarette on the stairs – Mr Loveland-Hall won't allow naked lights on stage either – and I saw Robbie running past to get fitted for the bad baronet's costume, but that's all I saw and are you going to do something? We'll all be murdered! I tell you, we're haunted! I've seen her!'

'Seen whom?'

'Her, the ghost!' screamed Miss Esperance. 'She smells of hyacinths and she steals gloves. One of my gloves went again tonight, out of a packet that had just come back from the cleaners. It still had the sealing wax, not broken, and there was a glove missing – a white glacé kid glove! She's always in

Rose Maybud's costume and she has eyes as black as the pit and she smiled at me! We're doomed!' shrieked Miss Esperance to the astonished ears of the entire cast of *Ruddigore,* and fainted dead away. Her black curls veiled her face as she slumped gracefully to the floor. It was the most decorative faint Phryne had ever seen.

CHAPTER FOUR

ROSE MAYBUD (TO ROBIN OAKAPPLE):
Ten minutes since my heart said 'white'–
It now says 'black'
It then said 'left' – it now says 'right'–
Hearts often tack.
I must obey its latest strain
You tell me so
But if I change my mind again
I'll let you know.

Gilbert and Sullivan
Ruddigore

By the time the police had completed their search, it was four o'clock and Phryne was feeling exhausted. There were too many people, too many voices, and too much inconveniently passionate emotion clouding the theatre. Commissioning Herbert to go and call for a certain taxi, she left by the stage door. She emerged into the icy darkness and waited under the streetlight, allowing the cold

69

wind to blow some of her tiredness away.

Someone was sharing the street with her.

A shadow detached itself from just around the corner of Little Bourke Street and began to drift towards her. She could not hear any footsteps and he or it moved quite quickly. Phryne retreated until she had her back against the wall of the theatre and unclipped her bag before remembering that she did not have her gun with her. She had not expected His Majesty's Theatre to provide her with such an engrossing and challenging evening. She peered into the darkness.

It was a he. A man, dressed in a dark suit, with only the gleam of a shirt at the throat to reveal him. A Chinese man.

She could not see if he was armed. She was waiting, calmly, for him to make a move so that she could break his arm when lights from an approaching taxi flooded the pavement and Phryne was distracted.

When she looked back, he was gone.

'Bert dear, what an opportune arrival,' she said gratefully, gathering her cloak and sinking into the front seat, 'I have had a really strange evening and I would like to go home.'

'You been to the Hinkler galah, Miss? Bit late, aren't you?' Bert's hand-rolled cigarette, as usual, was not disturbed by speech. 'Been a good day for the cabs. Every man and his woofer wanted to go out to watch that plane land. They had to put on special trains.'

Phryne always found Bert's company soothing. He and his mate Cec owned this taxi and drove it in shifts. Bert was short and square and dark,

70

Cec was tall and lanky and pale; Bert talked and Cec was taciturn. They had been through war and fire together and could handle anything.

'There've been two attempted murders at the theatre, Bert, and I've been retained by the Management. I expect that it will be explicable but there seems to be a ghost as well.'

Bert, unusually, did not reply. He hauled the cab around the corner into Victoria Street and trundled down towards a patch of lights. 'Need to go round the city,' he commented. 'Cops have closed Flinders Street – there's been a road accident. This way'll get us round quicker.'

'I didn't know the Market got up so early,' commented Phryne.

'Four o'clock in the winter, three o'clock in the summer, Miss. Them big drays block up the road something shocking, lucky they ain't travelling later when everyone's trying to get to work.'

He tooted and then passed a lumbering wagon, loaded with produce in sacks, which was occupying most of the roadway. A nodding Chinese man sat in the seat, the reins knotted to the bar in front of him, and a very well fed and polished cart-horse walked patiently between the shafts.

'The wholesalers get here real early, then the greengrocers' vans arrive to supply the shops. 'Course, the best grade stuff is always the Chinese, though the Italians run 'em close. Work like slaves, the Chows do. They don't want time-and-a-half or an eight hour day.'

'You don't like them, Bert?' Phryne was not at all sleepy, suddenly.

'I got nothing against 'em, Miss, as long as they

71

don't break strikes – and they don't. They're just trying to make a quid like the rest of us.'

Phryne reviewed the conversation and realised that Bert had gone silent on the subject of ghosts. She decided not to re-open it.

'Who's on the case, Miss?' Bert asked as the cab took St Kilda Road.

'Jack Robinson, Sergeant Smith, and a huge constable called Naylor.'

Bert whistled. 'Alias Smith, he's all right – all right for a copper, I mean, being as he is a tool of the capitalist oppressors and a running dog of the state dedicated to doing down the working man. His name really is John Smith, poor bu – blighter. His father must have had a funny sense of humour. And you get on all right with Robinson, who's not bad as cops go. But Naylor – you be careful of him, Miss. Big as a house and no manners. Beat the soul-case out of a couple of wharfies when he was supposed to be investigating some pilferage. Lucky not to be dismissed from the force. Not a nice man,' opined Bert, who only used this phrase for seriously dangerous persons. Phryne lit a gasper and thought about it.

'Can't see that he is a danger to me, Bert, but I'll take your advice and stay out of his way. He can't do much harm with Robinson there, I suppose.'

'Not nice,' repeated Bert. 'You be careful, Miss Phryne.'

Phryne agreed that she would be as careful as possible. She asked how the taxi business was going (it was no worse than usual), and was delivered to her house.

She let herself in quietly and climbed the stairs

to her own suite on the first floor. The house was silent. The Butlers slept in their room; under the autumn-leaf bedspread Dot slept in her tower. Only the black cat Ember was awake. He entered silently then levitated onto Phryne's lap as she sat at her dressing table, cleaning her face with precise licks of a wad of cotton.

'You gave me a shock,' she reproved him as the black nose nuzzled into her palm – Ember loved the taste of cold cream. He purred briefly, a rusty and absurd noise for a grown cat, then settled down in Sphinx posture along her silk-clad thigh.

Phryne brushed her perfectly black, perfectly straight hair, considering her reflection, and Ember raised his chin and looked into the mirror.

A stylised young woman draped in an ivory silk nightdress, with the slim, stylised black cat on her lap. Both pairs of green eyes considered the spectator, coolly. The *art decoratif* frame of the looking glass – leaves and garlands in delicate ceramics which wreathed artlessly around it – made them look like a very fashionable 1928 nymph and transformed suitor reflected in an Arcadian pool. An aphorism came to Phryne's mind.

'If pursued by a satyr, always contrive to be captured near the softest available moss.' Phryne chuckled, blew a kiss to mirror-Phryne and put nymph and panther to bed in something warmer than Daphnis' drift of leaves.

Morning brought coffee, Dot, and the news that Dr Fielding, Detective Inspector Robinson and Sir Bernard Tarrant were all downstairs and clamouring for an interview.

Phryne groaned. Ember had departed from her

73

pillow, leaving a small round patch of warmth, as soon as Mrs Butler had reached the kitchen and put on the kettle, a noise which signalled milk and a warm stove to sit by. Dot was drawing the curtains.

'What's the time?'

'Ten, Miss, and there's a crowd downstairs.'

'They can wait. Run me a bath, Dot dear. Then call and tell Mrs B to give them all tea and I'll be with them in due course.' Phryne stretched. 'I'd better have the black skirt and the plum Russian top, the walking shoes, and a large coat – it looks cold,' she observed. 'Dot, there were two attempted murders in the theatre last night – at the Hinkler gala, of all things!'

'Not attempted murder, Miss,' said Dot from the bathroom. 'Real murder now. The older chap's dead.'

'Oh, dear.' Phryne remembered a light, pleasant voice singing:

My boy you may take it from me,
That of all the afflictions accursed...
A diffident nature's the worst...
You must stir it and stump it and blow your own
     trumpet
Or trust me you haven't a chance.

Good singers were rare enough. They should not be wantonly removed. 'What about the other one?'

'He's out of danger – he took less of the stuff, it seems. You aren't going to work in the chorus, are you, Miss, like you worked as a rider in that cir-

74

cus?' Dot looked anxious. Phryne got up and stripped off the nightdress as she walked to the bathroom.

'No, Dot dear, I shall be entirely myself and I'll come home every night,' she said soothingly. 'Well, almost every night. I have had enough of performing. I don't know how Jack Robinson is going to react to me being involved in his murder inquiry and I really don't know what I can do, but I'll try – I promised Bernard.'

'Dr Fielding's downstairs. Is... I mean, you broke off with him, Miss?

'And I will not resume. A lovely man but he needs a wife and a dog and some children and a settled home, and you know how I feel about settled homes, Dot dear. I don't think he'll be difficult. And he has a face which is pleasant to contemplate. No, the main problem is the theatre. All those people are trained to be charming, delightful, fascinating, and to laugh or weep on command. That makes all poor Jack's usual ways of judging if someone is telling the truth or lying quite useless.'

'There's something else, Miss, it slipped my mind. This note was under the door.'

Phryne, pulling on crepe de Chine underwear, scanned the crumpled paper. It was part of a playbill. Someone had printed *'Yore irregler is redy'* and signed his name with a cross.

'That's my accomplice, Dot, a boy called Herbert of angelic countenance and no education whatsoever. He tells me he is going to be a great actor and it is distinctly possible. He's about four foot six and dark and if he turns up I want to see him right away. Now, I need a big bag, and I'd better have handkerchiefs, salts, cigarettes, a flask and...' she reached into the drawer of her dressing table, 'a new notebook.'

Dot watched with disapproval when Phryne added her small gun to the contents of the Florentine leather bag. 'You're expecting trouble,' she said slowly.

'Possibly.'

Phryne smiled at her maid. Dot was dressed in her favourite brown woollen dress, with an ochre jacket and ochre shoes. Her long brown hair was strained back into a plaited bun skewered with a vengeful hairpin and her brown eyes looked worried. 'Don't worry Dot dear, I'm just being careful. You're always telling me to be careful, aren't you? And it's time I listened. Now, a final sprinkle of "Jicky" and we can face the day.'

The parlour, which was spacious, did not seem large enough to contain Sir Bernard Tarrant, who was standing in the gentleman's position with his back to the fire, Dr Fielding, looking stricken, and a policeman drinking tea and eating muffins with the deep concentration of the unbreakfasted.

'Phryne darling,' said Sir Bernard, 'you look absolutely ravishing. Do be an angel and help us. I don't know what to do.'

'What else has happened?' Phryne sat down on the arm of Dr Fielding's chair.

'Why, poor Walter's dead, that's what's the matter. Wouldn't you say that's enough?' returned Bernard hotly.

'And no one saw anything useful, or if they did they are not telling me,' added Robinson, reaching

76

for another muffin. 'I've been up all night, and I've nothing to show for it. Well, not much. Naylor searched the dressing rooms, but found no drugs. Lots of other things, but no drugs. The chorus and the stage crew saw nothing. The analysis of the pills and the ... er ... evidence isn't done yet. I wish we could get a police surgeon who didn't go crook at being a police surgeon. Then there's this ghost. Miss Esperance says she's seen it, so do a couple of other people. There are no ghosts, so there's a trickster at work as sure as eggs. They're always awful – like anonymous letter writers. Do a lot of damage and when you catch them butter wouldn't melt in their mouth.' Reminded of melting butter, Robinson reached for another muffin and Mr Butler refilled his teacup.

'I think I can help you with ... with the ghost,' said Bernard reluctantly.

'Good. And you shall tell us all about it directly. Do sit down, Bernard, and have some tea and a muffin. You need fortifying,' Phryne ordered, and nudged Dr Fielding.

'What's the matter with you, old bean?'

'He shouldn't have died,' said Mark Fielding, looking up at Phryne. 'When I got them to hospital they were both past the recovery point. The young man's all right, just as I would have expected. The older man had taken more poison, and it was longer before he got treatment – but I could swear, Phryne, I could swear that he was recovering. I even got a light-stimulus response from the pupil.'

'You're upset that you lost a patient,' she said gently, and he replied, 'Of course I am, I hate

77

losing a patient, every doctor hates losing anyone, but this is wrong, Phryne, there's something
wrong with this death.'

'Jack, did you order a post-mortem?' she asked.

'Of course,' said the policeman, putting down
his cup. 'Should know what killed him by tomorrow.'

'Right, well, there's nothing to be done until
then, is there? If it's any comfort, Mark dear, I
believe that you may be right, and in any case you
behaved in a very prompt and professional
manner and certainly saved Robbie's life. So have
some tea, Doctor, and we'll listen to a ghost story.'

Mark snorted, 'Ghosts!' but took a cup from
Mr Butler. Suddenly hungry, he slipped the last
muffin out from under Jack Robinson's hovering
fork and ate it.

'I was in the 1898 production of *Ruddigore* in
London, have I ever told you that?' asked Sir Bernard. 'Yes, there we were – the Savoy season, new
costumes, new production – all of the best. Thirty
years ago. It seems like yesterday. And here I am
the Management – when I think about how I used
to complain about Management! Ah, well.' Now
launched, Sir Bernard seemed to be unwilling to
get to the point. Phryne prompted him.

'Who was in the company, then? What part did
you play?'

'Richard Dauntless, the Jack Tar – Gilbert genu-
inely admired sailors, you know. It's a very good
part.' He put one hand behind his back and
adjusted an imaginary straw hat with the other. 'I
shipped d'ye see on a revenue sloop,' he sang
softly, and Phryne saw the slimmer, less confident

Bernard of 1898 and reflected that he must have been very attractive. 'Yes, well, Robin Oakapple, who's later Sir Ruthven, was played by Charles Sheffield, and Rose Maybud was Dorothea Curtis.' He paused, his eyes full of memory. 'She was so beautiful, was Dorothea. Small – can't have been above five feet, a proud beauty, with midnight black hair in curls all down her back and dark eyes which burned holes in me. Buxom, but I could span her waist with my hands. She could sing like a lark and dance like an angel on the head of a pin. And she was ... alive. Dorothea was all alive, from her tiny hands to her neat little feet. She was proud of her small hands – size three, she had to have her gloves specially made, and her boots. Everyone was in love with her. She had mash notes by the crate and her dressing room was always full of flowers – her favourites. You could smell her hyacinths all the way out into the street when they were in season. The flower girls in the Haymarket used to order them in by the basket.'

'Were you in love with her?' asked Phryne softly.

'Oh, yes, of course. So were Sheffield and the chorus boys and half the orchestra. She could charm the soul out of an audience. I could stand on stage with her and watch them melt.'

'Whom did the lady favour?' asked Robinson.

'No one. She wasn't interested in people, only the effect she could have on them – it amused her. She carried Sheffield in the part, he was weak, couldn't dance, and his voice was not really strong enough for the Savoy. But I don't think she loved him, either – or me, though she favoured us in

79

turn with suppers and sometimes let us stay in her dressing room while she changed. I loved sitting in her armchair and watching her face, her eyes, the perfect curve of her white throat – she was altogether lovely. In a way the part of Rose Maybud was perfect for her. She had force and passion but she really didn't have a heart. Or so I thought. Poor Dorothea.'

'What happened to her?' insinuated Phryne.

'She used to say that she was a vicar's daughter,' said Sir Bernard, 'but she wasn't. She was born Dot Mobbs and her father was a coal heaver. She had to work when she was a child, hard work in a hotel, fetching and carrying and possibly other things as well – things were different for women then. She had a weakness for madeira, though I never saw her drunk, and that early work had hurt her back and her legs. She was often in pain, for which she took laudanum. You know what that is?'

'Alcoholic tincture of opium,' said Dr Fielding, drawn outside his own disquiet by this strange story.

'I wanted to marry her,' said Sir Bernard sadly, 'but she wouldn't have me. She sent me a note, refusing my proposal, telling me not to call for her after the show. I didn't – I didn't want to press her – but I should have. I've blamed myself ever since.'

'Why?' asked Phryne, as Bernard paused and stared into the fire.

'Why, because she hadn't refused. That bastard Sheffield had intercepted her note and sent another telling me no. She had agreed to marry me, and she waited for me – sat all night in her dressing room, waiting for me to come and I didn't. She must have been so joyful, then joy turned to despair when I didn't come and she thought me faithless. And when they found her in the morning–' Sir Bernard groped for a handkerchief. Tears were running down his face. 'She was dead, sitting in her chair, her head on her arm, my poor Dorothea. She'd taken enough laudanum to kill three men, then laid her head down in a nest of hyacinths and passed away. Her beautiful black hair was scented with the flowers. I never forgave myself.'

'What did you do to Sheffield?' asked Robinson, professionally interested.

'The call boy found the original note where he had thrown it into the fire; it had fallen behind the grate. I taxed him with the forgery and he admitted it. I beat him half to death with my cane. But it didn't help. I could have killed him, but it wouldn't have brought the dear girl back again. He went downhill after that. He wasn't very good, Dorothea had carried him; with her gone he couldn't manage. He went back to the chorus and took to the drink and I don't know what happened to him. Died in the gutter, I expect, which was too good a fate for him. It's an old story,' he added, wiping his eyes, 'and my Dorothea is thirty years dead. However, consider the happenings in the theatre. The missing gloves – she was always proud of her hands. And the hyacinth perfume, her favourite flower. Leila says the ghost has black eyes and is dressed as Rose Maybud. It looks like Dorothea hasn't forgiven me.'

'Nonsense,' said Robinson instantly. 'There are

81

no such things as ghosts.'

'Jack, please.' Phryne did not like generalisations. 'Let us consider this dispassionately. Why should she come back now, Bernard? Why not before, if she's returning to haunt you?'

'First time I've had anything to do with *Ruddigore* since 1898,' he replied. 'It isn't played much, because the sets are so expensive and hard to move. It's not a show you can easily take on tour – the second act has the ancestors in their frames, it's got to be a solid construction because the actors have to stand in it. Large cast and musically complex and audiences don't go out whistling it like they do *Pirates* or *Pinafore*. It hasn't been played in Australia before and I doubt I'll ever do it again.' He buried his face in his white handkerchief, overcome with emotion. Presently he blew his nose and continued, his voice cracking. 'She died playing Rose Maybud. She's still playing her. Besides, who knows how time goes on the other side of the veil? It may have been just the blink of an eye to Dorothea while I've dragged through thirty years since she left me. What's more, I bought a few things from the Savoy when I came over. One of them was the Rose Maybud costume. Leila is actually wearing Dorothea's dress. Not the one she died in, of course, but a dress Dorothea wore.'

'It's interesting–' began Phryne, when Jack Robinson growled, 'Spooks! It's not enough to have actors but I must have spooks as well.' He looked up to heaven as if remonstrating with the Deity and snapped at Mark, 'What do you think, Doctor? You're a scientific man.'

'I don't know, but it seems very unlikely.'

'Unlikely does not mean impossible, gentlemen,' said Phryne. 'If someone else knows about this then it gives our trickster a script, doesn't it? Think about it. Excuse me,' she added, and went to the door, where Mrs Butler was beckoning.

The kitchen was warm and bright, Ember was sleeping on the rag rug in front of the stove and Mr Butler was pouring boiling water into the kitchen teapot.

'Sorry to interrupt, but you told me that you wanted to look at the fruit, Miss,' said Mrs Butler. 'This is what he has.'

A Chinese man stood at the back door, a flat woven basket in his arms. He was dressed in the standard dark suit with shirt but no collar, and he had a shapeless felt hat on his head. She could not see his face.

'The Chinese have the best fruit, Miss. Always the earliest, and brought right to the door. 'Course, they never carry seconds or yesterday's or specked fruit, but we don't use them anyway,' said Mrs Butler. 'Which would you like, Miss?'

The basket held a variety of perfect fruit, a handful of peas and beans, a head of cauliflower, a carefully polished carrot and a flawless onion. The trader broke a pea pod with one hand and slit it with his thumbnail. Peas as firm as pearls gleamed through the shell.

'Pound of peas,' said Mrs Butler instantly. 'Pound of carrots, please.'

'White peaches,' Phryne picked one up and sniffed the furry skin. 'Divine! Get me an oodle or so, Mrs B.'

83

Mrs Butler gave the order for five pounds of peaches, and Phryne watched as the man trotted out to his cart, weighed out the vegetables and fruit, then came back to tip the basket gently onto the table. Peaches rolled and Phryne caught one.

The Chinese trader took the money and went; Phryne had not heard him speak.

'The best fruit, Mrs B?'

'Yes, Miss, but it has to be washed. They use night soil on the fields.' She took the peach out of Phryne's hand and rinsed it under the tap. It looked depressed.

'I believe I'll wait until it fluffs up again, Mrs B. Have you always bought our fruit from the Chinese traders?'

'Yes, Miss, except for the heavy stuff, potatoes and onions, they get delivered by the greengrocer,' Mrs Butler told her a little stiffly, as if her house-keeping might be in question. Phryne smiled.

'I leave it all in your capable hands, Mrs B, you know that. I'm just curious. Now I'd better get back to my conference. They may have got to fisticuffs by now.'

A heated argument about the reality or other-wise of ghosts had resulted in Sir Bernard calling Robinson a bone-headed rationalist and Robinson retorting that Sir Bernard was credulous. Dr Fielding seemed bemused. Phryne walked decis-ively between them.

'Gentlemen, please. Jack, I'd remind you that Shakespeare believed in ghosts. Bernard, you are not to insult a policeman who is trying to help. Now, I suggest that you all go home and get some rest, and I'll see you tonight at the theatre. Five

o'clock – that should give us time to talk to everyone again, without keeping the poor darlings up
all night. Even actors need their sleep, you know.'

Sir Bernard bowed, and Jack Robinson, recalling
that he was full of this lady's tea and muffins, said,
'Sorry, Sir Bernard.'

'Until five o'clock, then,' said Phryne, and saw
them all to the door with a certain relief.

'Dot,' she called up the stairs, 'I'm not going out.
Come down to lunch and then I favour spending
the afternoon in some research. Find me those
books we were given by Madame Stella. I feel a
call to the other world coming on.'

CHAPTER FIVE

MAD MARGARET (To ROSE MAYBUD):
*And he loves you! No, no! If I thought that, I would
treat you as the auctioneer and the land agent treated
the lady-bird – I would rend you asunder!*

Gilbert and Sullivan
Ruddigore

After skimming seven books on the subject, rang-
ing from the grave proceedings of the Society for
Psychical Research to some extremely individual
tomes penned by those in constant contact with
the other world, Phryne came to two conclusions
about ghosts. One was that they demonstrably
did appear, sometimes, in a place or for a reason,

or at least a lot of otherwise sane people had encountered one. The other was that there was no scientific way to demonstrate their existence, if they had any. These theories being entirely unhelpful she shelved the topic along with the books and drove into the city.

She was met at the stage door by Herbert Cowl.

'What do you want me to do, Miss?' he whispered.

'I want you to tell me everything you know about all the people in this theatre.'

'Might take a while, Miss. I know an awful lot,' he said dispassionately.

'Well, then, find out where everyone was last night. Was anyone out of their place? You know where everyone should be. Find out if that's where they were.'

'All right. When do I report?'

'Come to my house when you can. Here's a quid in advance. Is it a deal?'

The boy nodded, stowed the bank note in his pocket and vanished up the stairs as the doorman came wheezing out of his cage.

Phryne climbed the stairs to Sir Bernard's office to find it uncharacteristically messy and, for once, empty. He had recently been there, for she could smell his cigar.

She took a chair and began to make notes in the silk-covered book:

1. Who poisoned both Sir Ruthvens? Laudanum in the blue pills?
2. Tricks: missing gloves – Leila's, found in Mr

Alexander's room. missing bag, missing hyacinth perfume – chorus's bag, Mr Alexander's room.
notes which brought Dupont and Evans to Leila's room. Leila's destroyed telegram – chorus?
something in the whisky – Sir B.
3. Did Leila really see the ghost of Dorothea? Consider Dorothea's story. Is she really dead? Ask Sir B. If it is Dorothea, why is she haunting Leila?

All good questions, Phryne thought, and not an answer to her name. She added 'Who hated Walter Copland? Who hated Robert Craven?' to the list and contemplated it.

When the manager came in she asked abruptly, 'Bernard, are you sure that Dorothea is dead?' Sir Bernard seemed taken aback by the question, but answered readily, 'Yes, of course I'm sure. She's buried in Melbourne Cemetery. She was born in Richmond – the family shipped the body home in a coffin packed with hyacinths. You can go and look at it if you like. What a question, Phryne darling.'

'Just a thought,' she said. 'Now, let's go and grill someone. Who hated Walter Copland, Bernie?'

'Just about everyone,' he said gloomily. 'I didn't like the fellow myself.'

'We'll assume that you didn't do it. Tell me what he was like.'

'Well, he was always complaining about something. The theatre was too hot or too cold, too dark or too light, the chorus was out of key or the orchestra out of time. I mean, the chorus is often

87

out of key and the orchestra is usually out of time, especially if you insist on showing off by singing patter songs too fast just to show you can do it. Which he did. He hogged the stage, even though it's already a meaty part, Robin/Sir Ruthven. He tried to upstage Evans, which is silly – no one can do that. He reminds me of the way my Dorothea could convince every man in an audience that he was the only one – Gwil can do that, to the ladies of course, in his case. Dear me, I am babbling. Gwil has great talent. Walter also interfered between Selwyn and Miss Esperance – told Sel he was making a fool of himself over a heartless piece, which might be true but is never a good idea. Leave the fools to their folly, I say. Leila took umbrage and Sel nearly called him out. You know, Phryne, sometimes I think of that little farm I'll have when I retire. Nice and quiet. Out in the country. No music, no quarrels, and no people. Just Jersey cows. I find cows so restful.'

'You'd be bored to screaming point in a week,' commented Phryne truthfully. 'So who was in love with Mr Copland?'

'In love with him? You jest.'

'What, no one? Well, whom did he favour?'

'No one, as far as I know. Come along, we'll have a chat with Hans.'

'Hans?'

'James Hansen, naturally called Hans. He is ... he was Walter's dresser. Dressers know everything.'

Phryne followed him to the principals' dressing rooms, which were on a level with the stage. Bernard explained the layout of the theatre.

'Two staircases, one on either side,' he pointed. 'First level up are the chorus's dressing rooms, one for the ladies and one for the gentlemen. Then up another flight is wardrobe and storage. Down from here is the stage carpenter's shop. And of course you can go under the stage. You can do that later. Come along.' He opened a plain door and said sympathetically, 'Hans, my dear chap, how are you?'

A kneeling man with grey hair was shovelling a number of small flat bottles into a shoebox. He sat back on his heels and croaked, 'Just cleaning up. You'll...' he paused, looked away, and said flatly, 'You'll want the room again and I can't bear the idea of anyone handling any of Walter's things but me.'

'Yes, yes,' said Sir Bernard soothingly, 'leave it for the moment, Hans. This is Miss Fisher and I've employed her to find out what's been going on.'

'But the police—'

'Yes, we've got them as well. We'll find out who did it, don't worry.'

'I don't care who did it.'

Phryne took a good look at his face, which he kept turned away, unaware that she could see him in the large lighted mirror. It was a weak face, she decided, prematurely old and marked with lines so deep that they were almost like scars across the high forehead and gashes down each cheek. He was now hunched in the actor's chair, one shoulder higher than the other. His knobbed arthritic hands were clasped together as if for comfort. Tears were trickling unregarded down his face.

'We were together for twenty years,' he said in his

soft, cracked voice. 'Twenty years, Walter and I, in theatres all over the world. London and South Africa and New Zealand and Australia. Such a long time and now it's all over. Walter's gone.'

Sir Bernard laid a hand on the crippled shoulder. 'I know, my dear chap.'

Phyrne saw the reflected Hans twist away under the consoling touch.

'He was going to retire,' mourned Hans. 'We … he was going to live in Bendigo, he owns … owned a house there. And now, he's gone. I can't believe he's gone.'

'What happened last night, Mr Hansen?' asked Phryne briskly. This wreck of a man was going to collapse altogether under any more sympathy. The dresser pulled himself together.

'It was just as usual. He came in about six, we had a cup of tea, then he put on his costume, that's the shepherd's smock for Robin Oakapple. He had a touch of sore throat, he used to suffer terribly with his throat. I made him a lemon and honey drink and he did his makeup.' He gestured at the wastepaper basket, which contained a squeezed lemon and pads of cotton wool stained with grease-paint and powder.

'Did anyone come in?' asked Phryne. Hansen thought about it, passing a shaking hand over his eyes.

'No … I don't think so … yes. Mr Evans came in and said something nasty about Walter clipping his lines. He was smoking a cigarette, the insolent puppy. Walter ordered him right out. Cigarette smoke made him ill. Evans knows that. Welsh wretch! And Miss Webb popped in to say

90

good luck. She is a nice girl, Walter asked her about his indigestion and she suggested the blue pills. No one else, but I slipped out to get him some cough medicine about six thirty. I was only away half an hour, less than that. Oh, Lord. Could someone have come in and given him the stuff? While I wasn't here to protect him?'

Phryne asked, 'Did Mr Copland eat or drink anything you hadn't prepared?'

'No, he never even got to take the medicine. There it is.' Hans began to cry again as he picked up a red-sealed chemist's packet. 'He only took tea and the lemon and honey. My Grandma always swore by that for throats. Oh, except his indigestion tablets. He always took a few of those before he went on. He had an acid stomach, and stage fright made him worse.'

'Stage fright? After twenty years?' asked Phryne. Both Sir Bernard and the dresser looked at her.

'Phryne darling, you never lose stage fright. It can happen to a veteran just as easily as a beginner. It's good. It gives an edge to a performance. I always think that when you've lost the butter-flies, you've been on the stage too long.' The dresser nodded. 'Yes, but it has been getting worse lately. He was almost sick before he went on, ever since he got Sir Ruthven. He was getting on, you know, for an actor. Nearly forty. It's a strenuous part and he used to get very tired.'

'He was a great actor,' said Sir Bernard. 'Well, we must find you another position, Hans, old chap. Can't waste a good dresser.'

'Oh, no ... no, Sir B, I can't. I can't do this again. I'm too old. Just let me go away.'

91

The grasp on Sir Bernard's hand was unexpectedly strong. He enfolded it in a warm clasp, saying, 'Well, well, my dear man, we shall see. Stay on for a few days, will you, until all this is sorted out?' Hans nodded, overcome. Phryne and Sir Bernard closed the door on the crooked man, once more on his knees, sweeping up broken glass.

'Bernard, if it wasn't in the pills, where was it?'

'I don't know.'

'Did you see all those little bottles? They were brandy flasks, weren't they?'

'And rum. Oh, dear. No one told me he had a tippling problem. Well. I can't see that it has a bearing on his death.'

'Yes, you can. The drug may have been in the latest of those little bottles and Hans there is busy destroying the evidence,' said Phryne impatiently.

'So he is,' said Sir Bernard helplessly, 'but I can't just go in and demand them, can I?'

'Herbert,' called Phryne. The boy shot out of his post at the head of the stairs.

'Yes, Miss?'

'Help poor old Hans with the rubbish, will you? Find a sugar bag and load all the stuff into it and leave it in Sir B's office, sealed up. Can you do that?'

The shrewd face knotted in concentration, then cleared. Herbert knew what was going on, but all he said was, 'Yes, Miss.'

'You seem to have had a remarkable effect on the call boy, Phryne. He's a bright little person, Herbert is. I expect him to be a good actor, if he is not distracted early by the Actor's Enemies.'

'What are they?'

'Alcohol and women,' Sir Bernard grinned. 'Where next?'

'Let's talk to Gwilym Evans.'

'Oh, very well.' Sir Bernard knocked on the next door, opened it, and revealed Gwilym Evans in the arms of a pretty blonde girl. She gave a squeak of dismay and exited at speed, her hair streaming behind her.

'I told you, Mr Evans, the chorus are out of bounds,' said Bernard sternly.

'What can I do, when the dear girls come and throw themselves at me?' asked the actor plaintively. 'I'm persecuted by the female sex,' he added complacently, glancing slyly at Phryne. She instantly resolved never to be added to this attractive man's harem.

But she could not help smiling. He had turned back to the mirror, smoothing on greasepaint with long, practised strokes across a straight nose, over the contours of a youthful cheek and down into the hollow of a columnar throat. His hair was a little too long, entrancingly wavy, and the pale makeup made his dark blue eyes glow like sapphires. He looked at the mirrored young man with deep pleasure.

'A bit darker, for that weathered look, and cherry cheeks for Richard Dauntless the sailor,' he commented. 'To what do I owe the pleasure of this visit, Sir B and delightful lady?'

'This is Miss Fisher, she's a detective.'

'I've already talked to all those policemen,' drawled Gwilym.

'What did you have against Walter Copland?' asked Phryne sharply. He raised his reflected eye-

93

brows. The painted mouth curved childishly.

'I didn't like him. He clipped my lines and tried to upstage me, which he couldn't do. Not on *my* stage. My audience.' His voice was precise, the only remains of a Welsh accent being a pure vowel sound and a habit of pronouncing the whole word – 'de-light-ful', 'po-lice-men'. It was a very sure voice, with no cracks or hesitations. Gwilym Evans, however unreliable with the persecuting female sex, was deadly serious about his craft. 'He was too old for Ruthven, anyway, and he tippled.'

'He did?'

'He always carried a little flask with him.'

'Do you know it was alcohol?'

'What else could it be? He was frightened. Stage fright. He corpsed three times on Thursday in *Pinafore*. Ask Prompt.'

'Corpsed?' asked Phryne.

'Forgot his lines and froze to the spot,' explained Sir Bernard. 'I had no idea that it was so bad. Why didn't someone tell me?'

'What, tell tales to Management?' mocked Evans. 'He was bound to make a complete ass of himself and get caught out. All I had to do was wait. I mean,' he backtracked hastily, 'I've sung Sir Ruthven before, and you've run out of under-studies. And my understudy is Eric Parry and he's word-perfect. I've been rehearsing him a little bit, see, on the side.'

'In preparation for Copland's collapse and disgrace?' Sir Bernard eyed the actor narrowly. 'Mr Evans, you are incorrigible.'

'I am,' he agreed, smoothing one finger down the perfect cheek. 'Do I get the part?'

'Before you get the part, my boy, I'll play it myself,' said Sir Bernard in a tight whisper.

'Who'll play him, then?' asked Evans, really wanting to know.

'We'll do another show,' seethed Sir Bernard through his teeth.

'Wait a bit.' Phryne inserted a word into the promising quarrel. 'Mr Evans, you went to see Walter Copland. Did you see him eat or drink anything while you were there?'

'Yes, he was sipping at a concoction of lemon which that unpleasant dresser made for him. I didn't stay long,' said Gwilym, 'just dropped in to wish him the worst of luck. But Sir Bernard–' the beautiful hand touched the manager's sleeve – 'who will play Sir Ruthven?'

'Not you, Mr Evans. We may be rogues and vagabonds,' said Bernard, removing the hand, 'but we are not dishonourable and we will strive to be gentlemen.'

He strode out of the dressing room. Phryne looked back at Gwilym.

The wavy head drooped onto the graceful hand, as though the neck was too weak to support it. The blue eyes were screwed shut and the pale lip caught between the teeth to quell a sob. As Phryne watched, a tear dripped through the fingers. He was the essence of misery and it was clear that his heart was broken.

Phryne had no doubt that the emotion was quite genuine. She was also certain that it would not persist past the appearance of the next attractive female.

'That chap,' said Sir Bernard, biting into his

95

cigar as though it was a stick of liquorice, 'is an absolute bounder.'

'Then who is going to play Sir Ruthven?'

'Hanged if I know. It may have to be him, after all. It's too late to change the show now. But tomorrow we give *Pirates,* a little under-rehearsed perhaps, but I'm damned if an actor should begin to dictate to Management in this underhand way!'

'Would he have poisoned Walter Copland?'

'I wouldn't put anything past the chap. Phryne, what have you in mind?'

'That the next Sir Ruthven might be in danger, too.'

'Oh, Phryne darling, you don't mean it.' He began to laugh heartily, then stopped when he saw her expression. 'You do mean it. That's insane. You mean that we may have someone with a what-do-you-call-it – a monomania about *Ruddigore?*'

'It's possible, isn't it?'

'But – a monomania about G and S? If it was grand opera I could understand it, but comic opera?' He began to smile, and relit the battered cigar. 'But that solves the problem, doesn't it? I can't think of a fellow I would rather see poisoned. Nip back, Phryne dear, and tell Mr Gwilym Evans that he is to find a costume. He's going on as Robin/Sir Ruthven. I'll go and have a slip prepared for the programme. Back in a tick.'

Phryne returned to the dressing room where Gwilym still sat mourning in front of the mirror.

'Mr Evans? I've a message from the management.' He looked up, like a man reprieved from death.

'You're to go on as Sir Ruthven tonight. Sir

96

Bernard says to get fitted for a costume.'

She was not prepared for the dawning joy on the mobile face. He shone with an entirely authentic joy, caught up her hand, and kissed it. She felt his mouth open as he touched the palm, and shivered pleasantly.

'I won't forget this,' he promised, then ran past her towards Wardrobe. She heard him call on the stairs, 'Mrs Pomeroy, are you there? Mum dear, I need Sir Ruthven's costume.'

Fascinated, Phryne walked up to the costume department.

It was full of steam. A sweating girl was pressing what seemed like a hundred miles of frilly petticoats. A stately woman was stroking Gwilym's head as he knelt at her well shod feet with his face buried in her blue apron.

'Now, Mr Evans, don't take on. I'm sure we can manage, though I hope that there aren't any more accidents, my pattern is getting worn out. No, don't hug me, dear, I'm all stuck with pins. Sit down over there and Gladys will start the fitting. The smock's finished and the frock coat can be altered. Can I help you, Miss?'

'Mrs Pomeroy, is it?' Phryne held out her hand. 'I'm Phryne Fisher, I'm investigating the problems in the theatre.'

'Hope you can work it out, dear, it's been very unsettling. And costume work is unsettling enough. One moment, Miss. Joan, you finish those petticoats and then help Gladys with Mr Evans. Alice, can you deal with this,' she handed over three dresses with long rips in the hems. 'Those bridesmaids are as clump-footed a gaggle

97

as I've ever seen. Now, Miss, come in here.' She led Phryne into a cubicle at the far side of the wardrobe, hidden by dress baskets and racks of ironed clothes.

She was a small, bright-eyed woman, with dark hair in a neat bun, her well-made clothes covered by a large blue calico overall which was, indeed, stuck with threaded needles and pins, making her embrace perilous in the extreme.

'Well, I hope you can solve the problem. This company's getting very nervous. Actors are always nervous,' she said indulgently. 'Spats and tantrums and kiss-and-make-up like children. I feel like I'm running a nursery sometimes. Bad enough having Mr Evans in the cast, with all of them falling for him, and he's a wicked one.'

'Who has fallen for him?'

Mrs Pomeroy settled down to a cosy gossip. 'Half the chorus, along with Miss Wiltshire, Miss Esperance, of course, and even Miss Webb, who's usually level-headed enough. But he's not really bad, Miss Fisher, not evil. If he was a horse you would have to say he had no vice in him. He just can't help charming anything female that crosses his path. And he dearly wanted to play Sir Ruthven. Don't make the mistake of thinking their emotions are all put on. They're real people underneath, just exaggerated. They talk to me,' she observed, 'because I care for them. They call me Mum. They're quivering little things, under all that glamour. They're always afraid that no one really loves them, that they're going to fail. But they're addicted to applause. You can tell by the light in the eyes. Even that boy, that Herbert, he's got it.'

'What about Walter Copland?'

'Worse than any of them. Scared almost to death that he'd corpse. He used to stand in fittings and tremble. Miss Esperance could tell you about that. I was making up her change – the bride's costume – and she was talking to him about stage fright. She was carrying on something fierce about the Rose Maybud costume. The trouble with G and S is that it's under licence, so it has to be produced in exactly the same costumes and script and sets and music as the original. Fashions have changed since then. I was glad that she was talking to Mr Copland because it distracted her from how much she hated her smock. It does rather overcome her – she's best in tight-fitting clothes, she can wear those glove-satin or angelskin evening dresses that need hip-bones to wear, as you can, Miss Fisher – but Rose Maybud's got to look like a village maiden as Gilbert envisaged her.'

'Did you hear what they were saying?'

'Yes,' said Mrs Pomeroy, and shut her mouth tight.

'Well, what were they saying?' prompted Phryne.

'I don't like to listen to other people's conversations,' said the wardrobe mistress carefully, 'but I heard one bit and I was so surprised I nearly stuck a pin into Miss Webb. I haven't stuck a pin into anyone since I was an apprentice.'

'Well, what did you hear?'

'Mr Copland asked Miss Esperance to marry him.'

'Did he, by Jove! And what did she say?'

'She laughed.'

'Oh. Was there more?'

'He said he had a good bit put away and was retiring from the stage and going to live in Bendigo, or was it Ballarat? Some gold town, anyway. He said he couldn't stand the strain any more and he needed a wife who could manage a great house and servants and so on and wouldn't she think about it?'

'And?' said Phryne, agog.

'She said she'd think about it. Mr Copland wasn't very ... well, lovable. He was cool and aloof and I never heard a scrap of scandal attached to his name. But the fright had got to him. Mr Evans was counting the days until he got a go at Sir Ruthven. I only hope he can manage the part. It's often the way with things you want very dearly. When you get them you can't handle them.'

'What about this talk of a ghost, then? What do you think, Mrs Pomeroy?'

'There are no such things as ghosts. We've got someone playing tricks. Don't waste your time chasing after poor dead Dorothea, Dorothea's safe in her grave and her soul is in Heaven – I hope. You want someone who is alive and making mischief. And see if you can find them quickly. This company is on the verge of breaking down altogether. They are forgetting cues and losing pitch and Sir Bernard was lucky that it was a gala last night or the audience would have noticed how scrappy the production was. Even Mr Loveland-Hall is getting jumpy and he's normally the calmest of men. The technicals are grumbling more than usual and it's not pleasant to work here, though I usually like the Maj. Now, Miss Fisher, if you'll excuse me,' she said, and stood up.

'I'll come back, if I may,' said Phryne, and Mrs Pomeroy patted her briskly.

'You do that, dear,' she said, and went into the racks as a female voice summoned her to alter the set of a frock coat.

Phryne walked out of Wardrobe and down the stairs. Someone was sitting on the top step and she almost fell over them.

'Miss Wiltshire?' she asked, recognising Mad Margaret. The actress was already arrayed in a tasteful collection of weeds and the face which turned up to Phryne was frenzied enough. 'Why are you waiting here?'

'Because he went into Wardrobe,' she snarled, 'and when he comes out I'm going to kill him.' Phryne grabbed her left wrist in a strong grip.

'No, you're not,' said Phryne, twisting until the knife fell into her other hand. 'You're coming back to your dressing room and having a nice cup of tea and brandy. And then you are going to talk to me about ghosts and laudanum and green whisky.'

'I am?' asked Miss Wiltshire, coming quietly.

'You are.'

CHAPTER SIX

In bygone days I had thy love—
Thou hadst my heart.

Gilbert and Sullivan
Ruddigore

Phryne hustled Miss Wiltshire down the yellow corridor and into her own room. It was empty of people and crammed with costumes, clothes baskets, a mirror stuck all around with telegrams and a dressing table ranked with cosmetics. It smelt of cigarette smoke so Phryne lit a gasper for the actress and took one herself.

'Sit down,' she ordered. 'I gather that you are in love with that scoundrel of a Welshman as well?'

'Yes,' Mad Margaret heaved a shuddering sigh. 'Yes. I know he's a rogue. Totally untrustworthy.'

'Part of his charm,' said Phryne authoritatively. 'He has a dangerous feel to him, like skiing on the edge of a ridge or driving too fast in a big car. Exhilarating but very wearing on the emotions. The only thing to do with scoundrels is to enjoy them while you have them and try not to regret them when they've gone. Who is his current amour, then?'

'Leila. Or maybe Mollie. But he thinks that Leila can advance his career, which is true – she is able to influence the choice of her leading man.'

Miss Wiltshire threw back the mane of chestnut hair and laughed bitterly. 'He swore that he loved me. And he lied.'

'Love-lonely?' quoted Phryne. 'Oh, my dear, don't waste your time. Plenty of pretty men, Miss Wiltshire. Some even prettier than Gwilym Evans, who would not be improved by a steak-knife in the heart.'

'He hasn't got one. A heart, I mean. I think that you had better call me Violet,' said the actress, heaving a sigh which seemed to come from her bare feet. 'You're right, of course. I ought to thank you for interfering. I'll be able to do that in a little while.'

'I don't want thanks, I want information.' Phryne sat down on a stool, moving aside some hanging weeds. A thin woman in a brown apron bustled in.

'Make us some tea, Kit,' said Miss Wilshire dully. 'This is Miss Fisher.'

Kitty Collins sniffed and busied herself with a spirit stove and a kettle.

'Did you know that Walter Copland was drinking?'

'Yes. Not my business. Gwil ... Gwil said that he was waiting for him to make a hash of Sir Ruthven and was sure that he would get the part.'

'He has got the part – for tonight, anyway.'

'He always gets what he wants,' she said with a brief spurt of anger.

'He will always get everything that he wants and never get the one thing which he really desires – that's how it works with bounders,' observed Phryne. 'I speak from experience. A life of misery

103

and frustration will be his. I've known a lot of Gwilyms.'

The first sign of independent thought crossed Miss Wiltshire's ravaged face.

'Yes, I think you have. The nicest thing I've heard in ages. Yes. Everything that he wants and not the one thing that he really desires. Very comforting. I'm glad I didn't kill him.'

Kitty made a shocked noise and produced two cups of tea spiked heavily with brandy. 'There, you drink that, Miss Violet, and you'll feel better,' she instructed. Phryne sipped. It was three quarters brandy with a little tea added and she put the cup carefully back into the saucer.

'You'll see,' Phryne promised, watching the actress recover her poise. Miss Wiltshire was actually very striking, with a strong bony face, high cheekbones, brown expressive eyes and a mass of curly brown hair. Properly dressed, Phryne reflected, she would be not pretty – she could never be pretty – but *jolie laide*. Paris, for instance, would find her intriguing.

'Mad Margaret is not the best of parts for me at the moment,' said Violet. 'I'm already miserable and she has that sad song about the violet under the bush and the lover gathering only roses. I'll be better as Ruth the piratical maid of all work or Little Buttercup the bumboat woman or as Katisha. In fact, I'm going to have a lot of fun with Katisha. "There is beauty in the bellow of the blast, there is grandeur in the howling of the gale,"' she sang softly. 'Gilbert really despised older women, you know – all his older women are ridiculous. But Sullivan was sorry for them, perhaps because he had a mistress who was older than him, so he gave them beautiful music in which to sing their degradation. That's what makes the elderly lady parts so sought-after. I'm alternating with Agnes in them.'

'Is that usual?'

'No, but we're good at different things – she has a better voice than me, I can sing patter better than she can – so the audience gets us both.' Kitty sniffed again.

'Now, what about the ghost and all the odd things? Tell me what you can. I want to solve this, preferably before the admirable Jack Robinson gets his paws on anything ... er ... combustible.'

'I don't believe in ghosts,' said Miss Wiltshire flatly. 'But someone is playing tricks and it seems to be aimed at Leila and at Selwyn Alexander. I especially don't believe in ghosts who write notes,' she added. 'Someone brought Gwil and Dupont to Leila's room together, and there was a filthy row. Someone is certainly nicking Leila's gloves, and someone is leaving things in Selwyn's room.'

'Any idea who?'

'Look, theatres are emotional places – that's our trade, emotions. The poisoning could have been done by anyone. Could be an ambitious member of the chorus wanting to move up. Could be me or Mollie or anyone attached to that bounder Gwil – could be Gwil himself, it's suspicious that both Sir Ruthven himself and his understudy were removed. As to the gloves and the other things – malicious mischief, trying to scare us? It's working. We're scared enough. Those who aren't scared of ghosts are scared that someone could hate us enough to play all these tricks to make us scared. Selwyn's terrified of the supernatural. He's been to a medium who says that ... well, you can talk to him about it. Load of rubbish.'

'What is he like?'

'Nice enough. Getting old and terrified of it. No money and a poverty-stricken old age staring him in the face. Have you met Tom Deeping, the doorkeeper?'

'Yes.'

'He's our nightmare. We all fear that we'll end up keeping a boarding house, fat and slopping around in down-at-the-heel slippers or muffled in a great-coat complaining about our bronicals and dreaming of the good old days. The theatre demands youth – there aren't many parts for character actors and not many stay on after their bloom has faded.' She stood up and quickly sketched an old woman, cigarette in mouth, leaning back to counterbalance her bulk, wrapping a greasy kimono round her waist and opening a boarding house door. It was both comic and bitter. 'Thirty shillings a week, dear, and no gentleman callers in the rooms, I run a nice respectable 'ouse.'

She sat down again and the old woman vanished. 'Well, that's fate. Poor Selwyn isn't old yet, of course, but Gwil shows him up. Gwil's young. And of course Selwyn, the silly fellow, had to go and fall for Leila, who has a heart of pure platinum. Have you talked to her yet?'

'No. I was on my way there when...'

'You fell over Murderous Meg on the steps,' she laughed. 'Well, you'll see. But she's a good actress,'

106

she added, lighting another gasper. 'Nothing wrong with her craft, drat her. Thanks, Miss Fisher. I'll be all right now. Excuse me, I have to put on my slap and go out and be Mad Margaret again.'

Phryne took her leave and knocked on the next door.

Selwyn Alexander was sitting in the chair in front of the mirror, muffled in a towel, while the short fat dresser combed what was evidently black dye through his thinning hair. Phryne perched on the edge of the table and the dresser glared at her.

'Finished in a moment,' he snapped at her. 'Can't you wait outside, Miss?'

'No, I need to talk about ghosts and poisonings and a lot of other interesting things before the cops come back.'

'Miss Fisher!' Selwyn's face appeared through the towel. 'Get on with it, Bradford,' he snapped. 'Talk to me, Miss Fisher. What do you want to know?'

'Did you know that Walter was drinking?'

'Oh, dear, someone told you, did they?' She could not see the actor's face but the voice was full of regret. 'Poor Walter. He hit the bottle a few years ago and then dried out. I thought he was still on the wagon until I caught him in the wings with a little flask. It can happen to anyone,' he said plaintively, as the dresser rubbed his hair with the towel and whisked it away, then stood behind him to comb the glossy hair over the bald patch. 'He was never drunk – not on stage, not even when he was at his worst. The Management can fire you instantly if you're drunk on stage. But he was scared – he had the worst stage fright I've ever seen. He was getting on and his powers were deserting him, but he still had magnificent presence. He was a better Sir Ruthven than Gwil Evans will ever be,' he added through his teeth.

'What happened to the bottle?' asked Phryne. 'It wasn't on him when the police searched him, and it wasn't in his costume.'

'I don't know. Let's see, the whole chorus was on stage when he collapsed, everyone is at the end of the act. The wings are always full of people coming and going – stage crew and technicals and dressers and actors.'

'And what do you think about the ghost?'

Selwyn's countenance, which had been pale, bleached.

'She's here. I've seen her. She seems to be singling me out for attention.' He laid his long artistic fingers flat on the dressing table to still their trembling. 'I don't know if she was behind the poisoning, I can't imagine why, but she's been taking Leila's gloves and I've seen her – Charles and I both saw her. Eh, Charles?'

'If you say so, Sel,' agreed the dresser. Phryne looked at him. His hands were deft as they arranged the hair and pinned it. He was short and paunchy and had some stiffness in his left side and arm. His face was round and his eyes blue and the remains of what had been fine blond hair were cut very short, like a tonsure around a shining scalp. His mouth was pursed in a scowl.

'Dammit, man, you saw her! A week ago, when we were rehearsing *Ruddigore*. In the corridor – at

108

the end of the corridor nearest the stage, Miss Fisher. A woman in costume, and the scent of hyacinths so strong it almost knocked us over. Black eyes, she had, angry black eyes.'

'What do you think she wants?'

'I went to a spiritualist. I don't think that one can ignore these things. If she's come back after thirty years then she must have a reason.'

'What did the medium say?' asked Phryne, watching the dresser who was exuding disapproval from every pore.

'She said to come back next week – that is, to-morrow. Will you come, too? No one else believes in these things and I'm sure that there are mysteries beyond the veil which are hidden from us. Bradford thinks I'm mad. He now says he didn't see anything. But I saw him when she appeared. He was as white as a sheet and shook like a willow. Didn't you, Bradford, eh?'

Selwyn was suddenly the dominant melodrama villain. His moustache bristled and his voice had dropped half an octave. Even though Bradford must have been used to these demonstrations of acting, he backed a pace.

'I saw a bright light and got a shock,' he muttered. 'And the rest is your imagination, Mr Alexander.'

'Oh, to hell with you,' snarled Selwyn Alexander. 'Get out! Out!'

He drove the small man out of the dressing room and slammed the door.

'What about Miss Esperance, then?' asked Phryne quietly. Selwyn Alexander flushed brickred.

'I won't have her brought into this. I like your impudence!'

'I like it too, it's my best asset,' said Phryne, not at all abashed. 'Do resume your seat, you are dripping hair dye on your dressing gown. Now, would you like to talk to me or the cops?'

Mr Alexander coughed in outrage and then began to laugh. 'You are a remarkable young woman. All right. What about Miss Esperance? I ... want to marry her.'

'And?'

'She hasn't made up her mind yet,' he said wretchedly. 'There's me and that bounder Evans and Dupont the chorus master with his French accent and frankly, Miss Fisher, I don't give much for my chances.'

'Do you want her that much?'

'Oh yes, she is utterly beautiful. Utterly. And she threw herself into my arms the other night when she could have had Gwil. That's a hopeful sign. I don't know how Evans works on all the women. To me he seems transparently a scoundrel.'

'He is, transparently. Therein lies his attraction,' said Phryne.

'Oh, not you, too!'

'No, not me. I admire his talent, that's all.' Selwyn Alexander barked a scornful laugh. 'Being a scoundrel is a talent,' Phryne explained. 'I'll join you tomorrow and we'll see what the spirit world has to say.'

'Oh, Miss Fisher...' Selwyn stumbled over the words. 'Miss Fisher, you don't need to tell anyone, do you?'

'About what?'

'About the crowning glory,' his mouth quirked.

Phryne promised on her honour not to tell anyone that he dyed his hair, and went out.

It was getting late. Not enough time for the chorus, but they could wait until tomorrow. Just time for a word with Agnes Gault and Mollie Webb if she was quick. Then she had to catch, somehow, the chorus master, Mr Franklin, who played Old Adam, and, of course, the much feted Leila Esperance.

She was spared the labour of choosing when an elderly woman shot out of a dressing room with a star on the door and grabbed her by the arm.

'Miss Fisher, do see if you can talk to her. She's working up to a fit of hysterics and she has to go on in an hour. I'm Mrs Black, her dresser. She won't put on her costume and she's refusing to make-up. Come along, dear, do.'

Phryne went where she was pushed and came into a large dressing room, festooned with telegrams and mascots and garlanded with flowers. It smelt like a hothouse. Roses appeared to be Miss Esperance's favourite tributes.

'Here's Miss Fisher, dear, now control yourself,' ordered the elderly woman. 'You talk to her, Miss,' she added to Phryne.

Miss Esperance was slumped whimpering over the table, her hair trailing down and hiding her face. Phryne observed that Rose Maybud's sunbonnet was screwed into a ball in one corner, where it had evidently been thrown. She touched the actress on the shoulder and she shrugged away from under Phryne's hand.

'Sit up,' said Phryne in a sub-zero voice. 'I

111

know that you are feeling persecuted but you will not impress me with tantrums and you will damage your performance.'

This brought Leila up with a jerk and Phryne looked at her. She was indeed utterly beautiful.

It was a beauty bred in the bones. Her face was heart-shaped, her complexion, bare of makeup, was mingled milk and roses. Her eyes were as brown as topaz, her mouth a soft pink cupid's bow, her throat and bared bosom smooth and sculptural. She put up a perfectly formed hand and shoved her black hair back from her unmarked forehead.

'I always give a good performance,' said Leila petulantly. 'Don't I, Ursula? Always.'

'Yes, dear, you do. Now take a deep breath and I'll brew some of that coffee you like while you talk to Miss Fisher. She'll sort it all out.'

'Tell me about Walter Copland,' said Phryne, feeling uncharacteristically plain. 'Have a gasper.'

Leila accepted a cigarette, saying, 'I shouldn't, they're bad for the voice,' and fitted it into a long holder. There was grace in her every movement and Phryne had to admire her. She was as liquid and smooth as a black cat.

'Walter? He wanted to marry me. They all want to marry me, except Gwil. Gwil hasn't got marriage in mind.' She preened briefly.

'And have you decided?'

'Me? Marry? Copland was a has-been, Gwil is a rotter, Selwyn is on his way out and Dupont wants to keep me in a cage. I don't want any of them. But it has been diverting.'

'Yes, you have offended or slighted almost

everyone in the cast. All the women in love with Mr Evans are heartbroken and Selwyn Alexander is a nervous wreck and Walter Copland is dead. Robbie Craven is still in hospital with opiate poisoning. Do you find spreading ruin and destruction amusing? Was it you, perhaps, who brought Dupont and Evans to your dressing room at the same time? You would have found a fight for your affections diverting.'

'If I had done that I would have been there to watch,' Leila giggled. 'I always liked fairy stories where the princess sends the suitors out on quests. That would have been fun.'

'Yes, I suppose so,' said Phryne, disliking the actress quite profoundly. 'And then they could all have got killed fighting dragons and climbing glass mountains and you could have started again with a new set.'

'You don't like me,' said Leila Esperance in a wondering tone. 'Do you?'

'What gives you that idea?' asked Phryne. 'Now, talk to me. Did you know that Walter was drinking? You said he had no smell of booze on him.'

'Yes, but I didn't want to ruin his reputation. He was alive then. Actually, he stank of brandy – positively stank. And had been for a week, I hated getting close to him. Poor Walter. It's a testing part and he was getting on. Sir B's production is all movement and he runs us ragged.'

'And you didn't see what he did with the bottle?'

'I think he gave it...' she caught her lip between white teeth. 'No, I didn't see what he did with it, but he must have had one. He might have given

113

it to Hans, that creepy dresser of his. How he hates me, to be sure!' she said complacently. 'He glared at me as if I was going to kidnap Walter and sell him to the white slavers. Hans was in the wings with a towel and powder and some water, all the usual things. Walter used to sweat like a pig under the lights. Hans probably has it.'

'And what about the other things? The gloves, the missing bag, the ghost?'

'I'm afraid that it is her, Dorothea Curtis. She played Rose Maybud first, you know. And Sir B says she looked like me. She's come back, she's haunting us. I've seen her.' Miss Esperance began to shudder as though she had been dipped in cold water. 'I saw her at the end of the corridor, at the stage entrance. She's smaller than me, but she had Rose's costume on, the bride's dress from the last act, shining white and her hair was curling all down her back. She does look like me, you know. She was famous in her day.'

'Why has she come back?' asked Phryne quietly.

Leila shook her head violently and gasped, 'She's envious of me. I'm playing her part, wearing her clothes. She wants to take me over. She wants to possess me.'

Phryne detected real fear. The young woman's hands were clenched in the soft hair and she was tugging it with force enough to hurt. Her movements were still graceful but that was nature, not art.

'No,' said Phryne decisively. 'I don't believe it. I've just been reading about ghosts. They are phantasms – that's what the Society for Psychical

Research calls them – and they are re-enacting past events or they come to reveal something important. Ghosts can't possess the living,' she stated with conviction, suppressing her memory of various case histories when that had been what they seemed to be trying to do. 'Even if it is Dorothea Curtis come back from the dead she can't harm you, Miss Esperance.'

'Are you sure?' Phryne could not see the face under the shadowing hair but the voice was a child's, desperate to be told that she was safe in her bed.

'Yes, I'm perfectly sure.'

Mrs Black brought a cup of inky coffee and said bracingly, 'Time to get dressed, Leila.'

Unexpectedly, Leila Esperance embraced Phryne, pressing her soft flower-scented cheek against her neck. 'Thank you,' she murmured. 'I trust you.'

Phryne, a little shaken, released herself, muttered something about another appointment and found her way into the corridor again. Interesting. The ghost had appeared as Rose Maybud both as maiden and as the last-act bride.

'Miss Gault, do you have a moment?' she called into the next room, where Agnes Gault and Mollie Webb dressed.

'Yes, do come in. How is the investigation going? Sit down, do, I've got to draw on Dame Hannah's lines.' Miss Gault was solid, plump, and had a merry face which she was presently transforming into an old woman's as she talked. 'I tell you, dear, I've been in theatre since I was a tot – first appearance as a babe in the woods at

115

the age of three – and I've never known such a blighted season as this.'

'What's the cause of it?' asked Phryne, watching as the actress smiled and frowned and sketched in the resultant wrinkles with eyebrow pencil.

'Combination of factors. There's having Leila and Gwil in the same cast. Leila breaks hearts for fun and Gwil does the same, so that's the men and the women accounted for. Gwil's not cold like Leila, though. He's like the defendant in *Trial By Jury*.' She began to hum and then to sing:

But joy incessant palls the sense
And love unchanged will cloy.
And she became a bore intense
Unto her love-sick boy.
With fitful glimmer burned my flame
And I grew cold and coy.
At last one morning I became
Another's love sick boy.

'That's Gwil. No harm in him but as self-centred as a gyroscope. People will keep falling for him and then when he's tired of them he is surprised that they just don't go away and find another lover like he does. Leila is cold – she doesn't understand love. And she finds that being so very beautiful, people just do as she wants. Whole world's a sideshow to Leila. Then there's this theatre, which is ill-maintained and hard to work in, as cold as charity in the winter and boiling in summer. There's the orchestra leader quarrelling with Dupont the chorus master who is French

116

and dispassionate, and in love with Leila as well. Then there's this ghost thing. Actors are very superstitious. That's what's pushed us over the edge.'

'Have you seen her?'

'I saw something. Just a light and a scent.' An old woman's mask turned to Phryne and Miss Gault's nervous smile appeared ghastly. 'Hyacinths. A pale shape. At the stage entrance. I haven't mentioned it to anyone. I'd be obliged if you wouldn't, either. Hello, Mollie,' she said as someone came in. 'Just in time.'

'Miss Fisher, I'm glad you're here. Hello, Agnes.' Mollie Webb began to shed her outer clothes. 'It's starting to rain again. Where's Jill?'

'Miss Webb,' said a funereal voice. Jill Collins, sister of Kitty, came in and wrapped Miss Webb's shoulders in a towel. 'Sit still now, you're late. Where have you been?'

'Been to see Robbie. He's getting better but he still can't talk. The cops have got a policeman sitting by his bed. Poor Robbie, he looks awful. I saw that nice Dr Fielding there, too. I'm having supper with him tonight.'

'Oh, are you?' teased Agnes Gault. 'Getting tired of the stage, are you, Nurse Webb?'

'Pretty tired,' admitted Mollie, taking the question seriously. 'I'm never going to get much more than this kind of part and I'm twenty-five. Time to think about settling down. And he needs someone who can help him in his practice. He's starting out on his own next month.'

Phryne felt a completely unexpected pang at the idea of so finally losing Mark Fielding, mentally

117

slapped herself on the wrist, and commented with more warmth than she intended, 'I think you'd be ideal.'

'That's right, you know Dr Fielding, don't you, Miss Fisher? Do you really think I'd be all right?'

'Perfect for the part,' said Phryne. Mollie beamed at her.

'How's the investigation going?'

'So so. I'm still collecting information. Have you seen the ghost?'

'There are no such things as ghosts.'

'Well, who do you think is playing tricks?'

'I'd say it was one of Leila's suitors – probably a rejected one. The place is littered with them. Or Gwil's. He's had a brief fling with two of the chorus, Melly and Marie-Claire, silly girls. Now he's laying seige to Leila, he's cast aside poor Violet like a soiled glove and...' She drew a breath, patted her hands together, bit her lip and said in a strong voice, 'And me. I really thought he loved me, I really did, even though I knew he was a bounder and a cad and a rotter and all that. But he only loves himself. So I might have done it all, Miss Fisher, except that it wouldn't be poor harmless unpleasant Walter who died, but Mr Bloody Gwilym Evans.'

'But he is alive and well and playing Sir Ruthven and Walter Copland is dead,' Phryne pointed out. 'Therefore unless something went horribly wrong, you didn't do it.'

'No, I didn't.' Mollie stood still as Jill Collins lowered the bridesmaid's dress over her head. 'And at least I don't have to dance off with him at the end tonight, exuding delight. I get Eric

118

Parry, who is quite ordinary, can sing and dance like nobody's business and is, bless him, quite devoid of charm.'

Herbert could be heard in the corridor: 'Overture and beginners five minutes, ladies and gentlemen,' he announced. 'Five minutes.'

In a whisk of skirts, the room emptied.

'Miss Collins?' asked Phryne. The woman bent on her a desiccated face to match her dry voice.

'I hope you catch her,' she commented.

'Catch who?'

'The trickster. It's not my ladies.'

'Who is it, then?'

'All that pinching of things and leaving them in the wrong place. I used to be a teacher, I've seen girls like her, sly smile and quick fingers. They steal things and play tricks just out of mischief. She's the spitting image of a girl at my last school. Found with three purses and eleven ribbons, stolen just for the thrill. She'll be behind it, mark my words, just to make herself important.'

'Who?' asked Phryne as she heard the overture begin.

'Why, her,' spat Miss Collins. 'The star of the show, but that's not enough for her – Miss Leila Esperance.'

CHAPTER SEVEN

It is absolutely essential to the success of this piece that it should be played with the most perfect earnestness and gravity throughout... Directly the actors show that they are conscious of the absurdity of their utterances the piece begins to drag.

W. S. Gilbert
Notes to the Engaged (Actors)

Phryne heard an argument in the manager's room, and waited outside. A loud coarse voice was protesting, 'I tell you, sir, it's the carpenter, Brawn. He looked shifty to me.'

'Oh, did he?' said John 'Alias' Smith caustically. 'Who gave you divine intuition, eh? Give you some lip, did he, Billy? Is that why you hit him?'

'He swung a clenched fist at me,' began a sing-song recital, which Alias cut off abruptly.

'I've heard that far too many times in your career, Constable Naylor. Remarkable number of people attack you, and then you just have to beat them to a pulp to protect yourself. I've seen that carpenter. Big bloke, but not as big as you. What did he do? Fail to appreciate the majesty of the law?'

'He was unable to account to my satisfaction for his movements on the night in question,' replied the constable stiffly.

Sir Bernard and a man in overalls, holding a paint-stained cloth to his face, came up beside Phryne and she hushed them.

'Look at your miserable career, Naylor. Chucked out of one station after another for excessive violence. On suspension for that bloke you almost killed when you thought he was a tea-leaf and he turned out to be a perfectly honest, bona fide innocent bystander – one of the few in Melbourne. If only you confined your homicidal actions to the ones who were really guilty it wouldn't matter so much. But you sniff out the one person who hasn't got anything to do with the crime and use him as a punching-bag.'

'I get confessions,' said the loud voice.

'Oh, yes. You get confessions all right. Useless ones. False ones. Ones where your commanding officer has to stand in court and listen to silver-tail lawyers tearing them to confetti. "And was the accused injured at that time? Why is his name scrawled in this uncertain way at the bottom of this bloodstained document? Did he have all his fingers when he signed this?"' The mockery of a barrister's public-school accent was merciless. 'I'll give you one last chance, Naylor. If you do this again, I'll bounce you out of the force so fast your arse won't graze the steps of Russell Street. Is that clear?'

'Clear,' muttered Constable Naylor. 'Sir.'

'Good. Now get your notebook out. Jack Robinson'll be here in a moment, and the theatre manager, I expect, who'll be hot-footing it up here to complain about you belting his employee. And what Jack'll say I don't care to think. He

121

can't stand strong-arm tactics.'

By this time, the said Detective Inspector Robinson had joined the crowd at the door. He looked very disturbed.

Robinson opened the door and ushered Phryne, the injured man and Sir Bernard inside. Constable Naylor leapt to his feet. His face was quite blank.

'Been up to your old tricks, Naylor?' observed the detective inspector unpleasantly. 'I recognise your mark. Sit down, Mr Brawn. We'll get a doctor to look at your face.'

'I think me nose's broken,' said the battered carpenter. 'He hit me!'

Sir Bernard was indignant. 'I must protest, Detective Inspector!'

'Yes, yes, Sir Bernard, we can only apologise for our over-zealous officer.' Phryne was rather impressed by Jack Robinson's defence of Naylor, though she considered it unwise.

'Naylor, tell me what happened.'

'Sir. I was asking Mr Brawn where he was last night. He said, "Here, where do you think?" He was fixing some apparatus and I told him to stop hammering and listen to me. He did so. I said, "Did you know Walter Copland and Robert Craven?" He said, "Of course." I said, "Did you see either of them eat or drink anything?" and he said, "No, I was behind the scene trying to prop up the Ruddigore castle." I said, "Did you see anyone give either of them anything to eat or drink?" and he said, "No, look, I've got to get this fixed." I said, "Listen to me and answer my questions," and he said, "Go away you stupid cop," and swung a clenched fist at me. In order to defend myself, I pushed his arm away, inadvertently striking him in the region of the nose.'

'That's not what happened!' exclaimed the carpenter. 'He accused me of working in the theatre only because of all the pretty girls. He asked me if I ... if they...' The carpenter paused and wiped his bleeding nose. 'I'm a married man with two little daughters! I never heard such a suggestion!'

'Did you try and hit the constable?'

'Me? Look at the size of him!' Phryne and Sir Bernard considered the six foot four, eighteen stone bulwark of the constable and nodded. 'I was wild enough, but I don't go round picking fights with blokes like him.'

'Did you make that suggestion, Constable?' asked Robinson with deceptive mildness. Constable Naylor looked at his commanding officer and visibly weighed up his chances of evasion, estimated them at nil, and threw in the towel.

'I might have, sir, just to get a reaction.'

'Well, you got your reaction. Right. If you'll take a seat in one of the rooms, Mr Brawn, the doctor will come and look at your face. Sergeant, see him settled, will you, and get, oh blimey, not the police surgeon again. See if you can get that nice Dr Fielding to come out. Constable Naylor will pay his fee. You're dismissed, Naylor, go down and talk very nicely to the stage doorkeeper, he's the only one we haven't spoken to, and if you lay a finger on him I'll see you shot at dawn. Now, Sir Bernard, Miss Fisher, let's have a nice chat.'

'Hello, Jack dear. What an interesting evening we are having, to be sure.' Sir Bernard took the stopper out of his crystal decanter. He stared into

123

the contents with deep suspicion, then poured out two glasses of the good whisky.

'What have we got, then?' asked Robinson.

'I think we have the container for the drug.' Phryne pointed to a sugar bag in the corner of the office – Herbert had fulfilled his trust. 'Walter Copland was drinking heavily and he always carried a flat flask of brandy or rum with him. Miss Esperance now says that he was reeking of spirit and his dresser and several other people say that he was afflicted with crippling stage fright. What was in the indigestion tablets?'

'Chalk and bismuth. The report says that both men were given heavy doses of laudanum, which is an alcoholic tincture of opium with a strong sweetish taste. The medical examiner says that it can be concealed in something like port or brandy but not in tea or water. He found no injection sites. I've got the post-mortem on Copland, by the way.'

'Anything surprising?'

'Not really. Weak heart, that's why he died. And he was an alcoholic. Liver like a hobnailed boot.'

'Good. That confirms my information. I'm told that he took a cure and dried out but just recently he fell off the wagon with a resounding crash and has been soused ever since, though it never affected his performance.' Phryne glanced aside at Sir Bernard, who nodded. 'He always carried a little bottle with him, but he must have either hidden it on the stage or given it to someone. My best bet is Hans, his dresser – he was waiting in the wings for Copland to repair his makeup. The poor little man is heartbroken about Copland's death, Jack.'

'Why?' asked the detective inspector. 'He was just a servant, wasn't he?'

'He was his dresser for twenty years. An actor's relationship with his dresser is closer than a brother, it's intimate.' Sir Bernard sensed that he was not getting through, and elaborated, 'The dresser encourages, consoles, hears lines, and of course dresses the actor and makes up his face. Some of the most famous actors and actresses have the same dresser for their whole career. They are mother and father and friend all in one, in the closest professional sense.'

'Like a nanny?' asked Robinson. 'Or a ladies' maid?'

'Approximately,' Sir Bernard gave up. 'I agree with Phryne. Hans was getting rid of all the bottles when we went to see him. He would not want Mr Copland's reputation injured.'

'All right, we'll have the bottles tested and then we'll talk to Hans again. What else, Miss Fisher?'

'Well, we should see if Mr Copland left a will. He sounds like a man of property. He proposed to Miss Esperance and said he had a house in Bendigo, which Hans confirms.'

Jack Robinson made a note.

'I haven't talked to them about Robbie Craven yet, but no one seems to have even noticed him. He was Walter Copland's understudy but he was basically in the chorus and I haven't questioned them yet. As to the rest, Mr Evans might have done it because he was desperate to play Robin/ Sir Ruthven. He knew that Mr Copland was an alcoholic.' Sir Bernard stirred and muttered something about bounders. 'Robbie Craven might have done it to get the part, but something must have gone very wrong if he got a dose as well. Have you talked to him yet, Jack?'

'No, they say I can see him tomorrow.'

'Well, then, he should be able to say who gave him the bottle or the pill or whatever. As for the others, Mollie Webb, Violet Wiltshire and two girls from the chorus are in love with Mr Evans, which hardly seems germane to the poisoning but is of general interest. Mr Evans, Selwyn Alexander and Mr Copland, plus the chorus master Monsieur Dupont, are in love with Miss Esperance, who does not seem to care for any of them but who plays them off against each other for amusement. Between Gwilym Evans and Leila Esperance the cast are kept in a fine state of emotional ferment, which is, as you know, productive of those gestures which make the world so uncomfortable. A dresser told me that the tricks were being played by Miss Esperance, though she has no proof. But Miss Esperance probably didn't play the trick which brought Dupont and Evans to blows outside her door because she wasn't there to watch it. She might have stolen her own gloves, torn up her own telegram and planted it in the chorus's room, and she might have stolen the bag and planted it on Selwyn, though I can't imagine why.'

'But she can't have doped my whisky – what was that, anyway, Detective Inspector? – because she was on stage at the time and so were all the others.'

'Green food colouring, quite harmless,' said the detective inspector.

'Anyway, she's seen the ghost. And I would swear that she was frightened of it. Quite childishly and unaffectedly frightened.'

'What about the ghost, Miss Fisher? I'm assuming it's another trick, of course.'

'Everyone who has seen it says it is Rose Maybud. Although his dresser now denies that he saw anything, Mr Alexander saw her in her maiden's costume, at the entrance to the stage. Miss Esperance saw her in the same place, in bride's costume. Miss Gault didn't see a figure, just "a light and a scent" – the scent, of course, of hyacinths.'

'And do you think it is Dorothea Curtis, back from the dead?'

'No,' said Phryne. 'No, well, I don't think so. But I'm going to a medium tomorrow with Mr Alexander.'

'Why?'

'Why not?' Phryne smiled enigmatically, smoothed down her velvet top, and refused to explain further. Robinson refrained from comment and opened his notebook. 'Well, this is what I've got. I spoke to Mr West, the stage electrician – they call them "technicals". He explained how the lighting worked, most ingenious. He says that he saw nothing but he's in the lighting box and wouldn't notice anything short of a grenade. Unfortunately I sent Naylor to talk to Mr Brawn the carpenter and he got nothing out of him before the regrettable incident.'

'Why haven't you got rid of that bruiser, Jack?' asked Phryne.

'What can I do with him? If I let him out on the street he'll be inside in a month for manslaughter. Best to keep him under discipline.'

'Get him to join the army,' suggested Phryne.

'Army discipline is stricter than the police. He'd spend all his time in an army jail and that's not a fate I would wish on anyone.'

'But he hit one of my staff!' protested Sir Bernard.

'Yes, I know he did. I'll think of something,' sighed Robinson. 'What else? Ah, yes. I talked to the stage manager, Mr Loveland-Hall. He says that he saw Mr Copland drinking from a small bottle as he stood in the prompt corner, ready to go on. He did not think it his business to comment because the drinking never affected Mr Copland's performance. To the best of his recollection, Mr Copland gave the bottle to someone standing beside him in the wings.'

'Who?'

'He didn't see. There was a crowd of people there – the bucks and blades, he says, and the sailor Dick Dauntless.'

'Gwilym Evans,' said Phryne.

'Surely even Gwil would not be so stupid!' protested Sir Bernard.

'He wanted to play the lead very badly,' Phryne reminded the manager. 'And he is a Celt, you know.'

'But he was willing to wait until the booze caught up with Walter. You talked to him, Phryne darling. He's a rotter but I can't believe he would poison anyone.'

'Where do you get laudanum?' asked Phryne.

'It's a scheduled drug under the Poisons Act,' said Robinson, who had looked it up. 'It's not often used these days, being addictive, and mostly replaced by morphine and cocaine as a pain killer, or so that nice Dr Fielding tells me. You can get it from a chemist but you have to sign for it. Old people still use it for headaches and the like. I'm sending Naylor to search the Poisons Register in every chemist in the city and then, if we don't find it, in Carlton. That's where most of the company are staying. That will, with any luck, keep Constable Naylor out of mischief.' He smiled grimly. 'Anything I can do for you, Miss Fisher?'

'No, Jack, I don't think so. I've got a lot of ideas but not one provable fact so far. See if the bottle is in that sack, and test it for fingerprints. I want to know who handled the one with the poison.'

'So do I. What are you working on?'

'The murder of Dorothea Curtis, among other things.'

Bernard leapt to his feet. 'What?'

'Look at the story you told, Bernard dear. Analyse it. You described Dorothea as beautiful, heartless and vain. Didn't you? A proud beauty with great talent and a sordid background. Even if Dot Mobbs had a heart to start with, she couldn't have got to be principal singer with the Savoy company unless she had abandoned it pretty early. Everyone exploits the poor. If she had been prone to falling in love she would have been a dolly-mop in a bloodtub theatre, bearing a child a year, going downhill until she was singing in the street. Eh? Isn't that what happened to the girls with hearts of gold in the good old days?'

'Yes, well, yes, I suppose so,' muttered Sir

Bernard, shocked by Phryne's plain speech.

'So. To get to that eminence in her career she must have fought off or indulged innumerable managers – sorry, Bernard – and used her beauty like a weapon. Yes?'

'Yes, though not the Savoy, Any manager who tried that in the Savoy would have been instantly flung into the street. Mr Gilbert was very particular.'

'All right, but earlier. She went through how many companies before the Savoy noticed her?'

'Three at least. She seldom talked about those days. But I know she was on the music hall when she was seventeen, and she used to sing in pubs before that.'

'Right. So your Dorothea had a heart of stainless steel. You said that she agreed to marry you.'

'Yes, Phryne, but I didn't come! Sheffield burned the note!'

'That sort of woman would never die of despair, Bernard,' said Phryne gently. 'Dorothea might sit all night waiting in order to perfect her rage and plot revenge. She would not kill herself. She might kill you,' she added, 'but Dorothea had made herself and would not mar her own creation. She would know that all she had to do was to let go of her standards and she'd be in the street in six months. It's different now. I come from those same origins but I had a choice. Dorothea had no choice. She had to keep going up or crash. Do you agree?'

'Yes, yes, I agree.' Sir Bernard took out his handkerchief.

'So either Dorothea is back, raging for revenge

like Caesar's ghost,' said Phryne, 'or someone is trying to recall her to mind. Did she sleep with you, Bernard?'

Sir Bernard turned plum coloured and choked. Phryne and Robinson waited for his answer. Phryne said impatiently, 'Bernard, this is no time to go all reticent about a lady's honour. She's been dead for thirty years, dammit! Now answer the question. I need to know.'

'You really think that someone murdered her?' he whispered.

'Yes, I do.'

'Well, all right, Phryne, I'll tell you. The dear girl graced me with her regard for almost a year in 1896. Happiest year of my life.'

'She left you?'

'Yes. No explanation. She just packed her traps and left. She was missing for almost two months, then up she popped again. Refused to explain where she had been. No one knew. She wouldn't tell me. Must have been a new man, lucky devil. But I never knew who it was. No one in the theatre, anyway.'

'What time of year?' asked Phryne.

'Summer – height of summer. June and July, 1897.'

'Good. Now, I want to look at the contracts,' said Phryne.

'I never married, you know,' said Bernard sadly. 'Never found another woman to come up to my Dorothea. You know, Leila is a dead spit and image of her. Temper and all.'

'The contracts, Bernard,' reminded Phryne. Bernard unlocked his safe and laid a heavy bundle of papers on the desk without speaking.

'Well, I'm going to catch some of the perform-ance,' commented Robinson. 'Coming, Sir Bernard?'

'Yes. I want to see how my new Sir Ruthven is getting on,' said Bernard, recalled to his duty. 'I'll be back after the show's over, Phryne.'

Phryne nodded and was left alone.

The documents were tied around with a blue ribbon. They were standard forms, committing the actor to six months' work with the company at a standard rate of wages, allowing for release in the case of illness and providing draconic penalties for breach. Phryne wished that she had paid attention when her lawyer friend Jilly was talking about con-tracts and leafed through them rapidly, looking for particular information and noting that the chorus had to buy their own makeup and stockings.

After twenty minutes she heard the closing song which marked the end of the first act and stared at her scribbled notes.

'Damn,' she said quietly, reordering the papers and tying the blue ribbon with a packing knot. She thrust them back into the safe and closed the door, spinning the combination lock. 'The only one who qualifies is bloody Gwilym Evans.'

The chorus flowed past the office on their way to their room and Phryne stowed the notebook and joined them.

The chatter was strained. This chorus was ner-vous. The young men separated from the young ladies at the second corridor and went into their own room. Phryne followed the girls. Dupont the chorus master stood outside their door, smoking a cigarette. He had a large, comforting bourgeois presence.

'*Bonsoir,*' said Phryne and introduced herself. Monsieur Dupont, it seemed, wished to display his excellent English.

'Mademoiselle, I am delighted that you are here. You may be able to solve these mysteries and render the theatre calm again. My chorus is very nervous.'

'I have a question. What are your relations with Miss Esperance?'

He did not even blink. 'Of course, you must ask these things. And I shall not deny that there was ... an attraction. But the young woman has no heart, only beauty – very great beauty – and that fades, does it not? In any case I believe that she is in love with Evans, and there I cannot compete.' He seemed very relaxed for someone who had been cut out, and by a younger and prettier rival, so Phryne asked, 'And were you very upset by that?'

'At the time, yes. He gave me a mouthful of abuse and I lost my temper. But I did not hit him, for that would have led to my dismissal. And I have formed another attachment,' he said complacently.

'Oh? With whom?'

'Mellicent Hyland. She is young and has a good voice. With more training it may be great, a strong contralto suitable even for grand opera. She is willing to learn. I believe that she will go far – with me as her manager and, in time, her husband.'

'I'll come and see you at Covent Garden,' promised Phryne.

'La Scala,' corrected the chorus master. 'La

Scala, Milan.'

She left him dreaming of future glories and went into the dressing room.

'I'm Phryne Fisher,' she said to the crowded room. 'Can I have a word?'

'Oh, Miss Fisher,' cried one tall girl in bridesmaid's clothes, 'you're the private detective. Have you found out who poisoned Walter yet?'

'No, but I'm on the trail.' She sized up the ten girls. They ranged in size and weight from tall and thin to short and plump. Tea was being drunk and makeup repaired and there was an overwhelming waft of sweat and perfume.

'What about the theft of the bag and the torn-up telegram?'

'Could have been anyone. Miss Esperance is ... well, she's a bit hard to get along with,' explained the tall girl. 'I'm Jessie. We've talked about it, but we really don't know. None of us have a reason to go to her room and we wouldn't anyway.'

'Do you know who the telegram was from?'

'Selwyn Alexander, I think.'

'Good. And the bag?'

'Herbert's supposed to keep an eye out backstage,' said Jessie, who appeared to be a spokeswoman. 'But he's often busy and he's a lazy little rogue, always hanging about in the wings watching the show. Tom the doorkeeper is supposed to make sure that no one gets in, but he goes to sleep in his little booth. Someone could have come in from the street and pinched the bag. It needn't have been one of us.'

'Whose bag was it?'

'Mine,' said a plump blonde, 'I'm Melly.'

'Ah.' Phryne struggled to frame a question, and Melly blurted, 'Yes, I was in love with Gwil – with Mr Evans. And he did leave me for Marie-Claire. Marie and I were upset at the time, but then he dumped her for Miss Esperance, who is a cold-hearted bitch and will give him all he deserves so it's all right. And now I'm going to marry Monsieur Dupont and be an opera star and I don't love Gwil any more.' She burst into contradictory tears and was comforted by a press of bridesmaids. Marie-Claire, a slim dark girl, identified herself. It was on her shoulder that Mellicent was reclining.

'Yes, it is true, he is a scoundrel. But we did not go too far with him and we now loathe him so we have no reason to attack him, and anyway it was Mr Copland that was attacked,' she said carefully.

'Did anyone see Mr Copland eat or drink anything?'

'No, he entered from the other side of the stage. We are stage right – he's stage left,' explained Jessie. 'The boys might have seen him. He did drink, you know. Poor man. Pity he was so hard to feel sorry for. Never had a kind word for anyone, Mr Copland.'

And that appeared to wrap it up for Mr Copland. Phryne decided to watch from the wings as the overture to the second act began and the bridesmaids stubbed cigarettes, gulped their tea, and flowed down the steps and into the wings.

Phryne found Sir Bernard in the wings, watching Gwilym Evans talking to his ancestors.

'Dammit,' she heard him mutter. 'Dammit, he is good. He is damned good.'

Evans brought to the downfall of Ruthven Murgatroyd youth and freshness. He was not the standard melodrama villain, as the role was commonly played. The heedless confidence of Dick Dauntless was suppressed and in its place was a lurking horror; he was the epitome of a respectable young man finding out that his heredity was lethally compromised.

'The secret of G and S is that it has to be played perfectly straight; no winks, no asides, no "look how funny I am", no "see how absurd this is". It's very comic if it's played as though all the ridiculous conventions are true,' instructed Sir Bernard. 'And that's what that devil of a Welshman is doing.'

Sir Roderick Murgatroyd announced himself as the ghost of his father, and Gwilym dropped to his knees and sang on a pure double tone, 'Alas, poor ghost!' The attitude and the bent head conveyed pity and fear. It was stagecraft at its best. Phryne had to agree. Gwilym Evans, drat him, was a consummate Sir Ruthven.

Sir Bernard remained glued to his place in the wings, the ancestors sang about the ghost's high noon, and Phryne considered the stage.

The wings were situated in a gap perhaps four paces wide between two box sets. These were made of painted canvas over deal frames, held up by large brackets weighted down with sandbags.

They were crowded. Standing beside Phryne was Prompt, who had a book and a subdued light. Beside her was the stage manager, biting his beard because the orchestra was a beat out and gesturing furiously for a stage hand to get a broom and remove the sand leaking from one of the bags, which crunched underfoot. The call boy Herbert was staring fascinated at the stage, where Sir Roderick Murgatroyd was complaining that his portrait had been hung in a bad light.

Phryne peered across the stage, but could not see into the matching wings, partly because of the angle of the sets and partly because of the brightness of the stage lighting.

She looked up. A gantry held the lights; a double rank of metal spotlights, hung on a metal frame which boxed in the whole stage. She wondered how anyone knew which lights were on or off, and how they could be changed in performance from the sunlit village to the gloom of the Ruddigore castle. To make the floor of the stage a real death-trap, along with the sandbags and brackets it was festooned with important looking electrical cables, some of which were taped in place.

The wings also held a bevy of bridesmaids, three dressers, and Leslie Franklin, Old Adam. He had not straightened out from his arthritic crouch. Considering his real age, Phryne thought that this showed a commendable devotion to his part.

The ghosts ritually cursed Sir Ruthven, and then began to torment him. The circle of ancestors in wigs and caps hid the writhing young scion from sight, and Phryne, along with the whole popu-lation of the wings, found she was holding her breath. Evans clutched his head and rolled on the floor-cloth, whimpering in what seemed to be real pain.

Had the curse really landed on another Sir Ruthven?

Then he struggled to his knees and cried his line, 'Stop a bit! Stop it will you? I want to speak,' and clambered to his feet.

There was a general exhalation of relief.

'Fellow's too good an actor,' said Sir Bernard, getting out his lighter, catching Mr Loveland-Hall's eye and putting it back in his pocket.

Old Adam received instructions to kidnap a maiden and exited again. He stood still while Jessie mopped his face, powdering thickly over the sweaty greasepaint.

'Phew!' said Leslie Franklin, observing Phryne, 'I thought he was gone as well. Good actor, isn't he? Pity he's such a bounder – but what a performance he is giving!'

His voice was young, light and incongruous. When this accomplished young man had a little more experience then Gwilym Evans would have some competition.

After completing the patter song and stating with deep feeling that the title was too dear at the price, Sir Ruthven staggered into the wings, straightened immediately, and was supplied with a drink of water and a towel by his dresser John Rhys. Phryne overheard him say in an ecstatic whisper 'Oh, Shonni, it's going well!' as his face was repowdered.

Despard and Margaret were taking the stage, exchanging their lines with effortless facility. Selwyn Alexander, without the cruel competition of Evans' brash Dick Dauntless, looked younger and more in control, and Miss Wiltshire was sedate and calm in sober Victorian black.

Gwilym took the stage again. When Margaret

138

threw herself into his arms and he handed her politely to Selwyn, some sort of pact seemed to have been made. Phryne was fascinated. By the time they launched into the patter trio, they were in accord. Proceeding at an inhuman pace, they carolled that it really didn't matter, and it seemed not to.

Agnes Gault was dragged on stage, fighting Old Adam, and the play proceeded. Miss Gault finished her ballad about the little flower and the great oak tree, the whole cast emptied onto the stage, and the finale began.

Robin/Sir Ruthven abandoned villainy and barony and reclaimed Rose. Dick Dauntless took hold of Zorah. They launched into 'Happy The Lily' with a collective consciousness that this had been a very good performance of *Ruddigore*, which might have brought a smile even to the face of Mr Gilbert himself.

Applause washed over them and crashed like a tide. Phryne had not realised how loud it was, up on stage. She saw tired faces enlivened as curtain call after curtain call summoned them back to be loved and appreciated. No wonder actors could not bear to leave the stage, she thought. She felt elevated, although she had had nothing to do with it.

Finally the red curtain descended and did not rise. The cast sighed, sagged a little, and began to break into groups to leave the stage.

A sudden, earth-shattering crash deafened them. Dust billowed and the stage shook and rang like a drum. The curtain counterweight, which weighed a quarter of a ton, had broken its rope and fallen.

Phryne, holding her ears, spun around.

She saw through the blinding miasma of a hundred years' dust the leaden ingot, the size of a bale of wool, which was sewn into a huge wooden frame with a canvas cover. She stumbled on a trailing line snaking across the floor and fell to her knees in a pool of blood.

Shaking, coughing and sick to her stomach, she realised that there was someone underneath it.

CHAPTER EIGHT

GROSVENOR: *A curse on my fatal beauty, for I am sick of conquests.*

Gilbert and Sullivan
Patience

The cast screamed, cried, or went blank, depending on temperament. Miss Esperance fainted and was borne away, and the stage manager, after swallowing to regain his hearing, banished them all to the wings, driving them out like a flock of chickens. Only Gwilym Evans remained.

'You'll want to lift it,' he said shakily. 'The stage crew will have gone home. I can help. Shonni, we need to rig a line.'

'Leave it,' ordered Detective Inspector Robinson. 'No one could be alive under that. Someone fetch Dr Fielding out of the audience, will you?

140

John, go and get him. Tell him he'll get to sup with Miss Webb tonight, I promise. Miss Fisher, are you all right?'

Phryne found herself leaning on Gwilym Evans, at the same angle as he was leaning on her. His arms were holding her up, and his forehead was on her shoulder. He was drawing shallow breaths, and Phryne was rubbing at her eyes and suppressing shudders which shook her whole body.

'No,' she said, hearing her voice trembling. 'I'm not. I'm going to sit down,' and she led Gwilym down the stage steps into the empty orchestra pit, where she found the table next to the timpani and lowered herself and the actor down. There they clung to each other as if for warmth.

Phryne looked down at the head which burrowed into her shoulder. Dust coated his makeup and greyed his hair. His arms around her waist were muscular and he seemed to exude a grateful human heat. Phryne became aware that she was shaking as if she was desperately cold.

She held the actor closer and clenched her teeth. This was shock, she was familiar with it. The clinically shocked became deathly chill and she was aware that what she needed was an infusion of fluids and a blanket, but somehow she could not loose her hold on Gwilym.

John Rhys the dresser clattered down into the pit, draped them both with what appeared to be a quilt and observed, 'Don't let go of him, Miss. Always been high-strung, Gwil has.' He had a lilting accent and kind brown eyes.

'Yes, all right.' Phryne began to warm in the embrace of the covering. 'Get us some tea, hot,

141

lots of sugar. My God, did you see it?'

'Yes, missed you by a whisker. Missed Gwil by a hair. I'll get the tea.'

'You aren't affected,' observed Phryne rather resentfully.

'Come from a mining town, I do. It'll hit me in a few hours then I'll cry my eyes out. Delayed, see? In case we have to rescue someone. Back in a jiff.'

Phryne and Gwilym began to warm and relax. He shifted to get closer to her. Phryne felt no sexual attraction. She reflected that this must be instinctive – something like the clinging together of apes and pre-hominids back in the aeons when cave-dwelling creatures had been attacked by volcanoes and sabre-toothed tigers. Her own shock was lessening. Her shivering was coming under control and she freed one hand to wipe the tears and dust from her face.

Gwilym had not uttered a word. His thigh was aligned with hers, his arms locked around her, and she felt the heat of his breath in the hollow of her throat. She slid a grimy hand onto his chest and felt his heart beating wildly under Sir Ruthven's torn frilly shirt.

He raised his head and kissed her, smearing her with greasepaint and dust, and she was instantly flooded with heat. His fist clenched in the hair at the back of her neck and she strained to get closer, closer, locked mouth to mouth.

This would not do. She had no intention of being listed as yet another of Gwilym Evans' conquests. Phryne drew away with a great effort, kissed him lightly on the cheek, and said ambiguously, 'Well, that was close.'

'It was,' he agreed. He sat up out of her embrace and ran both hands down his body, flexed his fingers, wiggled his toes, and shook his head. 'I'm alive,' he announced.

'And so am I.' Phryne brushed at the greasepaint coating the breast of her Russian blouson and combed her fingers through her hair, shedding dust.

'Thank you,' he said soberly, the blue eyes deep as pools. 'I meant no disrespect, Miss Fisher. It was ... it was that...'

'That you are alive,' she said. 'The contemplation of death is a great aphrodisiac but I am not minded to join your harem.'

'Oh, God, my harem!' he said sadly. 'That was a kind kiss,' he added. 'God, I thought I was dead.'

John arrived with two mugs of very hot tea. Phryne, who usually hated sweet drinks, was not aware that it was sugared until the second last mouthful. Warmth and certainty sprang in her insides and she stood up and shook herself.

'I'm going back on stage,' she said.

'Wait – Miss Fisher–' Gwilym touched her arm. 'Sup with me tonight?'

He was floured with dust and his makeup was runnelled with tears. He was shaking with reaction, and white where he was not grey, yet he was still exceptionally attractive.

'All right. If I can,' she said, resolving to get a wash first. 'See you then.'

The stage contained Mr Loveland-Hall, picking bits of set out of his beard, three policemen, the bruised stage carpenter Mr Brawn and Dr Fielding.

'What do you want me to do?' Mark asked plaintively.

'Certify death,' replied Jack Robinson, and Mark looked at him. 'Yes, I know it's silly under the circumstances but we still have to do it.'

'All right, I certify that the poor fellow under that weight is deceased. He could hardly be alive, could he?'

'Good,' commented the policeman. 'Haul away, Naylor.'

The weight rose, revealing a crushed form underneath. Phryne looked away. She made it her policy not to see horrible things that she did not need to. Her sleep was haunted enough with the mouthing dead.

'It's Prompt,' exclaimed the stage manager. 'Miss Thomas. Poor girl.'

'You seem unmoved,' said Robinson, who was trying not to observe the puddle of ruined flesh and splintered bone which had been Miss Thomas.

'I was a stretcher bearer in Loos,' said Mr Loveland-Hall. 'Dead people are just dead. Poor Prompt! No one could have had anything against her. What a dreadful accident! Sir B, we have to inform her parents.'

'Give the details to my sergeant,' said Robinson. 'We'll handle it. Now, Doctor, we don't need you any more. Thanks for coming.'

Mark Fielding walked off the stage and down the stairs to wait for Miss Webb. He hoped that the doorkeeper might have a few swallows of port to spare. Even doctors, he reflected, are not immune to horror.

144

'Is the ambulance coming, Sergeant?' asked Robinson, watched for the nod from a shell-shocked Alias, and observed, 'After they scrape her off, we'll have all that gear down and bagged for the examiner, Naylor.'

'Jack, really!' exclaimed Phryne. 'You are a callous beast.'

'I am not allowed the luxury of being shocked,' said Robinson tersely. 'That's for civilians. Mr Loveland-Hall, can you tell me who was standing near Prompt when the weight fell?'

'Mr Evans and Miss Fisher. Excuse me, I should inform the doorkeeper to expect the press and to keep them out.' The stage manager exited rather precipitously.

'So, it was either meant to kill that poor girl,' reasoned Robinson 'or–'

'Me,' said Gwilym Evans, still draped in his quilt, who had come up unnoticed from the orchestra.

'Or me,' concluded Phryne, resisting the urge to join the actor in his covering to still her renewed shivering. 'You don't think it was an accident, Jack?' she asked hopefully.

'Not a chance,' said the policeman, holding up an end of rope which had been cleanly cut. 'No sign of fraying and good solid hemp.'

Phryne could think of no further objections. Someone had tried to remove either herself or the charismatic Mr Evans from the world and she did not know what to make of it.

Someone touched her shoulder and she turned.

'Come on, Miss Fisher, bit of a wash, eh? Gwil's all right here for a bit. Mrs Pomeroy says she can get the face-paint off your blouse and our dressing room has hot water laid on. The women are all still screaming and fainting and you don't need to go into that sort of carry-on.'

'Thank you.' Phryne accompanied the compact Welshman to a large room with a sink and tap. She stripped off the soft velvet top and unaffectedly removed her stockings, which were bloody at the knees. Shonni supplied her with a washcloth, a towel and a cake of expensive soap before he left. She stood on a mat and looked at herself in the mirror.

Her hair was capped with dust and her face was white under the smears of greasepaint applied when she kissed Evans. She slathered on cold cream from a big pot and wiped it off with cotton wool, glad to see her own features emerge un-scathed.

Hot water was a wonderful invention, she thought, as she rinsed off dust and blood and brushed her hair vigorously with one of the actor's brushes. She rubbed hard with the towel and restored her circulation, then applied a flick of powder, a dash of rouge, and a sprinkle of Gwilym's eau-de-Cologne.

It was a Phryne Fisher cleansed of adventure who sat down in Evans' chair and lit a gasper.

Shonni tapped and entered with a new pair of stockings, her own in a paper bag, and the blouse. There was a sticky patch on the shoulder but it was passable under her coat. Phryne reflected that she had been restored by someone else's charity twice in two days and decided to stop doing this.

She had just pulled on the stockings and re-assumed the blouse when Shonni ushered Gwilym inside, and Phryne stood up to leave.

'I'll wait outside,' she said, and went.

The chorus's dressing room was shrill with voices, and Phryne did not want to go in, but she knocked nonetheless.

'Oh, Miss Fisher, who was it – who was it?' demanded Melly.

'Prompt – Miss Thomas.'

'Prompt? It must have been an accident,' decided Jessie. 'No one could even get a word out of Prompt except in the way of business, I mean. Well, that's it, girls, I'm quitting.'

'Me too, this is too dangerous,' agreed several voices.

'Think about it,' said Phryne. 'You're on contract and you need the work, and the run at this theatre only lasts another week, then you'll be off to New Zealand. I suggest that you all go home and have an early night and you can think about it in the morning. What time is rehearsal?'

'Eleven,' said Marie-Claire doubtfully. 'Yes, that is probably the best thing to do. Come along, Mel. See you tomorrow, Miss Fisher.'

The chorus filed out, subdued. Phryne heard shrieking from Miss Esperance's room and felt unequal to any more temperament tonight.

As she left the theatre with Gwilym Evans, she saw a Chinese man hovering at the corner, and stalked past him with determination. Anyone who attacked her tonight, she decided, would be a dead man.

No attack followed. The figure drew back into the shadows of the doorway and did not speak.

The Ritz Café was entered through a corridor lined with wine barrels. It smelt agreeably of roasting and garlic and Phryne took a deep sniff.

'Back to life,' commented Gwilym, seating himself on a bench and drawing her down beside him. 'We need rare steak and mushrooms,' he said to the waiter, smiling with automatic charm. 'It's been a long night, Miss Fisher.'

'Call me Phryne. Yes, it has.' She roused herself to conversation. 'You gave a great performance tonight, Mr Evans.'

'Since we have shared a blanket, I think you should call me Gwil,' he grinned.

Phryne looked around. The Ritz was bohemian, fashionable, and nearly full, despite the lateness of the hour. Wine could not be legally purchased after ten o'clock, but a polite fiction allowed late diners to have a bottle on the table, which the management would solemnly swear was opened before the designated hour. Waiters in evening clothes dashed through the maze of wooden tables, carrying plates with effortless ease. The room was low, dark and wood-lined, and although it did not precisely resemble the Tuscan farmhouse which the Management fondly imagined, it was warm and felt safe. Phryne began to thaw.

Gwilym had already melted under her praise.

'Yes. I could feel it all coming together, I could feel it happening. Poor Robin finding out he is actually a wicked baronet and despairing. I felt his despair.' The blue eyes fixed on Phryne like a blow-lamp. 'That line, it's pure opera, Sullivan must have been thinking of Hamlet.' He sang,

148

very sweetly and softly 'Alas, poor ghost!' and several diners swung around to look at him. Three recognised him and he smiled and bowed to his public. 'And the music – it's almost folk song, almost Elizabethan.'

'But not quite. Sullivan must have known that authentic early music would be too much of a shock for his public,' said Phryne, who had heard Dolmetch in London and numerous amateurs on crumhorn, a sound which she could not like. She had also been taken entirely against her will and better judgement to several English Folk Song and Dance Society concerts. 'The closest he dared get was Purcell.'

Gwilym Evans appeared a little taken aback. 'You're well educated for a detective,' he commented artlessly.

'If we are going to make personal remarks, you're a long way from home for a Welshman!'

'Ah, yes, thousands of miles. I come from a little village half way up a slate mountain in the range the English call Snowdonia. You couldn't even pronounce the name, Phryne. A long way indeed. Have you ever heard of *hiraeth?*' he asked, his eyes staring sadly across endless seas.

'No, what is that?'

'A Welsh thing, hard to translate. "Yearning", perhaps. "Longing" is more like it. All of us have it, however happy we are. The yearning for home, even if we shook the dust off our shoes in loathing and swore never to return to the cold damp streets and the cold narrow people and the flat beer and the chapels fulminating endlessly against sin.'

'Are your parents still there?'

'I never knew my parents. I'm a foundling. Shonni's mother opened her door one morning and there I was on the doorstep, wrapped in some-one's apron and not another rag to my name. She had no children then, thought she was barren. She took me in and God rewarded her by giving her Shonni and Gwen and three others of her own after them. So I was a gift to her; a present from heaven, for all the chapel folk called me a mark of shame. Call a child a mark of shame and a devil's offspring, tell him he's bound to be evil, and he will become a bad boy – a *mwchyn*, chasing after the little girls and stealing their hair ribbons, then trying the drink and the weed and still singing like a bird. They resented my voice, those chapel folk. Said that the devil had given his own more skill than all the dutiful little Mam's boys.'

'How did you get to the Savoy, then?'

'Attracted the attention of the mine-owner, who thought it a pity that I should die choked with coal dust before I was thirty like the good boys. He sent me to London to be trained and I came here with the company. I like Australia so I stayed. But I never saw her again, my Mam. She died three years ago. Shonni went back when they told us that she was ill and stayed for the funeral but I had a part in a Sydney show and couldn't leave it. Oh, well,' he said cheerfully, blinking away tears, and picked up his knife and fork as two steaks smothered in mushrooms arrived.

Phryne realised that she was famished and tucked in heartily. The Ritz cooked an excellent steak.

She was deciding between pavlova, airy and

150

light as a sunset cloud, and a really excellent apple pie for dessert before the actor spoke again.

'The food's better here, too,' he commented. 'Australia has the best meat and the best fruit, and so cheap that no man need go hungry. This meal in London would cost me a prince's ransom, and no one in Wales would ever see that much steak on one plate – it's almost indecent. So you liked my Sir Ruthven?'

'You must know it was brilliant, Gwil. Partly because you took him entirely seriously.'

'That's the way to play G and S. Old Tom was telling me that he remembers hearing Gilbert rebuking George Grossmith the famous patter singer for adding a bit of business to his part. "The audience laughed," said Grossmith, and the old man thundered, "So they would if you sat on a pork pie. Stick to the part, Mr Grossmith, and no embroidery." Fascinating man, old Tom. But that's not Gwilym's end, coughing out his lungs on cheap port in a draught.'

'What will your end be, then?' asked Phryne, deciding on apple pie.

'I'll save,' he said. 'Every penny.'

'Then you should stop taking people out to supper,' said Phryne.

'Next week. I'll start next week, prompt,' promised Gwil, and Phryne laughed, then remembered the dead Miss Thomas. It was clear that Gwilym had been struck by the same thought, for his hand met hers across the table, clasped and clung.

'By God, I'd almost forgotten,' he whispered. 'God forgive me. Was it you or me, Phryne, what

151

do you think? Who was he trying to kill?'

'He or she, and I don't know. Someone may not like my poking about in the theatre. One of the four ladies you have recently slighted may have decided to make an exactor out of you. Or it might have been the ghost.'

'Dorothea? Tom's been telling me about her.'

'Did he know her?'

'Yes. He was with the Savoy from 1881 to 1914, when he went off to the Great War and never sang again. He was gassed. He started as a call boy and then went into the chorus. Voice wasn't strong enough for a principal and he says he can't act. But he remembers Dorothea Curtis. Says she was very like Leila.'

'Yes, that's what Sir Bernard says.' Phryne took a swallow of red wine to clear the aftertaste of fear out of her mouth. 'What else does old Tom say about her?'

'Says she threw a vase at him once in a tantrum and he's still got the scar. I haven't seen her, thank God.'

'Why? Are you frightened of ghosts?'

'Absolutely. And if you want to call me a coward you can go ahead. It's only because I'd give anything to play Sir Ruthven that I'm not breaking the track record to Sydney this very moment. I've been terrified the whole time she's been around. Leila saw her, says she was a bride. I've been shooing Shonni out into the passage to see if she's there before I leave the dressing room.'

'You don't think she's a trick?'

'Can't see how. Don't care, anyway. Leila's really frightened of her, and she's the only one who could play her. God, I'm shivering again. That was so close, Phryne, so very close. And I'm not ready to die yet. Not till I've played Hamlet. After that he can kill me, but not until then.'

He passed a shaking hand over his dark hair. Phryne thought that he would make an unusual but very attractive Hamlet, and the first one she had seen whom Ophelia could credibly fall in love with. The hand in hers was strong and beautifully formed, with long fingers only marred by chewed fingernails. He noticed what she was looking at and curled them under Phryne's palm.

'That's what *Ruddigore* has done to me,' he said self-consciously. 'Haven't chewed them in years and now I've nibbled them down to the nub again. Will you come home with me tonight?' he asked, staring pleadingly into Phryne's eyes. 'I don't want to sleep alone.'

'No,' she said, fighting down a treacherous urge to say yes. 'You've lovers enough, Mr Evans.'

'Not one that loves me, though. Not one with any brains or courage. That society Ffoulkes woman, she's been hounding me, wanting to make me the ornament of her salon – for a while. Otherwise my harem is composed of actresses clawing their way up in the profession who think me a useful stepping stone.'

'And you think Leila useful for the same reason,' Phryne released her hand, despite the pleasure of his touch. 'It's been a trying evening, Gwil. Don't make me argue the case with you.'

'Why not?' the mouth turned down. Phryne was tired and tempted and her voice became sharp.

'Because anyone so self-involved as an actor,

153

Mr Evans, makes a bad lover. I don't have the time to waste.'

'Ah well, it was worth a try,' he sighed, quite uncrushed. 'But I'll remember you in my dreams,' he added with a wicked grin. Phryne returned it with interest.

'And you may well feature in mine.'

They finished dinner with small cups of black coffee and a mint each.

As Phryne walked with him to her car, parked in Bourke Street, she had a strong feeling that she was being followed. She turned abruptly once or twice but could see no one. The streets were empty, dry and cool, and a light wind blew dust into her eyes.

She dropped Mr Evans at his boarding house in Lygon Street, refused a pressing invitation to keep him company, and drove home to put herself to bed uncharacteristically early, sober, and alone.

CHAPTER NINE

We've a first class assortment of magic
And for raising a posthumous shade
With effects that are comic or tragic
There's no cheaper house in the trade.

Gilbert and Sullivan
The Sorcerer

Phryne settled back in her chair next to Bernard

Tarrant in the front row of the stalls.

Eleven in the morning is not the ideal time to be in a theatre, she thought. It was cold, smelt stale, and the lights were sodium lamps which cast a bluish glare. This had the effect of making the tired faces of the company look deathlike, exaggerating every wrinkle and bleaching the pink out of even Miss Esperance's complexion.

'*The Pirates of Penzance*, Act 2,' said Sir Bernard. 'We seem unable to get away from Cornish fishing villages.'

A group of Cornish daughters were bidding a collection of lacklustre policemen to go and die in combat. They seemed unimpressed with the chorus, who told them that every maiden would water their graves with tears.

'No, no, no!' shouted Bernard, leaping to his feet. 'Terrible! Go back to the beginning, "Dry the glistening tear", and ladies, for God's sake try and keep in tune. Police, you're supposed to be marching, not dancing! I want to hear the thud of boots. Mr Evans, try bringing Miss Esperance to the front, on "I will try, dear Mabel". I can't hear a word out of her. Miss Esperance, are you well?'

Leila clutched at Gwilym Evans' hands and nodded forlornly.

'Then let's get on!' Sir Bernard resumed his seat, nodding to the orchestra leader. The musicians seemed nonabundant and Phryne wondered if this was just an effect of needing fewer players for rehearsal or whether a number of them simply had not turned up.

She noticed that the violinist was wearing a greatcoat, and that first trumpet was sniffing. The

155

chorus managed to come in almost in unison, and Mabel talked to her father about being an orphan. The cast appeared to know their lines, Phryne observed, wondering if the general vagueness of actors was produced by stuffing their heads full of someone else's words as a profession.

'Then Frederic,' announced Selwyn Alexander, 'Let your escort lion hearted be summoned to receive a general's blessing, ere they depart on their dread adventure... Sorry – ere they depart *upon* their dread adventure.'

Sir Bernard stirred but did not protest and a line of men came marching onstage. They were dressed in a collection of cast-offs. One was wearing a muffler and two were sucking cough drops and altogether they were the least likely collection of policemen that Phryne had ever seen. In the middle of the line was a young man whom Phryne did not recognise as Leslie Franklin until he began to sing.

'When the foreman bares his steel,' he sang robustly and the chorus echoed, 'Tarantara! Tarantara!' with no enthusiasm and very little volume. 'We uncomfortable feel,' continued Mr Franklin, wondering if there was anyone on stage with him and only partially reassured by the next 'Tarantara!' which had a little more force. 'And we find the wisest thing,' he went on bravely, 'Is to slap our chests and sing "Tarantara!"' Not a tarantara followed and Leslie stopped and looked at his director for guidance.

'Boys, what is the matter with you all?' demanded Sir Bernard. 'Castrated in the night? These are policemen; I want beef, I want a big strong sound.'

'Sir B...' ventured a tenor timidly, 'I think we're a bit *distrait*.'

'*Distrait*, are you?' said Sir Bernard Tarrant with withering scorn, taking on a pre-heart attack hue, 'You'll be *distrait* when I get hold of you. What's the matter, then? Do you realise that we are going to take this show on tour exhibiting the sorriest lot of policemen who ever disgraced Gilbert's words and Sullivan's music? Even New Zealand is going to notice!'

'The ghost...' said the same young man, emboldened by the rest of the group who were clustering behind him. 'Poor Prompt's dead, Sir B! It's too much. We're worrying about whether we are safe and that's never good for the performance. What's happening? Isn't someone doing anything about it? Someone hates us!' and the rest of the men gathered the speaker close, closing their ranks with what looked like military precision. Heads nodded and eyes were fixed on the director.

'Yes, all right.' Sir Bernard rubbed his cheek. 'Yes, I suppose you ought to know. The police are investigating, and this is Miss Phryne Fisher – the Honourable Miss Fisher. She's a private detective, employed by me. Together we will get to the bottom of the problem.'

Phryne stood up and the cast looked closely at her. She was dressed in a dark suit and the big tiger's eye brooch which secured her scarf winked reassuringly.

'I'm working on several things at the moment,' she announced. 'One is the ghost. Have you seen her?'

157

'Louis has seen her,' said a bass. 'So he says. And I saw something – a figure and a light and a scent.'

'Where?'

Louis, the tenor, emerged from amongst his fellows and said, 'I agree with Col. That's what I saw, too.'

'Where did you see her? What was she wearing?'

Louis plucked up his courage. 'At the stage entrance – stage left. She was Rose Maybud – first act.'

'Yes, sunbonnet and all,' agreed Colin.

'Were you frightened? Did you feel cold?' Phryne was recalling her textbook, in which the Society for Psychical Research had measured the drop in temperature when some supernatural phenomena occurred.

'Cold? My word,' said Colin, 'I felt like I'd been dipped in ice water.' Beside him, Louis nodded.

'Right. Did she speak to you?'

'Phryne, are you taking this seriously?' guffawed Sir Bernard, with an edge to his voice that she could not quite identify. Anxiety, perhaps?

'You asked me to investigate, Bernard dear, and I'm investigating.' The director subsided. Colin answered after consulting his colleague.

'No, she didn't speak and she didn't move – thank God, I would have died on the spot if she had.'

'Have you ever seen a ghost before?' asked Phryne, and both men shook their heads.

'And I don't want to see one again,' added the bass with perfect certainty. 'Eh, Louis?'

'No,' whispered Louis.

'I'm on the trail of whoever is playing these tricks,' Phryne assured them. 'I've never failed yet. I shall find out what is going on and I shall stop it, and you have the admirable Jack Robinson of the police force as well. You'll see me around – if there's anything you think might help me, please have a word. Just a chat, and unless it's germane to the issue, my confidence is absolute. All right?'

There was a general sigh of released tension and some of the actors grinned. Gwilym Evans had been fixing his hypnotic gaze on Phryne, and he smiled wickedly once he had made her look at him.

'Right, good, then can we get on?' asked Sir Bernard with restrained violence. 'From "When a felon", Mr Franklin and policemen, if you please.'

Phryne wandered away as she heard the young man announcing that a policeman's lot was not a happy one. The chorus were putting a lot more effort into their tarantara, and it echoed in the empty theatre.

She found the stage electrician, Mr West, puzzling and muttering over a pad of paper covered all over with arcane shorthand.

'Hello, I'm Phryne Fisher, whatever is that? It looks like Babylonian cuniform.'

'Patch sheet,' grunted Mr West.

He was a short, stout man in a foreman's dustcoat, under which he wore a suit – presumably to keep up the respectability of trade, Phryne concluded. He had brown eyes and thinning dark hair and a pencil was lodged behind his ear. He looked Phryne up and down and held out a hand covered with bits of sticking plaster.

159

'You're investigating, are you, Miss? Well, I can tell you about the lights and that's all. I don't do anything else but lights. Me and my assistants, we're just lights.'

Phryne said that she would be delighted to learn about stage lighting and Mr West softened noticeably.

'See, this diagram tells me where all the lights are, and what connects with what, and when I put it next to my running sheet on the circuit board,' he led Phryne down into his little box and waved a hand at a large board made of bakelite and covered with switches, 'it lets me alter the lighting. See, this bank of switches is marked A to L and numbered. So if I want to know what colour gel is on light A6, this sheet tells me it is sunshine yellow and is one of the bank which are lit for the village scene, Act 1. Then if I want to know how to produce the blue and white of the Ruddigore castle, I look at the sheet and it tells me that M7 is midnight blue. So all I need to do to change the lighting is bring down A to L,' he slid the switches of the top bank to zero, 'and bring up M to Q and there's your dark and haunted hall.' The corresponding slides went up. 'Light strength is from one to ten,' he explained. 'We dim the light by increasing the resistance, but that makes the resistors hot. You could boil a kettle on them.' Phryne realised that the heat of the board explained the sticking plaster on Mr West's hands. He must have permanent blisters.

'So all the lighting is worked out and arranged before the performance?' she asked, and Mr West scratched his head with the pencil.

'Of course,' he said patiently. 'We decide on the lighting with the director and then the stage manager and then we are up all night rigging the lights and doing a lighting rehearsal.'

'How many lights do you have? Can I see one?'

'Fifty-eight. Tim, lower a spot,' yelled Mr West. Someone answered from above. Phryne looked up and saw a figure twenty feet above the stage, perched on the iron gantry which boxed in the stage.

A large metal object was lowered gently down into Mr West's arms.

'See, this is the bulb – don't touch it, now, a smear of fingermarks on the globe'll break it, once it gets hot.'

'Does it get very hot?'

'Yes, Miss, far too hot to touch. This box has shutters at the side to allow us to narrow the beam and direct it. See, here's the place where we put in a slide – a gel holder, it slips in here. The gel is made of dyed gelatine, to make a coloured light. All the globes are just white, but if we put a slide over them it can be any colour you please. Undersea is green, sunlight is yellow, gloomy is blue. A lady's boudoir in a Feydeau farce is pink,' he added, smiling for the first time. 'All right, haul up, Tim.'

The unwieldy metal box rose as the invisible minion hauled on a line, and there was a clunk as it was fixed in its place again.

'There are the other lights,' Mr West pointed at the dress circle, where Phryne noticed a bar from which several lights were suspended, 'controlled from the board along with the others. Did you see that aeroplane we had for Hinkler? You ask the carpenter Leonard Brawn about that. Didn't he go crook!' he chuckled. 'And so did I, they wanted to hang the bl ... blighted thing over my lights. You can imagine how the management would have liked a bl ... blasted huge shadow flicking over the stage during the performance. And when Bill told 'em about it they carried on like two bob watches. You see,' the thinning crown bent and the voice became conspiratorial, 'no one notices us, Miss Fisher, and no one appreciates us. I can have been up all night fixing the lighting, half dead for lack of sleep, so tired I can't see me own hand in front of me face and it all goes bonzer, then no one says a word. But if a change is a second out they're round here howling for blood. Technicals, they call us. Just technicals. But if it weren't for the technicals their show wouldn't never go on.' He cocked an eye at the singing policemen on stage. 'They don't know what we do for 'em. Have you seen 'em up close? Hags, most of them actresses. But give 'em the right makeup and lighting and they look like princesses. The brighter the light on the face the fewer lines it has – electric light evens out the features. Only reason Mr Selwyn Alexander is still getting away with playing boys is the extra-bright Maj lights. Oh, well,' he shrugged, 'there it is. Now, Miss, was there anything you wanted to ask me?'

'Have you, or any of your assistants, seen the ghost?'

'Nah,' a sneer lifted the corner of his mouth. 'Only players would believe in such things. There ain't no such thing as ghosts. They're just work-

162

ing 'emselves up to a tizz, a tantrum and a pay rise, you watch.'

'And what about the curtain weight?'

'Rope must'a frayed. Poor old Prompt. Never a cross word out of her – never a word, to tell the truth. Look, Miss, theatres get like this. One thing goes wrong and then another, as it will in the way of things, and then everyone starts jumping at every sound and expecting the end of the world. We've only got another week and then we're on the boat and it will all be forgotten by the time we sight Auckland.'

'So you think I'm wasting my time?'

The electrican grinned. 'Your time, but the management's money,' he said.

Phryne wandered behind the set and tripped over a tall man in overalls who was mending a sand-bag. He grabbed her as she fell and set her back on her feet.

'You're Miss Fisher?' he said, unsmiling. 'Leonard Brawn. I'm the stage carpenter.'

'And what do you do?'

'Everything that Jim West don't.' He was thin, about forty, and had a thatch of blond hair with paint in it and hands like spades. They were curiously out of proportion to the rest of him and also bore sticking plaster and smudges of iodine. Phryne took the offered hand and observed that the thumb looked like it had been hammered too many times. His voice was deep and pleasant. 'I make sets, fix machinery, paint cloths, rig scenery, make and repair furniture and props. I'm the one who gets lousy jobs like flying that blasted plane.'

'Yes, I saw it. How did you manage it? Mr West told me they wanted to hang it over his lights.'

'Yair, and then over the stage, till I put the mozz on that bright idea. There was an airforce chap here lording it over us mortals but I stopped him smartish. I dropped a line down through the dome, Miss, found the point of balance and hung it; then I had a couple of light ropes tethering it so it couldn't swing out too far. Then one of the boys just had to stand there and give the thing a little tug if it slowed down. After a few circles the propellors caught and it buzzed around good-o, though what the Gods would have seen of the stage is more than I can think. Still, they came to see Hinkler, not the show.'

'Tell me, can we really go down under the stage?'

'Yair, you've been there, lighting box steps are there.'

All Phryne had seen was a vast cavern which was lined with iron pipes and painted that depressing shade of rancid cream.

'I'll show you once I've got this rip sewn up. Sand makes a noise underfoot and they're all high-strung as it is. And I don't want Mr Love-land-Almighty-Hall on my back.'

He knelt down again and drew the bag-needle through the canvas. On stage, a strong sad voice was lamenting:

Ah, leave me not alone to pine
Alone and desolate
No fate seemed fair as mine
No happiness so great!

164

Phryne saw that, the carpenter had stopped sewing to listen to Leila Esperance's voice. When she was answered by Gwilym Evans' rich tenor, 'Ah, I must leave thee here/In endless night to dream,' he dragged the thread with a sawing motion through the canvas and finished his mending with a deft double knot, snapping off the waxed thread.

He beckoned Phryne to follow as he went down a flight of stone steps at the side of the stage. The lighting box was on the left and she was in a cavern floored with cobbles and roofed with bricks some twelve feet high.

'You can come down through a trap in the stage itself,' said the carpenter, 'like the devil does at the end of *Faust*. But this is where all the sets are stored, the ones that aren't flown up into the flies – that's up above the stage. You saw the lighting gantry. Above that is the flies. We can lower sets down and haul the old ones up. That's why you must never touch a rope. Lay a finger on it, move, it or undo it, and you could kill...' he stopped abruptly.

'Kill someone? Is that what happened to Prompt?'

'No. That rope frayed. Now, here is the warehouse – through those double doors. We own this bit of Little Bourke Street, before the Chinks begin.'

'You don't like them?'

'Yellow scum.' Mr Brawn was only restrained from spitting, Phryne felt, because he had to clean the floor. 'The stink from their bloody bananas can turn a man's stomach. Well. That's all, Miss Fisher.'

'It seems to be as big and complicated an operation as staging a major war,' she commented.

'But no one notices us. Stage crew are just hands. Only when something goes wrong. Then they go crook fast enough. My word they do!' His eyes blazed with sudden fury. 'Then they come down on us like a ton of bricks. "That set was crooked, Mr Brawn." "There is a rip in the scenery, Mr Brawn." "There is sand on the floor, Mr Brawn, pray have it cleared away – the stage sounds like Brighton Beach." Fair go, sometimes I'm ready to throw it all in, I can tell you. How would their bloody theatre run without us? That mob wouldn't recognise a hammer if it hit them. And they get all the applause and all the glory, and we do all the work. Got big heads, actors. All of 'em.'

'What about Management?' ventured Phryne. Mr Brawn snorted.

'They want it all done yesterday and it shouldn't cost an extra penny, even if I've got to go all over town matching paint or go dotty mending sets that are past it.'

'Why do you work here, Mr Brawn?' she asked gently, 'If you loathe them all so much?'

'Because it's magic, Miss – when it works, it's magic.'

There was a brief silence.

'Have you seen the ghost, Mr Brawn?' she asked, and the stage carpenter snapped, 'No,' and walked away out of the warehouse into the street, leaving Phryne wondering why no one did appreciate technicals.

Phryne dined quietly at home with Dot.

'How's the investigation going, Miss?' Dot asked, picking up her knife and fork to attack a lamb chop. Dot liked the theatre. Also, Phryne was unlikely to be in much danger in such a relatively civilised place, unlike say, a circus, which was populated by freaks and gypsies.

'I haven't the faintest idea what's going on, Dot dear. There seems to be a ghost, lots of people have seen it. There is a trickster pinching gloves and making mischief, and now there is a murderer. And I think he was intending to murder either Mr Evans the lead singer or me.'

Dot's belief in the safety of theatres was dashed. She shook her long plait back over her wool-clad shoulder and asked, 'Would you like to talk about it, Miss?'

'Dot, I'd love to talk about it, I really would, but I don't want to weary your ears just now.'

'No, Miss, really, I'm interested,' protested Dot, who saw the theatre as a glamorous and slightly wicked place (though not, of course, as wicked as The Movies).

'Good. All right. The ghost is supposed to be Dorothea Curtis, who had a brief affair with Sir Bernard Tarrant in 1896, and who was found dead in her dressing room in 1898 in the middle of a production of *Ruddigore*. The only persons at the Maj now who knew her then, as far as I can tell, are Bernie himself and a decrepit stage door keeper called Tom Deeping, who's been with G and S all his life.'

'Then she's come back to haunt Sir Bernard?'

167

asked Dot, who had no conceptual difficulty with ghosts. 'Have some more of this creamed potato, Miss, it's really tasty.'

Phryne took more *pommes duchesse* and waved her fork in the air for emphasis.

'No, all the tricks seemed to be aimed at Miss Esperance and Mr Alexander. Neither of them have any connection with poor dead Dorothea. Of course, when old Bernie confessed that Dorothea had been having an affair with him and then vanished from the stage for a couple of months, I immediately leaped to the usual conclusion.'

'A baby,' agreed Dot. Devotion to the doctrine of the Catholic Church did not preclude a girl knowing what's what, her mother had considered.

'But the baby would have had to have been born in 1897, probably when she vanished from the stage, that is June or July. I went through all the contracts and the only birth date that matches is Gwilym Evans, and he is Welsh. Then when I asked him about it he revealed that he was a foundling, but what would Dorothea be doing abandoning a baby in Wales, of all places? I know these Londoners. They think going to Chiswick is travelling abroad. If Dorothea was going to abandon the child, she would have left it in London. Besides, she would have been noticed. Any London lady turning up in one of those small mining villages would have been watched by the enthusiastic peasantry from the moment she set foot to ground. Of course, she may have had a child earlier in her career, but how I can find it now is beyond me.'

'Hmm,' said Dot, taking another chop. 'That's a puzzler, Miss.'

'Then there are the appearances of the ghost. What do you think about ghosts, Dot?'

'You should get onto the church. You should call Father Ryan. It's their business,' said Dot firmly. 'All this spirit talking and table-turning, it's mortally sinful.'

'Now, I suppose, is not the time to tell you that I am going to the Spiritualist church tonight with Selwyn Alexander?' asked Phryne with a smile.

'Oh, Miss, you be careful.'

'I'll be safe with Selwyn, Dot. He's in love with Miss Esperance as who wouldn't be. She is perfectly beautiful.'

'It's not your virtue I'm worried about, Miss, I reckon you can take care of that. But Father Ryan preached about it only last week. Possession, he said, possession is the great danger of spiritualism and he was talking about an exorcism he had performed. Some silly madam was playing with an ouija board and got herself possessed. He says they aren't the spirits of the dead, who are with God, but the temptations of the Devil.'

'Dot dear, I'm sure that the Devil has other things to do.'

'No, Miss, he's got plenty of time – he "walks to and fro upon the earth, seeking whom he might devour" – that's what the Bible says.' Dot was in deep earnest and Phryne patted her hand.

'I don't think you can be possessed unless you want to be,' she soothed. 'And I don't want to be. It can't be that bad, Dot dear, lots of people go to these spirit readings – it's been popular ever since

169

so many young men didn't come home from the War. There are many lost souls.'

'Souls,' said Dot firmly, 'are with God.'

'You know what I mean. If it makes some poor bereaved mother feel better if she thinks that her son is somewhere with a lot of flowers and happy singing – much though that might not have suited him in his earthly form – what harm does it do?'

'It's dangerous,' said Dot mulishly. 'I don't like it, Miss.'

'Then I'm sorry, but I'm going.'

'Will you wear your St Christopher medal?' bargained Dot, and Phryne nodded. 'Then I'll just say a rosary, Miss, until you're safely home.'

Phryne reflected that knowing that Dot was telling her way solidly though her beads would hardly ensure that she returned home promptly, recognised that she was being blackmailed, and smiled.

One could never have too many prayers. And it would give her nervous maid something to do.

The Spiritualist church smelt exactly like an ordinary church, old hymnbooks, cough lollies and brass-polish. It was sparsely furnished and crowded. Phryne, sitting on a hastily bagged front row bench, scanned the audience as Selwyn Alexander sat down with his dresser Bradford beside him.

'He wanted to come,' he apologised. 'I didn't think you'd mind.'

'Not at all.'

The congregation, it seemed, were mostly female. About half of them were in deepest mourning. There was a sprinkling of children and several men. It was not like a church gathering, but buzzing with excitement.

The table on the dais was draped in a blue velvet cloth and massed flowers banked the steps. A stout woman was assisted onto the stage by two helpers and there was some applause. 'It's Mrs Price,' said the woman beside Phryne. 'She's really good.'

'Now, we will all sing "Shall We Gather At The River",' said the stout lady. 'So the spirits will know that we are all here and in the right frame of mind.'

A harmonium groaned the chorus and the voices rose. They were a good deal more enthusiastic than the Maj's policemen and most of them were in tune.

Shall we gather at the river,
Where bright angel feet have trod?
Flows the crystal stream forever,
Flowing by the throne of God.

The audience responded that yes, they would gather by the river, and Phryne began to feel warm and excited.

Those sitting in the front pews had flowers in their hands. Phryne had a small gold button, one of a set which Bernard had given Dorothea Curtis and which he had retrieved from her belongings after she had died. He had not wanted to lend it to her but she had insisted.

'Spirits of the other world,' began Mrs Price, 'hear us and come to us. We are open to you; we want to talk to you.'

Unlike a trance medium, Mrs Price seemed to require no spirit guide and no props. The helpers received things from the audience, placed them in paper bags and handed them to the medium as she stood on stage.

'Is there a Susan? Someone who says you are his daughter says that the paper you are looking for is behind the kitchen drawer.' There was a gasp in the body of the hall. 'This flower comes from a woman who has lost her son. You haven't lost him. His name's Bill and he's standing behind you. Bright eyes. He's calling you bright eyes.' Someone sobbed. The medium picked up another fruit-bag. 'Liz, he isn't dead. He's in South America and he isn't coming back, love,' she said sadly. 'There's a woman and a baby. Sorry,' she added as Liz screamed in outrage. 'But there's another man for you,' said the medium hastily. 'You'll meet him in three weeks' time. Tall man with black hair and he'll make you happy. Now...' Phryne saw Mrs Price lay the hand holding a bag on her corseted middle and wince. 'Go and see a doctor right away, dear,' she said. 'Name of May ... no, not May ... Maisie? Maisie. Your Grandma's here and she's saying "It's serious, make her go to the doctor."'

She walked along the stage, holding a bag. Her voice was no longer sure. She sounded shaken and puzzled. 'There's three people here. This is a strange one. There's a Greek woman and a man and Dorothy. Dorothy?' The medium's eyes unfocused. 'Dorothy but not Dorothy. She passed on last century, she's a ghost. The other woman's here now. And the man. Someone killed her. Can Ph ... Psy ... I can't get it. Stay and see me afterwards.' She laid down Phryne's bag and rubbed her hands as if wiping off dough, resuming her former calm. 'Tom, here's Tom saying that his Mum is here. He says, "You still like ginger biscuits, Mum." He's smiling. He's wearing overalls ... he fell off ... fell off a ladder?' Another little cry broke through the silence. 'Then there's a girl, a pretty girl holding a bunch of roses. She says they're her favourite flower. No, that's her name. Rosie. There's a boy with her; her little brother. They passed on together. She's talking to John. She says, "Johnnie, you have to forget me and marry someone else. I'm happy here and I can't come back and I'll wait for you."'

Someone in the audience fainted and was borne out. It was getting hot in the hall, and Phryne fanned herself with a spare paper bag. This was most impressive and she did not know what to make of it.

After ten minutes, the medium, who had been flagging, sat down and one of the helpers announced, 'That's enough for tonight. Now, we will all sing "Bringing In The Sheaves". Good night and God bless you.'

Phryne stood up to sing the hymn, waited until the audience had gone and gathered her male companions. They went with the waiting helper behind the dais and into what had been the vestry, where the stout woman was drinking tea and putting her feet up on a hassock left over from the Church of England's occupancy.

'Are you Greek?' asked the medium. Mrs Price was as broad as she was tall, with a no-nonsense manner completely devoid of mysticism.

'No, but my name is Phryne.'

'I couldn't get it – it's harder when I haven't heard the name before. Well, you've brought me a puzzle! I don't know what to make of all these people. I'll have to try a trance and I don't like trances, they give me a splitting headache. Is this important, dear? I don't want to pester the spirits out of idle curiosity. This isn't a parlour game, you know. I never make anything up and I don't get any fee for this. I'm not one of those performing mediums with dark closets and a lot of tricks. I've been able to see spirits since I was a child and they trust me and I trust them. If I fake it, I lose it.'

'No, it is very important,' Phryne assured her.

Selwyn Alexander and Bradford stood by the wall as the medium closed her eyes and began to speak softly.

'Come along, Dorothy, there's people who want to talk to you.' Nothing happened and Selwyn began to fidget. Phryne hushed him. The helper whispered, 'It's too much, trying a trance when she's so tired.'

'Dorothy, where are you?' said the medium crossly. 'I'm tired and I don't have time to play games. Come here, there's a good girl.'

'Call her by her real name,' suggested Phryne, 'Dorothea.'

'So that's what it was. Dorothea, Dorothea, come along and talk to us,' Mrs Price said coaxingly. 'That's a good girl. Now, what have you to say?' The face changed eerily. Muscles seemed to writhe and rearrange themselves. It was like watching the surface of a boiling pot. Then the movement, which had been making Phryne feel quite seasick, settled down. On the medium's pink triple-chinned countenance a pouting, cross, very pretty face was visible.

'Poisoned,' said a petulant, light voice. 'Poisoned me!'

'Who poisoned you?' asked Phryne, deciding to behave as if she was talking to Dorothea and sort out the reality of the situation later. 'Why?'

'Jealous,' snapped the girl's voice, then dropped into weeping. 'My baby,' she mourned. 'My little baby.'

'Where did you leave the baby?' asked Phryne. The medium sat bolt upright and pointed a finger at her audience.

'Murderer!' she screamed. Selwyn Alexander's eyes dilated black with shock and he clutched his dresser, who was sweating. Mrs Price collapsed, rubbed her face, and said, 'I hate trance. Ouch. I feel like a rubber band snapped back into place. She was a pretty one, though. Black hair and such dark eyes. What did she say?'

'She called us murderers,' said Phryne.

'You don't feel like telling me about it?' asked Mrs Price, her eyes glinting with ravenous curiosity. 'I never get to hear the end of stories.'

'Sorry,' said Phryne. She opened the bag and retrieved the gold button. Then she offered the helper a banknote.

'For your work,' she said. Mrs Price waved it away, closing her eyes on her headache.

The helper accepted it on the way out.

Selwyn Alexander and Bradford, clinging to one another and trembling, got into Phryne's car and

175

she drove them to Carlton. They did not speak all the way home, which, Phryne reflected, was an indication that they were seriously shocked.

When she returned to her own house, she saw a shadow on the foreshore directly opposite; a man leaning on a tree, smoking a cigarette. He could have been there for any number of legal or illegal purposes, but he was unusual in that he was definitely Chinese.

CHAPTER TEN

Now let the royal lieges gather round
The Prince's foster mother has been found!

Gilbert and Sullivan
The Gondoliers

Dot, as promised, was sitting in the parlour telling her rosary. Phryne walked quickly into the room and shed her coat.

'Amen. Well, Miss?' Dot asked, examining her employer narrowly for signs of foaming at the mouth or speaking in tongues. 'How did it go?'

'Odd, Dot, weird and strange. Mr B, a cocktail, if you please.' Phryne flung herself down onto the sofa and smoothed her stocking, where the wooden bench had roughened the silk. 'There was nothing in the performance which she couldn't have got from a person at the theatre but ... it was convincing. Not a thing about the delights of the

176

spirit world and she didn't want money.'

'You were endangering your immortal soul,' said Dot severely. 'I was worried about you.'

'Well, my soul escaped unscathed, Dot dear, I am just puzzled. What would you like to do this evening, eh, to make up for being so concerned about me? I do appreciate you, Dot.'

'I would like to mend stockings and listen to the wireless,' said Dot, hauling out her sewing basket. Phryne summoned up a smile and turned the bakelite knob.

A flood of dance music filled the parlour. Dot threaded her needle. Phryne eased off her hand-made black leather shoes, sipped her cocktail and tried to think.

Shelving the whole *Ruddigore* question for the moment, she concerned herself with what the Chinese thought they were doing, following her around. Tomorrow night, she decided, she would ask the delightful Lin Chung for an explanation and a whole bolt of the best silk in compensation. Sky blue, she thought, enough azure silk to drape the walls of her parlour.

Dot woke her two hours later and put her to bed.

Morning brought Jack Robinson to breakfast.

The underfed policeman encouraged Mr Butler to load his plate with eggs, bacon, ham, and tomatoes. He buttered toast with a lavish hand and ate solidly for ten minutes while Phryne nibbled at a tea-cake and drank black coffee.

When he was sipping his second cup of tea, she asked, 'Who dropped the weight, Jack?'

'Hanged if I know.' Under the influence of well-cooked food and hot tea the detective inspector began to look less haggard. 'I've asked everyone and no one saw anyone near the rope. I can't tell if everyone is lying or everyone is telling the truth, in which case it never happened and poor Miss Thomas only thinks she's dead. Half of them think it was the ghost and the other half are convinced it was an accident. I can't believe it was the ghost and I don't believe it was an accident. Then there's the question of whether it was aimed at the person it killed or whether it was meant for either Mr Evans or you. Opinion's divided on that, too. Lot of them would be glad to see Mr Evans dead if he wasn't such a good actor, but because he is, they seem to be able to digest his being such a bounder. Have you got anything?'

'I've been working on the ghost. I went to a spiritualist meeting last night with Mr Alexander and the medium called him a murderer.'

'Is that possible?'

'I don't think he could have cut the curtain-rope, he's too stiff to climb. He might have killed Dorothea, I suppose, if he happened to be in London and was a very precocious child.'

'So that's no use.'

'No,' said Phryne. 'I'm still convinced this ghost is a trick, but I can't see how it is being worked.'

'I don't need to know about the ghost, there are no such things as ghosts,' said Jack Robinson impatiently. 'I need to find a murderer who's accounted for two people already before he kills another.'

'You mean that the person who poisoned poor Robbie and Walter Copland is the same as killed Prompt?'

'Unlikely to have two murderers in the same theatre.'

'Different methods. Don't murderers usually stick to their *modus operandi?*'

'Yes, but this is a theatre, they're very odd folk.'

Phryne was unconvinced. 'I think that's going too far,' she said. 'But you go your way and I'll go mine.'

'All right. What are you doing today?'

'I'm going back to the theatre, to see what people will tell me.'

'They might tell you more than me, if you can stomach them. I'm going to the hospital – they might let me talk to Robert Craven today.' Jack Robinson levered himself to his feet. 'Oh, by the way. You'll never guess who Walter Copland left all his money to – and a tidy bit, too. House in Bendigo and a nice little financial cushion behind the fire-brick.'

'No, I'll never guess,' said Phryne, who hated parlour games. 'Who?'

'House to Hansen the dresser "for his devoted service" and fifty quid to the doorkeeper, Tom Deeping "in memory of the old days". And a small legacy to Miss Esperance and the rest to that boy, Herbert "who shows such promise". Not surprising, but enough to be a motive for murder. We have to talk to old Tom again. Thanks for the breakfast – it was good-o.' He called into the kitchen, 'Thanks, Mrs B, I was perishing for some good tucker and a cuppa. Well, I'll probably see you later, Miss Fisher,' he said gloomily, and Phryne conducted him to the door.

'Put your coat on, Dot dear,' called Phryne.

179

'I'm taking you to the theatre.'

The theatre was silent when she and Dot arrived. The old man said, 'No rehearsal today, Miss, there's a matinée. You've got the place to yourself for a couple of hours.' He smelt even more strongly than usual of cooking sherry, and he leaned close to Phryne, so that she had to squeeze against the wall.

She placed a hand on his chest and said softly, 'You knew Dorothea Curtis, didn't you?' and he sprang away as though her touch was electrified.

'Knew her?' he croaked. 'Knew 'em all. She was a haughty piece, she was. I knew where she came from, see, for all she behaved like Lady Muck. I knew her when she was singing for pennies in pubs and selling kisses to drunken sailors for the rent.'

'Did you, indeed? Were you one of her customers?'

'I couldn't afford Dorothea,' he laughed unpleasantly. 'She was too dear for me, little Miss Dorothea with her black curls and her bright eyes and her airs and graces. But she offended all them nobs. Got on one goat too many and someone killed her. And she was so beautiful,' he said, and Phryne hastily extracted herself and her maid from the stage door corridor before he started to cry. The last she saw of Tom Deeping was a crumpled yellowing face, the bloodshot eyes overflowing with tears which ran down his wrinkles and soaked the collar of his dirty ex-army greatcoat.

Hammering could be heard onstage, and when

they climbed to the next level Phryne and Dot found several young man and women playing pontoon in the ladies' dressing room. They leapt to their feet, spilling the pack.

'It's all right, it's Miss Fisher,' said Jessie to the others. 'Don't tell on us, will you? Just a friendly game, only the blokes aren't supposed to be in here.' Phryne promised not to tell. 'We're on this afternoon, and it's not too nice where some of us are staying, so we come in here and play cards.' Phryne said, 'That seems innocent enough.'

Colin the bass gathered the cards with rather worrying expertise and began to shuffle them. 'It takes our mind off performing and all the strange things that have been happening,' he explained. 'Closest thing to pure thought is card play.' There was a groan at this.

'Don't get him on to gambling as a path to Pure Thought,' urged Melly. 'We've heard that speech several times and it's boring.'

'Very boring,' agreed Marie-Claire.

'I'm just going to have another look around,' said Phryne. 'You haven't seen me.'

'No,' Colin agreed, dealing out cards. 'We haven't seen you.'

'But you'll try and get it all sorted out, won't you?' Melly grabbed Phryne's velvet sleeve. 'We're doing our best to be brave, but we're in such a state that one loud sneeze and we'll all burst into tears.'

'I'll do my best.' She closed the dressing room door and said decisively, 'Right, Dot dear, we are going to search a couple of rooms. I've brought you because you'll know instantly if anything is

181

out of place. One room is Mr Evans' and perhaps I'd better do that one, you know what gentlemen are like, and particularly that gentleman. The police have already searched for anything overtly criminal or related to the murders. But we are looking for anything odd, anything peculiar. Perhaps you could begin with this one.'

She opened a door with a star on it. Dot shrugged off her burnt-orange coat and peeled her gloves down as her eyes examined the room.

Phryne searched in the time-honoured Pinkerton method for an hour and came up with a healthy respect for Gwilym Evans' love life – he had bundles of love letters, all tied with pink ribbon, in the same drawer which held a packet of contraceptive devices – and none of the things for which she was tentatively searching. She noted with interest that Miss Diana Ffoulkes, queen of the flappers, had an exceptionally combustible prose style. She was promising to follow Gwilym to New Zealand, if only he would grant her – what was the phrase Bernard had used? Ah, yes. His regard. Phryne folded the letters into their original creases and replaced them. He had a British passport which confirmed his date of birth and some letters written in an exceptionally foreign tongue which must have been Welsh. These seemed to be missives from home, laboriously lettered with a leaking pen on cheap paper. She stole one from the middle of the bundle and returned it to its hiding place at the back of a drawer.

Then she joined Dot, who was straightening up from an inspection of the dressing table bottom.

'Several things, Miss,' she said in answer to

Phryne's unspoken question. 'A box of white powders in paper, like a Bex. I think they're prescription, by the label.' Phryne examined the chemist's packet. 'Morphine. Miss Esperance, one to be taken if the pain is severe.' She nodded at Dot to go on.

'This,' said Dot, blushing, exhibiting a diaphragm in its little box. Phryne nodded again. 'And these. I found them at the bottom of that dress basket. Why would anyone keep single gloves there, when the mates to them are in that glove box?'

'Why indeed?' Phryne looked at two gloves, differing slightly in colour and degree of wear, which had been knotted together. 'Put them back, Dot, very well done! How did you know where to look?'

'I had a lot of sisters,' said Dot, restoring the spoil to various niches. 'We got good at hiding things from each other.'

'Right, now we look at the other ladies,' said Phryne, and led the way.

Apart from revealing that Miss Wiltshire was a smoker and that Miss Gault had a taste for Dr McKenzies' Menthoids, an empty packet of which lay in her wastepaper basket, Phryne found nothing of interest in that room until Dot, questing behind the hanging rack, found several sheets of brown wrapping paper, carefully folded. Phryne spread them out. On the edge of one, which had been cut into an irregular shape, was a fine line. Phryne touched it and it smudged. Eyebrow pencil.

She rolled up the marked sheet, restored the

others to their place, and led Dot to the manager's office.

The notes which had brought two rivals to their lady's door were in the drawer. She laid them and the sheet together and Dot said, 'Yes, they fit.'

'So, it was one of those women who called Evans and Dupont together. I wonder if she was watching? Miss Wiltshire or Miss Webb, I think – Miss Gault is otherwise interested.' Phryne folded notes and paper together and stowed them in Dot's basket. 'Right, now the chorus rooms. Then I have to find Herbert. He has a report to make.'

'I'll search, Miss, you find him.'

Phryne agreed and walked back onto the stage, where she found the boy staring up at the lighting gantry. He jumped when she touched him.

'Hello, Herbert!'

'Oh, Miss Fisher, you gave me a surprise. I've been waiting for you.'

'Good. Come along and tell me what you've found.' She led the way to the manager's office. 'What are you doing here, when you ought to be minding the stage door?' Herbert avoided her eyes and hung his head.

'Tom, he's ... he's...'

'Drunk?' suggested Phryne.

The boy's fine hands were twisted together. 'My dad, he's like that when he's been having a few, and then he comes home and bashes my mum if lunch isn't ready.'

'He must start very early in the morning.'

'Yes, Miss, he's a pastry-cook.'

'Yes, I thought he might be. Herbert, why did you put green food colouring in the whisky?'

The face screwed into an expression of such wronged innocence that Phryne almost laughed.

'You'll have to work on that expression, Herbert dear, it's overdone. The really innocent look blank.'

The boy's face changed as if by magic. Now he looked astonished and a little affronted by her outrageous suggestion.

'Perfect. Now answer my question.'

'You going to tell Sir B?'

'No, not if you explain.'

'I can't, really. It was one of them...' he paused thoughtfully, gathering words, 'irresistible compulsions.'

'Irresistible compulsion, Herbert?'

'I ... saw Miss Esperance slide the ribbon off a pair of new gloves, then hide one and then scream about some ghost stealing her glove. So I thought—'

'So an irresistible compulsion came over you to play a trick and blame poor dead Dorothea?'

'Yes, Miss.'

'Right, have you done any of the others?'

'No, Miss.' The face was shiny with virtue and he held Phryne's gaze unflinchingly. She dropped the eye contact and looked at his hands. They were loosely clasped, without tension. Either Herbert had mastered the art of lying in one short lesson or he was telling the truth.

Then again, he was a very quick learner.

'All right. For God's sake don't give way to any more irresistible compulsions, Herbert, this case is muddled enough without you adding your six-penny-worth to it. Promise?' The boy nodded.

185

'Now, Tinker, what have you to report?'

Herbert, delighted at being addressed as Sexton Blake's assistant, leaned forward and said confidentially, 'Where do you want me to start, Boss?'

'Begin with Walter Copland, Robbie Craven and the bottle.'

The boy sat down on a velvet chair and began in a fast, mechanical undertone, obviously copied from a radio serial, 'I asked everyone who was on stage at the time and three people saw the bottle and saw Mr Copland drinking from it. Then he passed it to someone in the wings and that someone gave it to Robbie Craven. So there was only one bottle and the poison was in it and it went from Mr Copland to Mr Craven and Mr Craven was later so he got less of the laud-an-um and so he didn't die.'

'Yes, but who handed it to Mr Copland in the first place?'

'No one, Miss, I mean Boss, it was his own bottle. He brought it with him. They say he was a real old boozer and used to drink all the time. The chorus says when he got to that bit when he confronts them in *Ruddigore* the smell of his breath made 'em sick.' The boy had cheerfully forgotten the terror which a drunken man evidently invoked in him.

'And who took the bottle from Mr Copland and gave it to Mr Craven?'

'Can I whisper, Boss?' Phryne inclined her immaculate head and the boy leaned close to her small, well-shaped ear, breathing in the scent of her perfume. He whispered a name, tickling her

186

neck. Phryne sat bolt upright, to her assistant's regret. He hadn't been that close to a lady before.

'Are you absolutely positive, Tinker?' Phryne's eyebrows shot up. 'Sure?'

'Certain sure. I got four people who saw it. And one of 'em's Colin,' said the boy. 'He's not likely to have made a mistake.' Phryne remembered the large economy-size bass with the deceptively placid manner and agreed. Well, well, well, she thought.

'Now, as to the ghost, Tinker?'

'She's always been seen at the entrance to the stage, Miss, and she's always in Rose Maybud's village costume, except when Miss Esperance saw her as a bride. Two of 'em say that she was just a light and a scent. Hyacinths, Miss. Real strong.'

'Any idea who's doing it?'

'No, Miss, I reckon she's a ghost all right. I've drawn up this.' He shyly produced a notebook and opened it. Phryne saw a list of times and people, painstakingly ruled and meticulously clean, as though it had been rewritten many times. She scanned it quickly.

'I found out where everyone was for each time the ghost was seen, Boss,' explained Tinker/ Herbert proudly. 'I didn't put anyone in until I could prove they were there by someone else's say-so. No one was in the right place to play the ghost, not more than once.'

'This is a beautiful and invaluable chart, Tinker dear,' said Phryne slowly, 'but it means...'

'Either that they are working together or that she's a real ghost. And they'd never work to-gether, Miss. Not a whole lot of actors, 'specially not this company, which is either half in love with Miss Esperance or Mr Evans,' said Herbert with relentless logic. 'So she's a real ghost.'

'I can't,' confessed Phryne, 'at this moment, see another conclusion to be reached. Here, assistant, give me your chart, and take another quid for expenses. And listen, Tinker,' she reached out and took the boy's hand and the green eyes held him still, 'you be careful. Someone's already tried to drop a curtain weight on me – or it may have been me. You have a great career in front of you, I'd hate to see it ruined by premature death.'

'Can't catch me, Boss, I'm the gingerbread man. But I'll be careful,' he promised. Phryne did not for one moment think that this was the case, but let him go and he danced out of the office and into the corridor.

Dot returned, a little flushed.

'Anything, Dot?'

'No, Miss. Just a couple of the gentlemen giving me some sauce. Nothing in their room except what you'd expect. What now, Miss?'

'We wait for Sir B and I'm expecting Jack Robinson to have seen Robbie Craven by now. And I know what Robbie Craven is going to tell him,' she added. 'I know who poisoned him.'

'You do, Miss?'

'Yes.'

Dot's curiosity was roused. 'Who?'

At that moment the door opened and Sir Bernard came in, accompanied by the policemen. They looked grim.

'I've spoken to Mr Craven,' said the policeman. 'He told me who gave him the bottle.'

'Yes. I'll go and get the offender. But it may not be as helpful as you think.'

Phryne brought Gwilym Evans into the room. The actor was wearing a loose, open shirt and his hair was severely brushed back in preparation for wearing a wig.

'What's this all about, Phryne?' he was demanding, when he saw the ranked pillars of Management and Law and sat down rather abruptly.

'Oh, so you know,' he said.

'We know,' said Phryne quietly.

'But I didn't know it was poisoned!' he protested, doing 'virtue outraged' much better than Herbert, though of course, Phryne thought, Gwilym had had more practice. 'I took it off Walter because he seemed sozzled and I was worried that if he collapsed Management would find it on him and sack him. Then Robbie was so scared at going on as understudy he saw it in my hands and snatched it off me.'

'He says that you offered him a drink,' said Robinson quietly, 'and he took a couple of swallows. That was nearly enough to kill him.'

'And you did want the part of Sir Ruthven,' said Sir Bernard.

The actor hunted around the room for an ally and settled on Phryne with gratitude.

'Phryne, my dear girl, tell them I couldn't have done this!' His eyes were wild and the beautiful fingers disordered the curly hair. 'I wouldn't hurt anyone!'

'Wouldn't you?' asked Phryne. 'You break hearts all over the theatre without a second thought. You were waiting for a failing actor to lose his place in the same way vultures wait for a dying cow. I bet your beak watered when you saw Copland stumble onstage. Started seeing your name at the head of the programme, Gwilym?' She stared hard at him, searching for something – ambition, perhaps, or the pale flame of madness. 'Perhaps you didn't mean to kill, perhaps you miscalculated the dose – or perhaps you didn't realise that Copland was an alcoholic and would drink the whole bottle at one go. Did you give him the bottle, Gwil?'

'No, no, ask his dresser – ask Hans. Walter brought it with him. I swear!' His rich voice rose a few tones and took on a strong Welsh accent.

Sir Bernard rang the bell and told the attending Herbert to find the late Mr Copland's dresser.

'I tell you, I didn't know there was anything in that bottle but brandy. All right, I admit it. I hoped that Robbie would be too frightened to give a good performance and hoped that I'd get the part – but that's all, that's all, I swear. And that's the truth.'

Herbert came back with the news that Hans was not in the theatre.

'Gwilym Evans, I am arresting you on...' began Jack Robinson, and Constable Naylor closed a meaty hand on the actor's upper arm.

'No, no, my dear fellow, what shall I do for a Sir Ruthven if you arrest him?' wailed Sir Bernard. 'At least leave it until we can find Hans.'

'He'll run,' opined Naylor, tightening his grip. Evans winced in pain as he was lifted off the ground.

'What do you think, Miss Fisher?' asked Robinson, instinctively minded to oppose whatever his beefy constable thought.

'He'll stay,' said Phryne. 'He's an actor with a plum part. The prospect of execution immediately after he left the stage would not pry him away from this company. Take his passport and he'll be here when you want him.'

'Turn him loose,' ordered Robinson, and the large constable did so reluctantly. 'You will give me your passport as the lady suggests, and you will be here when I call for you, do you understand?'

Gwilym nodded. Phryne heard, to her amusement, manager and actor give identical sighs of relief.

The theatre was filling up. Phryne heard the usual chatter approaching in a wave up the stairs. 'Miss Fisher, I hope you're right about him,' worried Jack Robinson. 'Oh, by the way, I've got this for you.' He gave her a piece of paper with an address in Collingwood.

'What's this?'

'Only surviving relative of Miss Dorothea Curtis. Got in touch with us because she'd heard something about the ghost. Said she could see you this afternoon.'

Dot, still somewhat breathless from driving with Phryne in her Hispano-Suiza, which was always exciting, rang the doorbell of a small bluestone house.

A small woman in black answered the door.

'Miss Mobbs? I've come about Dorothea Curtis,' said Phryne. An old, old face turned to hers, both eyes bright as needles. Her scanty white hair was drawn back into a bun and she walked with a cane.

'Miss Fisher? Yes, I've heard the name.' The voice was not thready but strong, though much higher in pitch than it would have been when Miss Mobbs was young. 'An enterprising young woman – it's wonderful what gels can do these days. Now, tell me – is the ghost of Dorothea really walking?'

They had come into a painfully clean parlour, decorated with a print of two dogs. The fireplace surround was black-leaded to a jet finish and the hearth had a folding fan in it. The mantelpiece was loaded with ornaments and the air of the room was still, as though it was seldom entered. It smelt of beeswax and lavender water. Phryne perched on the edge of a horsehair sofa, evidently designed by members of the Spanish Inquisition in one of their more sadistic moments, and replied as honestly as she could.

'All reason is against it, but all belief is for it. Yes, she seems to be.'

'I see.' Miss Mobbs looked at Dot.

'Would you do me a kindness? My legs are getting old. Go into my bedroom and fetch the japanned box which sits on the night-table. It is under my Bible.' Dot did as she was asked and returned with a handkerchief box, which she put down on the old woman's lap. Miss Mobbs folded both knob-knuckled hands over it, however, and began to speak, calmly and clearly.

'I knew Dorothea Curtis when she first came to the Savoy – I was her cousin and I became her dresser. I had lately lost my husband and a child and I had no mind to marry again. She became,

192

in some ways, my daughter – the child I would never have. She was a wilful child – *just* a child. But very beautiful. There are always those who would take advantage of beautiful children.' The voice was still calm, as though all passion in it had been burned away by the years. 'She met some of them. Most of them she saw through and laughed at, but there were two – rivals. One was Charles Sheffield and the other Bernard Tarrant. Oh, they were wild for my Dorothea! But she could not make up her mind. She favoured Sheffield because he was weak, easy to turn to any purpose. But I think she loved Bernard – yes, I really think she did love him. She granted him...' the old voice paused, and Phryne put in, 'Her regard?'

'A nice phrase, Miss Fisher, yes. Then there was a child. One child gave birth to another. She gave the baby to me and told me to kill it. She was very young and she had been most cruelly used by those men – those two men. I took the baby and gave it to some friends of mine who dearly wanted a child and could have none. The baby thrived. I never told Dorothea, but I think she knew.'

'Whose baby was it?' asked Phryne.

'Bernard's – oh, yes, it was Bernard's baby. It had his eyes.'

'Why didn't she tell him about the baby and marry him?'

'He was an impoverished actor then – in no position to support a wife. And she wanted things,' said the cool voice. 'Money and position and a carriage and servants. I told her to follow love, because without it life is empty – who knew that

193

better than I? But she laughed and said that if she had the establishment she could find love elsewhere. Poor child. Poor Dorothea. Then she was dead. She had agreed to marry Bernard as was right, that jealous man Sheffield had interfered, and she was dead. I never believed that tale that she committed suicide, never. Not Dorothea. Someone murdered her, murdered the pretty child. I tried to tell them but they did not listen to me. So I left the theatre, came here, inherited this house and all the keepsakes as my relatives died one by one. I knew that it would come out, one day. And so she is back. Why, I wonder? She cannot be looking for me in the theatre. I would dearly love to see Dorothea again. But there, I am becoming foolish. I have been thinking of her all day, since that policeman said that you were investigating, Miss Fisher. Now,' she opened the box, 'here is all that I have of her.' Worn fingers felt over the familiar contents. 'Here is her locket. I put just such another around the neck of that baby when I took it to its new home.' She allowed Phryne to look at a heart-shaped gold locket with a picture inside. The pouting, pretty face of Dorothea Curtis smiled out of the gold frame. Three seed pearls were set in the initials on the cover. 'Here is her hair,' said Miss Mobbs, and Phryne touched a faded lock of springy black hair which still had a faint scent of hyacinths. 'And here is a photograph of the baby,' said Miss Mobbs.

Phryne turned the photograph of an undistinguished naked infant lying on a fur rug over and noted that it had been taken by Colonial Photographers, The Strand, London. She passed the photograph to Dot, who liked babies. Phryne always considered that they resembled rabbits in the market when newborn, and uncommonly alcoholic drunks when a little older. Also, despite the pride of their mothers, she could never tell one baby from another, except that some were ugly and some were merely exceptionally plain.

'Miss Mobbs, to whom did you give Dorothea's baby?'

'I ... can't recall,' said the old woman with perfect composure.

'Miss Mobbs, please. I believe that the baby is in danger. I think someone has found out something – Lord knows what! But there have been two murders and I need to know.' Miss Mobbs was silent for three minutes. Phryne watched the hand of the ormolu clock give a little shudder as each measured interval died. It was quite silent in the parlour.

'A family called Pearson,' said the old woman at last, laying a cold hand on Phryne's arm. 'They were emigrants.'

'Where to?' Phryne hoped it wasn't Canada.

'Australia, of course. Dorothea would have liked that. She was born here, you know. Her father was a failed emigrant, dragged his family back to Wapping and drank himself into his grave – and not before time, either. We brought her back – in a coffin full of hyacinths. She's buried in Melbourne Cemetery. It's an elaborate monument – she would have liked it. It has been a long time since I could walk that far.'

'Miss Mobbs – can you imagine why Dorothea has come back?' asked Phryne, and the old woman answered, 'Why, she's found out that he killed her. And she wouldn't brook anyone killing her, not my fierce Dorothea. She would be a very nasty ghost. She's come back to hound him to ruin.'

'Who?'

'Bernard Tarrant, I expect. I believe that Charles Sheffield drank himself to death years ago. Tarrant's the only one it could be. But I wouldn't have thought it of him. I think he really loved her, you know, though it is thirty years and my memory is not good. I thought that she loved him, too. My poor Dorothea.'

'Who looks after you, Miss Mobbs?' asked Phryne.

'A girl comes in every morning,' she answered with dignity. 'But I can manage most things. If your companion will do me the favour of filling my kettle that will be all I need. A full kettle is too heavy for me now.'

'Dot, would you mind? May I borrow this photograph, Miss Mobbs?'

'If you come back and tell me what happens. I'm very near the edge now – very near – I begin to see the shapes and the lights over the water, over the deep river that divides life and death. I expect soon to see some people I've been waiting for, waiting all these weary years. My mother told me that only the dying see ghosts. But I'd love to see her ... to see Dorothea ... again...'

The head drooped back against the back of the chair. Phryne stowed the photograph and went into the kitchen, which was also immaculate, cold, and clean.

'No wonder she can't handle that kettle, it

weighs a ton,' said Dot, banking the slow combustion stove and rattling the fender until the flames subsided. 'There, that'll be hot come tea-time. How is Miss Mobbs?'

'She's asleep,' said Phryne. 'We'd better go, we're tiring her out.'

'Miss Mobbs,' said Dot, 'we're going now. But we'll come back and tell you what happens.' Miss Mobbs muttered an assent and they left the house.

'Lockets and missing babies,' said Phryne as they got into the cherry-red car and she pressed the self-starter. 'Dot, I have the strangest feeling that I'm caught up in a Gilbert and Sullivan plot.'

CHAPTER ELEVEN

Did ever maiden wake
From dream of homely duty
To find her daylight break
With such exceeding beauty?

Gilbert and Sullivan
The Pirates of Penzance

Meanwhile and regardless of ghosts, there was a bath, and the necessity to dress for dinner. It was Thursday and a certain young Chinese man was coming to dine and, with any luck, to explain.

Phryne poured a generous dollop of essence, which smelt bewitchingly of chestnut blossoms, into her deep bath and lay back in the hot water, thinking.

If Gwilym Evans was not Dorothea's child, and it seemed unlikely in view of what Miss Mobbs had said about the destination of the adoptive parents, then baby Pearson was not involved in the problems at the Maj, which came as a relief. Phryne hoped that Dorothea's child had taken up a nice safe trade like plumbing, preferably in Tierra del Fuego or even Yarraville, and had never been tempted near a playhouse.

Herbert had put the dye in the whisky and Leila had secreted her own gloves. Either Miss Webb or Miss Wiltshire – thinking it over, Phryne favoured Miss Wiltshire as having a much sorer heart – had arranged the meeting of the two rivals and had undoubtedly hoped to watch the taller and stronger Dupont beat the faithless Gwil to a pulp. Phryne could only applaud this attempt to extract something out of his hide.

However. She rubbed languidly at her knees with the sponge and considered further. If Leila was hiding her gloves then perhaps she had also torn up her own telegram and done the other things. She could certainly have stolen the bag and planted it on Selwyn Alexander – but why? And why Selwyn Alexander?

This she could not answer. She wondered if she could find a suitable alienist to diagnose the actress as having dementia praecox, which was the only motivation Phryne could see, and ducked her head under the warm green water.

By the time she came up she had hurled all the problems relating to the Maj into storage, whence she could retrieve them when she needed to consider them again.

'Is this a ... nice young man, Miss?' asked Dot, supplying underwear of the finest washing silk.

'Oh, no, Dot, not you too.' Phryne was at a loss dealing with those who considered other races to be inferior. She herself dealt with everyone from an attitude of effortless superiority, but there were no ranks in the rest of humanity. To Phryne, a stupid Englishman was just as much an affront to her as an obstructive Hindu or a foolish Greek. And while the world was positively littered with beautiful men of all races Phryne thought that it would be criminal to neglect one because he happened to be of a different hue.

'I don't know what you mean, Miss.'

'You don't consider the Chinese to be savages?'

'No, Miss. Just different,' said Dot innocently. 'But they're heathens. We send them missionaries.'

'This one has certainly been to university, Dot. Despite that, I doubt he's a heathen.'

'Well, that's all right then, Miss. Only I thought I saw a Chinese watching the house.'

'When?'

Phryne sat down to pull on her black stockings.

'Last night, Miss.'

'Yes, I saw him too. I think this has something to do with that fight that Bunji and I dived into. They haven't made any threatening moves, Dot dear, and I'd rather like to know what we have got ourselves into before we go calling the cops. I'm expecting that Mr Lin will be able to explain. If not, then I will have to do something – I can't have an escort everywhere I go.' She stood up

199

and Dot dropped the dress over her head.

Phryne turned to the mirror and saw a perfectly simple, perfectly plain gown of draped black crepe, which had cost a crown princess's ransom. Her neat head was crowned with a fillet of twisted silver wire, from which descended one black ostrich feather that curled down almost to her shoulder. She made up her face with speed and efficiency and blew a kiss to her reflection.

'Not too severe, Dot?'

'No, Miss.' Dot summoned up her laboriously learned French. *'Chic. Très chic.'*

'Bon,' said Phryne, flicking the feather back. 'Now, a little scent and down we go. Your accent really has improved. Dot. You've been practising.'

'Hugh,' said Dot, blushing. 'He learned French at school and he's better than me, so we talk.'

Phryne wondered what they talked about, Dot and her large and delightful police constable – French being notoriously the language of love and confidences – but firmly did not ask.

Lin Chung, waiting in the parlour, heard a step on the carpeted stair and turned quickly, then was frozen in his place.

Descending was the silver lady, all in black which caught no light. Her gown draped over breast and hip, artfully suggesting the body underneath. He was struck again by how Chinese she looked, except that she could never be Chinese. She was altogether unique and other.

Following her was a young woman who made no impression on him at all.

Phryne extended a hand, laden with a heavy silver ring, and he kissed it.

200

He was very good-looking, she thought, and well-mannered as he ushered her through the dining room door and stood until she was seated. On the other hand he was not talking at all and she did not want to have so great an effect that she rendered her guest mute.

As Mrs Butler's excellent bouillon was served, she said, 'Tell me, what should I call you? If you are Lin Chung then you ought to be Mr Lin, I suppose.'

'That is correct, Miss Fisher.' His voice was very English. 'But all the fellows at school called me Lin, Chinese customs being beyond them. I would be honoured if you would do the same.' The dark eyes bent on her, leaning over to touch the very end of the black feather. 'You are very beautiful, Miss Fisher. I thought you so when I saw you swooping to my rescue in the lane, but now...'

'Now?'

'You could almost be one of my own people,' he said, trying desperately not to give offence. 'The Manchu princesses had your carriage, the proud set of your head, and they had black hair and red mouth like you. But you have green eyes, and there is more colour in your hair, and yet...' He dried up again. Phryne decided that she could not get through dinner on compliments and said, taking up her spoon, 'How did you come to be at school in England?'

'Ah, well, my father is a follower of Sun Yat Sen. He believes in education. I was born here, Miss Fisher, and was sent to Cambridge to study. Then I went to live in Shanghai to practise my

Cantonese and to learn ... what may be learned in Shanghai.'

Phryne grinned. She had been to that notoriously wicked place on a cruise, and remembered the quasi-Western hotels, the walks along the Bund, the glittering dresses on the pretty girls for which the city was famous, and dancing the foxtrot in the Star Ballroom. And the slim young men in Western dress, avid for Western ways and Western women. Somehow she had avoided involvement, but they had been undeniably attractive. In fact, she was wearing, in honour of Lin Chung's visit, the silver ring she had bought in Shanghai's most exclusive jewellery shop.

With a shock, she also remembered a sign in the private park belonging to one of the embassies. 'No dogs or Chinese allowed.' Or was that Hong Kong? She felt a pang of shame that she had not even torn down the sign and jumped on it.

'China is a very old country, Miss Fisher,' Lin Chung was continuing. 'That does not mean that it is always wise. The pattern of history has been that the mandate of Heaven is withdrawn from a corrupt dynasty, a new regime takes over and the new destroys the old. Then it becomes old and wicked in its turn and is again invaded and destroyed. Western interference during the rebellion of Righteous Fists kept the Manchu on the throne when they should have been swept aside. That was bad for China. Now Japan is threatening us again – our old enemy – and where will help come from? In any case China has only ever depended on itself. My family came here when we still called Australia the Second Gold Mountain.'

202

'What was that?'

'The gold rush, Miss Fisher. The First Gold Mountain was California. We have been here ever since.'

'All that time?'

'Indeed. We try not to attract attention, Miss Fisher. Safety lies, the Elders taught us, in proper behaviour and in care. There were anti-Chinese riots during that gold rush and many of us died. There was an upsurge of nationalism in the 1890s, prompted by the *Bulletin* crowd, who said that they wanted a white Australia, though most Australians are white in the way that white elephants are white, and there might have been riots then, too. So we are always careful. We do not display our wealth. We try not to directly compete with Australians.'

'How do you mean?'

'You have seen the hawkers in the city?'

Phryne recalled a man in a collarless shirt and felt hat with a yoke over his shoulders, walking down beside the Queen Victoria hospital. 'Yes, I have.'

'What do they sell to the factories and the shops?'

'Tea and ginger and roasted peanuts. I buy them when I am shopping, sometimes. They warm the hands.' She recalled clutching cold fingers around the hot peanuts in their little paper bag. Delicious.

'And what do the barrows in the city sell?'

'Fruit and flowers.'

'Yes. We do not compete unless we have to. We import most of the tropical fruit in Melbourne; we also grow very good vegetables. These we trade in direct markets. Even there some people call us dirty yellow scum and complain that we are under-cutting their prices. My family, Miss Fisher, imports silk and porcelain. Others import paper products, china, and fancy goods, mainly to supply Chinese families already here. We try never to come up flat against opposition, because that is not the way to survive, and above all things we are required to survive.'

'I see.' Mr Butler brought in a fricassee of veal and attendant vegetables. Phryne continued, 'Tell me, Mr Lin, what did Bunji and I interrupt in Little Bourke Street the other night?'

He smiled nervously. 'Merely a family quarrel. You need not be concerned.'

'I am concerned, Mr Lin. I have been followed and I have been watched ever since. What is going on? You owe me an explanation.'

'Tell me first, Silver Lady,' said Lin Chung, 'how do you feel about us?'

She could not read the black eyes, but the voice was urgent.

'I like you,' she said, 'if you are pleasant, and I dislike you if you are not. Just as I would judge anyone. Is that what you mean?'

'Yes, I believe it is,' Lin Chung smiled again. 'My grandmother, once convinced that you were not a spirit, said you were a courtesan, Miss Fisher. By that she meant no disrespect. They were the only independent educated women in China, the only ones with freedom of action and their own honour. Then when I looked up your name in a classical dictionary I found that Grandmother was right. Grandmother is always right. It is one of her

204

most irritating qualities. Phryne, who offered to reconstruct the walls of Thebes if she could carve on them, "The walls of Thebes, ruined by time, rebuilt by Phryne the courtesan." And they preferred their ruins!' he laughed gently. 'So. I trust in your honour not to reveal what I am about to tell you. It is like this. There are two families who have both been here from the beginning, that is, 1845 – Hu and Lin. We have never been friends, always rivals. We have long memories, Miss Fisher. We remember that the Hu family carried off a shipment of gold, and the bearers of that gold were never seen again. They remember that one of the Lin uncles seduced a Hu woman and she drowned herself. There are many injuries but at last my father and grandfather said "Enough." They went to the Elders of the Hu family and said, "We all came long ago from Five Dragons village in the south. We speak the Cantonese tongue. We should be brothers." To this truce, after long discussion, the Hu family agreed.'

'I see. What went wrong?'

Mr Butler removed the plates and brought in apple crumble and cream, which Phryne ate without tasting.

'How did you know that something went wrong?' Lin Chung countered.

'It must have. I know enough about China to know that old people are honoured. It must have taken something really serious to cause that mob to beat your grandmother.'

'Serious, yes.' He ate some apple crumble and glanced to both sides, as if someone might be listening.

'After dinner we will go up to my apartments and you can speak freely,' she offered. 'Meanwhile, tell me about yourself. What is your profession?'

'I am a trader, though I trained as a stage magician – tradition in my family. I was one of the strong men, trained in the temple of the War God in Canton. By long meditation and constant practice, we can do many things which the West considers marvellous – dance on eggshells, for example, and perform feats of strength. I was only there for a couple of years and did not reach mastery, but it is a useful skill.' Lin seemed relieved at not having to talk about his family. His voice was light and pleasant, with a honey-coloured undertone which promised sensuality. Phryne noticed that he had an entrancing profile, high cheekboned, with a long nose and winged eyebrows. 'But when I came home I found that the stage was too precarious a life for the son of the Lin family, and I became a merchant. I trade in silk. This used to yield a good living, but recently the market has crashed. The price of silk has plummeted because of the invention of art silk – artificial silk. It is washable and very cheap and looks – vaguely – like real silk. Now bolts of top-grade, fine-quality brocade, or corded silk like the gown that Grandmother sent your friend Miss Ross, will fetch only half the previous price.'

'Is this disastrous?'

'No, Miss Fisher, we will sell other things. Though not bananas. I do not like bananas. Furniture, I think. The *art decoratif* uses many Chinese forms. We will adapt. We always have. If it gets really bad, perhaps I will go back on to the stage.

Acrobats and strong men and magicians are always employed, especially if they have trained in Canton.'

'What sort of tricks do Chinese magicians do?'

'Oh, there is the one where I catch a bullet in my teeth. That's dangerous – it killed the most famous of all Chinese masters, Ching Lin Soo. There is the one where I pour milk into a bowl and change it to water with gold fish swimming in it. There is the one where I call up spirits, though that takes a lot of preparation.'

Phryne was impressed. 'Does, it, by Jove?'

The young man smiled modestly, 'It is all tricks, Miss Fisher ... Phryne.' He used her name for the first time with becoming modesty. 'I will show you some of them, if you please.'

'Could you call up a spirit for me? I've been trying to find one lately and she is very difficult to locate.'

Phryne told him about Dorothea while he finished the apple crumble and sipped at one glass of wine – he had refused more.

'Well, what do you think?' she asked, in conclusion.

'It is ... difficult to say. Although my family are Christians, there is a lot of traditional lore about ghosts. They are always seeking something. Indeed, one way of gaining final revenge on someone is to commit suicide on their doorstep, so that your ghost will haunt them forever.'

'That's a very final revenge.'

'Yes, but Chinese belief says that you will be around to see it, free of the bonds of flesh. If she was Chinese, I would say that Dorothea has returned to wreak vengeance on her murderer. She cannot kill him – ghosts are not believed to be able to affect the material world which they have left – but she would drive him into death, into suicide, in his turn. Or she may have been a fox-spirit.'

'A fox-spirit?'

'"Do not give your heart to a fox, or she will bite it in two,"' quoted Lin Chung, finishing the wine. 'A fox-spirit is a pretty young woman with a beautiful smile and the heart of a demon. She will take your property and waste it, and then when you try to make love to her, she will turn and bite – then resume her fox-form and leap out the window, never to return.' He looked at Phryne's solemn face and laughed. 'It is only a tale, Phryne. Just a fairy tale.'

'Fairy tale or not, there was a lot of fox in Dorothea. What did you call to me, when you saw me in the street that night?'

'I said "Run!" in Cantonese. I thought you were one of us. Grandmother addressed you in Chinese because she thought that you were an ancestral ghost. Then I realised that you were a woman, the image of the Taoist Lady of the Moon, all silver.'

'The silver lady,' mused Phryne. 'And tonight?' she gestured to her sombre magnificence.

'Tonight you are the moon eclipsed,' he said softly, taking her hand and kissing it. This seemed to be a declaration, and Phryne was not going to waste it.

She led him up the stairs to her boudoir, set down the tray of coffee and champagne, then locked the door and sat down on the sofa.

'Drink with me,' she said, and supplied him with Veuve Clicquot in a long-stemmed glass. 'And tell me all, Mr Lin.'

'Silver Lady, it is not a romantic tale.' He paused, then went on. 'There is a way of cementing an alliance such as the Elders have suggested.'

'A marriage?' Phryne's mind reverted instantly to the sullen girl called Annie in the room hung with brocade.

'As you say.' The young man looked away, into the wreathed mirror. His skin was almost brazen in Phryne's pink light and his eyes were black. Small cuts, rapidly healing, were all that remained of the damage inflicted on him in that affray.

'The bride is that pretty girl called Annie,' she prompted, putting her hand on his.

'And the groom is me,' he made a comical grimace. 'Neither of us wish to marry the other. I do not wish to marry at all and poor Annie has fallen in love with another. Because she has told her family this and defied them, they do not wish to take her back and I don't want to marry her.'

'That doesn't explain that attack on your grandmother.' Phryne pointed out.

He said reluctantly, 'No, well, there is another faction, the Li family, who wish San-niang, Annie, to marry their son. They were hoping to kidnap Grandmother and hold her for ransom. They know that we would do anything to get her back.'

'Why does everyone want poor San-niang?'

'Because she is the only heir of her father, and he is very rich.'

209

'But this is Australia – she can't be married to you or anyone against her will.'

'There are ways to persuade,' said the young man, his hand sliding slowly over Phryne's. 'But I will not have her forced and neither will Grandmother, so it is insoluble unless she changes her mind, or I change my mind, or she is kidnapped, or...'

'She runs away.' The caress was sending pleasant tingles up Phryne's arm. 'Then who has been watching me?' she asked.

'Some of them are sent by Grandmother and are of the Lin family; they are there because she fears some attack on you and she owes you a debt. Some may be Hu and some maybe Li. Until this problem is solved it might be best to avoid Little Bourke Street, Phryne.'

'Can't, I'm investigating the Maj – His Majesty's Theatre. I'll just have to be alert.'

Phryne leaned across and unfastened his tie, opening the collar and unbuttoning the shirt. A perfectly bare chest was warm under her palm, and his hand came up to caress her cheek, moving down to the hollow of her throat.

'What is the Chinese phrase for making love?' she asked and he replied on a gasp, 'The play of clouds and rain.'

'Show me,' she requested.

They shed clothes and lay down on the moss-green sheets. He was slender and beautiful as he lay beside her and kissed very gently down the length of her body, sweeping his fingers in precise arcs across her flesh which seemed to leave sparks in their wake, electrifying each delicate place with a touch as light as a falling leaf.

'This is butterfly touch,' he whispered into her navel, 'Silver Lady, you are as white as white jade, and this,' his mouth touched and Phryne's hands came down to stroke his head, 'is the jade gate.'

Phryne was unfamilar with a sexuality which did not entirely depend on penetration. Her body glowed under his touch. His face was mask-like, concentrated, as beautiful as a carving, but he shivered under her fingers as she smoothed her hands down long flanks and scented, muscular chest.

When he finally drew her up into his embrace, half lying across her bed, she wreathed her arms around his smooth back and the warmth contracted to a fiery bead which burst and bloomed like a firework.

Phryne woke slowly and dreamily. Someone was kissing her, soft fast kisses in the curve of her shoulder, which moved gradually down to her breast. This brought her fully awake. She opened her eyes on the dark. There was a naked man beside her, lying close and warm.

'There remains yet some of the night, Silver Lady,' suggested the light voice and she turned into his arms. 'And the moon is not yet down.'

Phryne found, as the hands and mouth became more urgent, that this was true.

Lin Chung woke again and looked at the face lying on the pillow beside him. Strands of night-black hair strayed across her face. Chinese but not Chinese, he thought, like but not like. He saw their reflection in the large mirror which was

211

tilted to reveal the bed. A pillow-book etching, the woman naked and white as ivory, and himself lying beside her, covers cast off to reveal the lovers to the illustrator. He lazily enjoyed the artful asymmetry of their pose; her outflung hand curled empty on his chest, his arms around her, the bulge of muscle in one of his shoulders, the flat plane of the other. The golden-beige of his torso against the stark paleness of her thigh made a pleasing contrast. One of her small high-arched feet was shamelessly visible to make the picture unfit for general exhibition.

He regretted that there was no one to draw them, to make a delicately tinted, hand-coloured plate for a deluxe edition of *The Carnal Prayermat* or *The Golden Lotus*.

She stirred and the picture dissolved. The ivory woman stretched and rubbed one hand across her face. Lin Chung brushed away the silky hair.

'Lin?' she asked, then full remembrance flooded back and she smiled sensously and stroked the hand cupping her cheek. 'Ah, yes.'

'Yes indeed, Silver Lady.'

'Is it morning?' Phryne was never at her best in the mornings. 'Damnation. I have to get up. I've got to find out what is happening in that theatre.' She looked at her lover. 'Am I mistaken, or was that one of the most wonderful nights of my life? Ring the bell, Lin, I must bathe and dress,' she demanded crossly, sitting up.

He did as he was ordered, a little disconcerted.

'It was the most wonderful night of my life,' he agreed softly. 'Was I just an experiment, Silver Lady, Moon Goddess?'

'If so, you were remarkably successful.' Phryne found her feet with a flash of pale skin which made him wish even more for an artist. 'You were absolutely lovely,' she added from the bathroom, then he lost her voice over the roar of taps.

He joined her at the bathroom door, and she handed him a silk robe figured with dragons and pulled on a peacock garment which the Lin family must have imported. He recognised the embroidery of Tainan. Another link between us, thought Lin Chung.

'Will you dine with me tonight?' he asked diffidently. He had encountered experimental ladies before, ones who wanted to 'find out what a Chow was like' and was hurt to think that he could have made such an error regarding Phryne. The door was unlocked and the plain young woman came in without knocking, setting down a loaded tray on the small table in the main room.

'Yes. Of course. Where?' she asked. 'Dot, I'm going to need climbing-around-the-set clothes. A sturdy garment of some sort, thick stockings and flat-heeled shoes. I've got an idea, which is strange considering the hour. My God, it's afternoon. Ah, coffee,' she commented, breathing in the steam of a small cup evidently containing concentrated caffeine.

The maid went into the walk-in wardrobe and rummaged. Phryne offered him Chinese tea and waved a hand at a proper Western breakfast.

Bemused, Lin ate and drank, luxuriating in the comfort of the gown. Although he believed firmly in the Westernizing ideas of the semi-divine Sun, he felt that a Chinese gentleman ought to be able

213

to wear robes. It was Iron Goddess tea, he found as he sipped it, a strengthening beverage. He bathed in her undersea coloured bathroom and dressed in his discarded evening clothes.

'Tonight,' said the Silver Lady as he stood uncertainly at her boudoir door, 'come and get me at the theatre. Before the performance. Seven?' She pressed against him in a brief contact which caught his breath.

'Seven,' he agreed, and kissed her hand. The silver ring was a dragon and phoenix, he saw, entwined together. The symbol of the Emperor and the Empress, and of the King and Queen of Heaven. The symbol of a perfect mating of Yin and Yang.

It was a good omen, and he left Phryne's house and drove himself home, tired and elated.

Phryne bathed, dragged on a purple knitted dress and a black woollen jacket and pulled lisle stockings over her legs. She had woken with an idea which was now eluding her. Somewhere, sometime, someone had said something important and she had missed it. She groped after the elusive memory and it slipped away.

'Blast,' she said again, finished her coffee.

'Miss, you know that baby?' offered Dot. 'Eat a little toast, Miss, you can't go out with nothing but coffee and it's past lunchtime.'

'What baby? Oh, you mean Dorothea's child. Yes, what about it?'

Dot produced the photograph. Phryne looked at it. A baby lay face down on the rug, laughing, its head turned to the camera. It was totally bald and resembled all other babies of its class and age.

Phryne could see nothing unusual in it.

'Look at the back, Miss, just above its little bottom. There.'

'Yes, I can see a spot on the photo.'

'Not on the photo, Miss, on the baby,' urged Dot. 'It's a birthmark. Shaped a bit like a strawberry.'

Phryne stared, recognised that Dot was arguably right, and gave her back the picture.

'More than ever, Dot dear, I am convinced that we are caught up in a comic opera. A strawberry birthmark, oh dear, oh dear. Now how am I going to peel the shirt off Gwilym Evans without getting myself embroiled in...' Phryne caught Dot's reproving eye. 'Well, you know what he's like! I'll think of something. Perhaps I can drop in while he's dressing. Now, I've got to go and see the priest of the Methodist church, he's the only person in Melbourne who appears to speak Welsh and I need a translation of that letter. No, he's not a priest, he's a pastor. Or a reverend. Then I'm going to the theatre and I'm dining with Mr Lin. Depending on one thing and another, I may not be back tonight.' She loaded her bag with various useful things. 'And I promise I'll wear my St Christopher medal and not have any dealings with any unclean spirits, Dot.' She crossed her heart under the purple wool and Dot smiled.

Phryne pulled on a black suede cloche hat and pencilled in her eyebrows, patted her nose with the powder puff and clipped the compact closed. In the mirror, her eyes shone as green as Roman glass. She had been slightly cast down at the loss of Mark Fielding so firmly and forever. But there

215

were compensations, Phryne thought, definite compensations, and walked down the stairs to her car.

CHAPTER TWELVE

Box: *Do you have a strawberry coloured birthmark on your left shoulder?*
Cox: *No!*
Box: *Neither do I! You must be my long-lost brother!*

Maddison Morton
Box and Cox
(later *Cox and Box* with music by Sullivan)

Phryne found the priest, pastor or reverend of the Welsh Church of Saint David standing in the street waving a scrubbing brush at the fleeing forms of several street urchins, who had been painting rude words on his wall.

'There is no place for you in the Kingdom of Heaven!' he roared. He waited to see if this dreadful curse would fell them with a lightning bolt, then shrugged and began scrubbing. Phryne commented, 'Presumably God will get around to them later,' and he looked up. He was stout, robust and perhaps fifty, with a carefully cultivated white beard.

'To be sure he will. You are the young lady who called? I am the Reverend Daffydd Griffiths. Come in,' he said. His voice was like an organ, rich and deep. 'What do you wish me to read for you?'

'This.' Phryne walked into the chalk-scented dimness of a perfectly bare hall. One would only know it was a church from the plain wooden crucifix behind the altar.

'Ah, yes. Do sit down.' The Reverend's office was crammed with papers and books and he cleared a chair for her to be seated. 'This is a simple letter from a village in the north, badly spelled and not very well written.' He knitted his white brows. 'It says, "Dear Gwil, our boy is seven now and going to school. When are you coming home? I got the money you sent but things are getting dear. Mari." Do I know this man?' he asked severely.

'I think it very unlikely,' responded Phryne, opening her purse. 'Thank you for your translation. Could I make a small donation?'

'Thank you.' He bristled his brows at her. 'Do you like to sing?'

'Yes, I do,' she confessed.

'We have a service in English every week, no sermon. Just singing. A real roof-raiser,' he said proudly. 'Perhaps I will see you there?'

'I belong to the Church of England,' said Phryne, which was effectively true, as far as she belonged anywhere.

'That's all right,' said the Reverend, making an expansive gesture. 'As long as he had a voice, my congregation would accept a Heathen Chinese.'

'Thank you,' said Phryne, and was ushered into the street, where the Reverend Mr Griffiths resumed his scrubbing. Phryne was pleased that the children had been interrupted halfway through their rude word.

She walked briskly away. It was just a common saying. But she had just spent all night playing clouds and rain with a heathen Chinese, and he had been loving, delicate, skilled and terribly intelligent. Yet what she was thinking of – an alliance with a man of a different race – would be considered by all of society to be a vast and irretrievable degradation, making her of less value than a whore. Phryne closed her fists and stiffened her spine.

'To Hell with all racialists,' she said aloud. 'And to Hell with eugenics, degenerate heredity, miscegenation and frauds who pile up skulls like a conqueror as well. May they choke on their bones.' A passing gentleman boggled at her and crossed to the other side of La Trobe Street. 'There is no place for them in the Kingdom of Heaven,' she added, rolling the phrase over her tongue and filing it for future reference.

So Gwil Evans had left a wife and child in distant Wales. She considered this, turning the corner into Exhibition Street and avoiding a clutch of city gentlemen in pin-stripes and bowlers. No wonder he couldn't marry any of his lovers, though she questioned that he wanted to, except perhaps Leila Esperance. And he couldn't marry her, not with Mari at home in a cold little village somewhere in the mountains and a son seven years old. No wonder he had not gone home to his foster mother's funeral. And he might well be Dorothea's child, if he had a birthmark on his lower back.

She reached the theatre to find Herbert in

218

charge and Tom Deeping asleep in his little box. The boy touched a finger to his lips and led Phryne to the stairs. He looked strained and the dark eyes had shadows underneath. There was a bruise on his cheek and he had one hand tucked into his shirt.

'Your dad again?' she asked and he nodded. 'Can't your mum leave him?'

'No, there's all the others and there's nowhere to go. Anyway, she says it's what men are like. Grandad is a drunk, too. It's all she knows. He wants me to be apprenticed to a baker. I told him I was going to be an actor and...' Herbert shifted uncomfortably, as if more bruises were hidden under his cheap unravelling jumper and patched trousers.

'No reason for you to stay, Tinker. I can make some arrangements, perhaps, if you like.'

'I'm not going into any orphanage,' stated Herbert.

'No, that would not suit. I was thinking of a family to board with while you're learning to be an actor. Ah. Here is Dr Fielding. Mark, can you have a look at this young man?'

'No, I'm all right,' protested Herbert, 'and I'm minding the door.'

'I'll mind the door. Mark, take him into the gentlemen's dressing room and come back with a report. This is unacceptable,' said Phryne implacably. Mark Fielding knew that tone. He took Herbert's shoulder in a gentle grip and moved him upstairs.

Deeping lay back in his chair. Breath heavily laden with port puffed out between his lips, the only sign that he was alive. Although her own father had been a heavy drinker, Phryne had never seen him violent and was not afraid of alcoholics. She was musing on the lucky mistake that her father had not been himself at her christening, which resulted in her being named for Phryne the courtesan and not Psyche the nymph – a *felix culpa* if there had ever been one – when Mark came back.

He walked stiffly down and said in a voice of restrained anger, 'He's been beaten with a belt and punched and kicked. He has two broken ribs and the poor little chap is badly bruised. I've strapped him up and given him aspirin but he ought to be in bed. What are you going to do about him, Phryne?'

'I'll see Sir B as soon as he arrives and get him apprenticed or under contract today. Then you can find him somewhere pleasant to stay for the future and I'll pay for it. Simple.'

Mark Fielding smiled. 'Your solutions are always simple,' he said. 'Incomparable Phryne! Are you sure you don't mind?'

'About what?'

'Mollie Webb and me. I think – I think she...'

'I think so too and I hope you'll be very happy.' She kissed him gently and for the last time on his soft red mouth.

Sir Bernard arrived to find his office occupied by Miss Fisher and a snuffling call boy who seemed to have been in the wars.

'Ah, Bernard.' Miss Fisher fixed him with her glittering eye. 'Do you really think that this fellow can be an actor?'

'Yes!' Bernard was surprised into honesty, 'I do. Why?'

'Then put him under contract or whatever you do, there's a dear. If you want him to survive long enough to play in your panto. I'll bear the costs of his maintenance for the moment. Then he can pay me back, if he likes, out of his legacy from Mr Copland.'

'Herbert, is this what you want?' asked Tarrant severely.

'Yes, Sir Bernard,' whispered Herbert Cowl, his bruised eyes growing large with hope. 'If I can pay her back. I don't want to be no... I don't want to be a burden on anyone's charity.'

'You won't be, dear boy. You've inherited a tidy sum, they tell me, from Mr Copland, who said you had "such promise". Just what an actor needs, a trust fund. Well then, sign here and here. But I'll need the father's signature, too, Phryne.' Herbert stiffened his thin shoulders and said despairingly, 'He'll never sign.'

'Yes, I think he will. Dr Fielding will go around and see him this afternoon, when he's delivering you to your new home.'

Phryne did not think any drunk would stand up against a determined Dr Mark with an injustice to avenge. 'Now, is there anything you want to do, Herbert? You're a member of this company now.'

'I'll go home and get my things,' he said breathlessly, 'if the doctor will take me. Say goodbye to Mum. Oh, Boss,' he said with a rush of affection, 'you're bonzer.'

With that he launched himself regardless of his injuries at Phryne and kissed her moistly on the cheek. She hugged him gently for a moment. Then he released her and darted out of the office in search of Dr Fielding.

'That'll be a valuable contract,' she commented, as Bernard added it to the pile and stowed it in the safe.

'I know. If he lasts, the boy will be good. Has to learn his craft. But he has the makings,' said Bernard. 'And at least I've got his details when he's too young to change them.'

'Change what?'

'The date of birth, the time he began. If you listen to them, all actors were born in a trunk, were on stage at the age of three weeks and smash hits by the time they were ten. And trying to work a cabinet secret out of a member of parliament is child's play beside getting an actress to divulge her age.'

'So they lie about it in contracts?' asked Phryne tensely.

'Yes, dear girl, of course. The theatre is youth, and age is a handicap and the dreadful spectre that lurks behind each star's door.'

He was about to develop this promising metaphor when he looked up and realised that his audience had gone.

Just to be sure, Phryne marched into Gwilym Evans' dressing room where he was donning his rehearsal costume for *The Pirates of Penzance*, pulled aside the screen and stripped off the frilly shirt. He stared at her, grinned, then stopped grinning as she pushed him so that his face was to the wall and then peered closely at his back.

'Shonni, help,' he called, 'I think I'm being raped.'

'Never needed no help for that,' came the dresser's voice.

'What are you doing, Miss Fisher, and can I join in?'

'Look at his back,' she ordered, pinning Gwil to the wall with a firm hand.

'I'm looking.'

'Not a mark on it, is there?'

'No, perfectly clear,' Shonni agreed, humouring her.

'What about you?' she asked. After all, the children could have been changed at birth. That would be very Gilbertian. She released the actor, who pulled his shirt on as though he was cold.

Shonni turned away and allowed Phryne to bare his back and examine it.

'Good.' She turned and left, slamming the door behind her.

'Box on Cox,' said Gwil faintly to his dresser. '"Do you have a strawberry birthmark on your shoulder?" "No." "Neither do I! Then you must be my long-lost brother!" I've got to find out what she's doing, Shon, or I'll die of curiosity. Give me a coat and some shoes, and let's go.'

But Phryne was stopped short of her destination by Jack Robinson's sergeant.

'Miss, the D. I. sent me, he wants you right away in Mr Copland's old room. And the doctor, too, and Mr Evans.'

'Is it serious?' Phryne suppressed her anxiety for getting at a solution and laying it bare immediately.

'Boss seems to think so. This way.'

Dr Fielding, Phryne and a partly dressed Gwilym Evans crowded into the dressing room, where Jack Robinson occupied the dresser's stool.

There was a small man lying back in the actor's chair. He was gasping for breath and blue; Mark knelt by him and laid a warm hand to his pulse.

'He's taken something pretty rapid,' he said. 'If you want to talk to him, be quick.'

'Tell the sister and his mother that I'm sorry, and make sure Herbert gets the money,' whispered Hans, the dresser. 'I never meant to kill ... never meant to kill.'

Phryne knelt down on the other side and the sad, watery eyes fixed on her face. 'You'll understand. He was getting old, said he was going to retire, retire so that we could live together like he always promised. So I thought I'd spike his brandy, make him sleepier and more clumsy, he was too old for those roles, too old, when there were such good young men. I put laudanum in the brandy, but I forgot how nervous he was, how scared he was. He drank it all at once, it must have affected his heart. I just wanted him to retire!'

'And he had also declared that he was going to marry Miss Esperance,' suggested Phryne softly. The dying man heaved in his chair, his face distorted with emotion. 'Foolish! What good would he have been to her, or any woman? He was mine – I was a boy when he found me...'

'When you fell in love with him,' said Phryne in a low gentle tone. James Hansen nodded. 'We used to talk about sitting either side of the fire in his house in the country. "We two shall sing like birds i' th' cage," he would say. But he never lived to play Lear. He wasn't good enough for Lear. We were going to be so happy, but he wouldn't leave the stage – couldn't leave it. I sat beside him in that hospital and watched him die. He didn't tell anyone about his heart. They might have taken the roles away – the dancing and the applause, he couldn't live without it. I didn't mean to kill him, but he died. Poor Robbie Craven nearly died, too. And I was going to let you suffer for it, like you made Walter suffer,' he said to Gwilym, the enfeebled hand closing on the actor's wrist. 'But I saw you play Sir Ruthven. You put your heart into him, you played him right. Better I should die than you. The show ... must...' he convulsed and groaned. Then the head fell forward, the hands relaxed.

'He's dead,' said Mark Fielding, getting to his feet.

'And he went before he could complete the aphorism, which comes as something of a relief. Poor little man!' said Phryne. 'Well, that's one of your murders solved, Jack – one murder and an attempted murder. We are proceeding.'

Jack Robinson removed the sheet of paper from under the dead man's cheek.

'This is a full confession to causing the death of Walter Copland, and if the press gets hold of this my chief'll make a dog's dinner out of me. In relation to motive, of course. We aren't going to mention this to anyone, are we?' he asked the room, his unremarkable face set with purpose. Sir Bernard agreed and Mark Fielding nodded. Jack Robinson looked at Phryne.

225

'Depends. Are we still prosecuting Mr Evans for giving the bottle to Robbie Craven?' asked Phryne.

'No, it was an honest mistake. He's free to go,' said Jack Robinson. Phryne was impressed. She had not known that it was possible to deliver such a long speech entirely through the teeth.

'Good, but you can leave Mr Evans to me, Jack dear,' she promised in turn. 'He may not be the dog's dinner, but he can still be the cat's breakfast. Come along, Gwilym,' she said, leading him out of the room by the sleeve, 'I have something of yours which I would like to return.'

She led the bemused actor back into his dressing room and leaned on the door.

'He said I played well, and that's the reason he didn't leave me with a murder charge,' said Gwilym, sinking into his chair and mopping his face on a towel. 'I could have spent the rest of my life in jail, or even...'

'Danced on the end of a line,' agreed Phryne. 'Yes, but you are reprieved and Jack will not take any action against you.' She came a little closer and the actor stared adoringly up into her eyes. 'But I might. Do you recognise this?'

'It's a letter, it's mine,' he snatched it out of her hand, the loving look quenched like a spark. 'And I can't imagine why you stole it,' he said angrily. 'You can't read it.'

'No, but there are those who can. What about Mari and a boy seven years old? How can you go around offering to marry actresses when you have a wife and child in Wales?'

'She's not my wife. She was my landlady's

daughter in Aberystwyth,' he said disgustedly. 'She did the housework and made the beds.'

'And then she lay in one?' asked Phryne acidly.

'Yes, it's my child – I suppose it's my child. I send her money when I can. But I'm not going back. You heard that old man. I'm good – I know I'm good. I'm going to be great. Well, that's my dirty little secret, Miss Fisher, and I hope it amuses you.'

'Not particularly. Got any others?'

He was caught on the edge of laughing or raging, and Phryne saw the mood tip over. He laughed and seized her in his arms. He kissed her hard, and she returned the kiss. Sensual, tasting of coffee, but not a patch on Lin Chung.

'I already know that secret,' she said, freeing herself. 'Now I have another person to talk to. Keep well, Mr Evans, and try to send some money home.' And Gwilym Evans, whose celebrated charm had never failed before, threw a boot at her as his dressing room door closed behind the slim figure.

Phryne surprised Miss Leila Esperance in her robe, listening to her dresser Mrs Black describe Hans' death.

'Then he called in the policeman and that Miss Fisher and Mr Evans and the doctor, and he told them that because Mr Copland had deserted him and proposed to you, he had to kill him!'

Leila purred. Phryne said, 'He did not mean to kill, you know. Now, Miss Esperance, I am asking for information and it has to be the truth. Tell me your real name.'

'Leila Esperance.' She picked up an eyelash brush and began to apply it, staining the hairs deep black.

'What name were you born with?'

'None of your business.'

'Miss Esperance, I think you ought to answer my questions.'

'You may think so, but I don't.'

Phryne stared into the twisted, peevish face and laughed. 'I wish your admirers could see you now!' The beautiful face immediately blanked of expression.

'It would be to your advantage,' offered Phryne. 'It may have a great bearing on your future in the theatre.'

'My future in the theatre is secure,' snapped Miss Esperance. 'Now if you don't mind, I'm upset about poor Hans and I want to get on with my makeup.'

'Where were you born and when?' persisted Phryne. Miss Esperance said wearily 'London.'

'When's your birthday?'

'The twelfth of June, if you want to buy me a present.'

The voice was dripping with engraving acid. Phryne went on.

'What year?' The actress did not answer. Phryne went to the door and called, 'Bernie, can you come in here a moment?' She waited until the large rubicund form of Sir Bernard had joined them and asked again, 'What year?'

'Eighteen ninety-seven, if you must know. I was an orphan and my family was called Pearson and they came out here when I was a baby.'

'Look at this photo.' Phryne thrust it into Bernard's hand. 'That is a picture of Dorothea Curtis's child, the one she bore while she was away from you in the hot months of 1897 – June and July. Didn't you know she was pregnant, Bernie? Didn't you notice?'

'I teased her about getting stout,' he stammered. 'What with clothes being what they were, and corsets and all … I didn't know, I never suspected .. but do you really mean that, Miss Esperance...'

Phryne ripped the gown away from Leila Esperance's creamy shoulders and it fell to her waist. Around her neck, between sculptured porcelain breasts, was a golden locket the exact twin of the one Phryne had seen in Miss Mobbs' house.

Phryne took the locket in her hand and Miss Esperance wriggled. Suppressing the actress, she pressed the button and the locket popped open, revealing a pretty, pouting face. 'Dorothea Curtis,' said Phryne.

'I never knew it opened!' exclaimed Leila Esperance, and was pushed away as Phryne exhibited her beautiful back to Sir Bernard's astonished gaze.

Just where the slim waist curved in was a strawberry coloured birthmark.

'This is your daughter, Bernard.' Phryne perched on the stool as Miss Esperance stared open mouthed at Management. 'Dorothea never told you. She gave the baby to her cousin and dresser Miss Mobbs, who gave her to a couple called Pearson who were emigrating to Australia. Dorothea put the locket around the baby's neck – it was all she had to give it.' Phryne amended the story as she spoke. There was no sense in defying the melodrama conventions and it might hurt Bernie's feelings to know that Dorothea had ordered the baby killed. 'What happened to your parents, the Pearsons I mean, Leila?'

'They died. Five years ago.' The actress's voice was mechanical with shock. 'There was something Mother was trying to tell me when she died, but she couldn't get the words out... Something about London and the locket. So she came to find me,' said Leila softly. 'My true mother came to find me.'

'"By the powers,"' said Sir Bernard softly, holding out his hand, '"I do believe this lady to be my daughter."' Phryne tracked down the quotation – *A Winter's Tale*. Another hidden daughter. Jack Robinson was right; there was always a word for any situation in Shakespeare.

Mrs Black bustled forward and pulled Miss Esperance's gown up, covering her with a costume cloak.

'Now, we'd all be better for some tea,' she observed. Phryne vacated the stool and Sir Bernard sat down on it. He was holding Leila's hand as if it was a day-old chick and his cigar had gone out. Phryne decided that a little time would be necessary for everyone to adjust to their changing fortunes and left the room.

'Phryne, what is going on?' demanded Mark Fielding, rumpling his curly hair. 'The chorus want to know. They've had enough shocks lately.'

'Tell them that Hans is dead and that he killed Walter Copland because he was trying to get him

230

to retire. That's close enough to the truth without being too scandalous. They'll guess the rest if I know choruses.'

Phryne saw Mollie Webb shoot out of her dressing room and run straight into Mark Fielding's arms. He bent his head to whisper to her and Phryne felt a sting of jealousy, suppressed it firmly and walked away. Herbert caught her at the manager's door.

'Something else has happened,' he said accusingly. 'Listen to Miss Esperance!'

Phryne heard a murmur of soothing conversation, and someone sobbing.

'She's crying. That's not unusual, Tinker.'

'It's not the way she usually cries,' he said stubbornly. He was right. It was probably the first unaffected emotion which Miss Esperance had exhibited since she cried for her bottle at the age of eight weeks, thought Phryne. She mentally slapped herself on the wrist and led Herbert into the office. In a last toast to poor dead Hans, Phryne poured herself a drink of uncoloured whisky.

'There's an end of our investigation, Tinker,' she said. 'You're provided for, we've solved the murder and found the missing daughter – it's about time for the curtain.'

'No, Boss, you've forgotten the ghost.' The boy's eyes were indecently bright for someone who had been beaten to a pulp by a drunken man that morning.

'So I have,' said Phryne. 'Thanks, Tinker! Of course. The ghost.'

Mark Fielding had made several phone calls

and had found a family to board Herbert. He took the boy off to obtain his father's signature, farewell his mother, and see him safely installed. Phryne handed over a five pound note with instructions to purchase some gallons of liquid parent-persuader on the way.

Then she wrote down, from her invaluable assistant's chart, every sighting of Dorothea and every other strange thing that had happened.

She pored over this for an hour and gave it up. It was impossible and even Sir Bernard's whisky would not make the times fit. No one could have played Dorothea more than once. Either there was a theatre-wide conspiracy or she was a real ghost.

However, she went back to Leila Esperance's dressing room to ask a few more questions.

She found Sir Bernard beaming and Leila leaning on his shoulder, her black curls flowing down his back. Even his cigar was glowing with pride.

'Phryne, my dear girl,' he greeted her jovially. 'Knew I did the right thing, asking you to investigate. Best decision I ever made.'

'Good. I'm glad you're happy, Bernie. Can I have a word with your daughter?' The mere use of the term made the cigar glow brighter. Bernie bent and kissed the rosy cheek, said, 'Back soon,' and went out.

'Leila, I need to know about the gloves and the bag,' said Phryne. She had never seen anyone as beautiful as this young woman elevated with joy. She was almost angelic. The voice, however, was cold and sharp, like a whisky-sour.

'All right, since you know. It was me – the gloves. Well, two of the gloves. I didn't take all of them. And I didn't take the bag. I tore up the telegram. I don't know why.'

'Why gloves? Are you sure you didn't know you were Dorothea's daughter?'

'No, no, I didn't know – really I didn't. Oh, poor mother! She scared me – I was frightened when she came – I shouldn't have been, it was my mother, my beautiful mother, and I ran away, I screamed and ran away.' Her eyes brimmed, then tears ran down the soft cheek. Phryne wondered which part she was presently playing.

'She'd understand,' soothed Phryne. 'Anyone would have been frightened. But you stole your own gloves, and tore up the telegram, Leila, and that's all? You didn't steal the hyacinth perfume? You didn't plant anything on Selwyn Alexander?'

'No,' said the actress simply. Phryne, for some reason, believed her.

'It's lucky it took so long,' Leila said flatly. 'Lucky we didn't find out until now.'

'Why?'

'I'm a principal singer and I got here on my own. No one will be able to say that Sir B pushed me. I did it all on my own. And now I'm Management's daughter. Will she come again, my mother? I want to tell her I'm sorry I ran away. I won't be scared next time,' she said imploringly and Phryne was filled with pity, entirely against her better judgement.

'If she comes again, you can tell her so. But if she's here, perhaps she'll know anyway. And perhaps that's what she wanted to do – perhaps that's why she's come. To make sure that Bernie has a daughter to be proud of, and to stop you

233

making a foolish marriage – several foolish mar-riages, come to think of it. Now she's done that, she might be free.' Phryne was on exceptionally shaky ground and knew it, but she seemed to be comforting Miss Esperance.

She left the father and daughter to become acquainted and took herself into Sir Bernard's box, where she could hear a comforting noise of hammering and swearing on stage. There she fell into a doze, and woke on the stroke of seven o'clock with the knowledge that she had forgot-ten something terribly important.

Originally, it had appeared that Dorothea had not returned to ensure any happy endings. She was raging for revenge on her murderer. And he or she had still not been found.

CHAPTER THIRTEEN

Within this breast there beats a heart
Whose voice can't be gainsaid.

Gilbert and Sullivan
Ruddigore

Phryne met an immaculate Lin Chung at the stage door, where Tom Deeping had recovered and was once more at his post. Behind her, the stage echoed to the chorus trying to sing 'Hail the bride-groom/hail the bride' to the constant interruptions of the chorus master, who was yelling actionable things in French about their pitch and how it got like that.

She felt scratchy and irritated and silently took his arm. They turned down into Little Bourke Street. They had passed a banana store and the Chinese Mission building before she spoke.

'Sorry, Lin, I'm in an evil mood. I have solved two of the problems but there is this ghost and I don't seem to be able to get a handle on her at all.'

'Then we shall have a pleasant dinner and you need not think about her for a few hours,' he replied equably, as they passed Quong Hoong Wah, general store. The shopkeeper, sweeping his step with a short whisk broom, said, *'Wah! Jung gwok moh nui a?'*

Lin replied, *'Moh kam Gong, a pak! Pang yau che!'* and the shopkeeper laughed.

'What did he say?' Phryne demanded. Lin shifted his gaze and said, 'Oh, just a comment about women.'

'On the general subject of "aren't Chinese ladies good enough for you?"' she guessed shrewdly. He looked down at her, astonished.

'Yes, indeed. How did you know that?'

'That's what someone would say to me if I escorted you down Toorak Road. This is going to be a rocky and difficult road, Lin, if we want to walk it.'

'Yes, I had considered that.'

'And?'

'Difficult roads are so much more interesting, don't you think?'

'Picturesque,' agreed Phryne and began to look

235

about her.

Little Bourke Street was narrow and crowded. It was sliced across with lanes and all of them were full of people working. Each little grey stone house, she saw with pleasure, had a door and a doorstep where someone was sitting doing something. An old woman was shelling peas. A young man was splitting what looked like cane, laying the pieces in a water-filled dish beside him. A well-fed orange cat sat on a windowsill next to a pot of herbs, surveying the scene with distant eyes.

The air smelt overwhelmingly of fruit, with an underscent of saffron, garlic, dust, people and motor exhaust.

Lin and Phryne stood back against the wall as a large truck manoeuvred its way carefully out of Corr's Lane into Little Bourke Street and trundled past. It had 'Yee Tong, Fruit Merchant' emblazoned on its dusty side.

Little shops with tiny windows breathed forth a smell of herbs and strange spices. Each one appeared to be staffed by an old woman in dark loose trousers and tunic, her head wrapped in a white scarf, with an attendant cat sitting at her feet.

'Small tiger,' said Lin Chung. 'Every shop has a *mau*. For the mice and rats. They are also effective against demons.'

'"The cherub cat is a term of the angel tiger,"' said Phryne, quoting Christopher Smart, and Lin said 'Yes, that is exactly it. Who said that? I thought I knew all the Chinese authors.'

'Not Chinese, don't be so isolationist.'

236

'English?'

Phryne nodded. 'Eighteenth century. And mad. Where are we going?'

'A restaurant in Heffernan's Lane. Unless you are feeling uncomfortable?'

Phryne had been aware of the eyes as soon as she had entered Little Bourke Street on the arm of a Chinese man. Everyone was, indeed, looking at her, but the gaze was neither insulting nor intrusive. They were interested in her, and she was interested in them. It seemed fair. Phryne had been stared out of countenance in too many countries in the world to bother about a few glances in the heart of her own city. Plump, well-dressed and decorative Chinese children sat up in prams and goggled at her in a most satisfactory way, their hair carefully done in two straight plaits which stuck out at right angles from the wearer's head, giving them the appearance of dolls.

It was not as though she was the only foreigner in the street. She sighted a very un-Chinese Louis Orbuck and Co, jewellers, down one of the lanes. Along another lane, she saw the Domino Shirt Manufactory and His Majesty's Motor Garage, with the usual complement of greasy mechanics lounging about outside, breathing the same fumes as Petroleum and Oils in Star Lane. As they turned the corner of Heffernan's Lane, she heard the earthquake thud of a printery called City Service Press.

Altogether Little Bourke Street was as interesting and bustling as Shanghai, with the same bamboo washing poles which bannered laundry above the street, fewer sing-song girls, and the same strange scents.

'This is the home of Mr Li,' said Lin Chung. 'He is a doctor. A herbalist. It is surprising how many Australians come to him.'

'Why?'

'Chinese medicine and Western medicine have nothing in common. The theory is entirely different. Western medicine treats the disease – Chinese treats the patient. In Melbourne you pay your doctor when you are sick. But in China you pay him to keep you well.' A white-bearded old man was standing at his shop door, flanked by bunches of dried things which Phryne could not identify. And that surely was not a box of cicada shells which he was sorting?

'This is Miss Fisher, Mr Li,' said Lin Chung deferentially, and the old man looked at Phryne and bowed.

'Miss Fisher,' he said politely, 'I trust you have no need of my services.'

'No, thank you,' said Phryne, inclining her head in return, 'I am just here to dine with my friend.'

'I believe that there was some little unpleasantness in the street, in which you intervened with great courage,' he said, and Phryne disclaimed, 'It was nothing, really.'

'I believe, however, that the matter has been solved,' he said quietly, 'and that you have no further need to concern yourself.'

The words might have been directed at either Phryne or her companion. Lin Chung made a slight bow and the old man returned to sorting what were definitely cicada shells.

'What was all that about?' asked Phryne when

they were beyond hearing distance.

'What?' asked Lin Chung, absently. She tugged at his arm.

'Don't go all inscrutable on me, Lin.' He grinned and put his hands together like a stage Chinaman. 'So solly. Little missee has no need to wolly about poor ol' Sam Pan,' he chanted in a sing-song tone, and bowed from the waist. Phryne laughed.

'Tell me in your own time,' she said implacably. 'I can wait.'

He gave her a wary sidelong glance and they stopped outside the door of a restaurant. The name over the door was Mee Heong Guey, which sounded unlikely. Lin Chung commented that the Australian signwriter had undoubtedly misheard 'Kei' and had written 'Guey' as his next best guess. The small windows were fogged and Phryne could not see inside.

'This place makes real Cantonese food, such as you will not get anywhere else in Melbourne.'

He opened the door. The buzz of conversation, which had been considerable, was silenced.

Phryne retained her hold on Lin's arm, feeling a little disconcerted. The cafe was full of people, mostly family parties, sailors, and a group of unaccompanied young men in baggy blue suits. Everyone, from eldest grandfather surrounded by his family to the smallest child perched on three red cushions, was staring at Phryne as though she had recently arrived from Mars. She stood her ground and stared back.

What good-looking people they were, she thought, the girls with their long plaits and the young men with their smooth skin and straight backs. The faces of the aged were lined with wisdom; settled, unhurried, full of authority.

An elderly lady picked up her chopsticks and said something sharp to a young woman nursing a baby, who dragged her gaze away from Phryne and spoke to her children. An old gentleman nudged his son and he called his brothers to attention. In an instant the whole restaurant had returned to normal and the new arrival was henceforward ignored.

Though she was positive that most of the regained voices were speculating about her, Phryne was relieved at their courtesy. No Australian pub crowd would have been as polite to a visiting Chinese woman, she was sure.

Lin Chung looked at Phryne and said, 'I didn't think – I am very sorry.'

'There is no need to be sorry. Are we going to get something to eat? I'm famished.'

'*Doh je leung wai*,' said Lin to a greasy person in an off-white apron, and they were conducted to a table covered in checked red and white oilcloth.

The waiter immediately filled two blue and white china teacups with pale scented tea and Lin Chung asked, 'Will you let me order?' Phryne nodded and sipped the tea. It smelt like jasmine, and was clear and hot.

'This is a modest place, but the owners come from Szechwan, which has the best food in the South. I have ordered the specialities. I hope you will like them. Phryne, I ... possibly I should not have brought you here.'

'Why? Is it going to get you into trouble?'

'No, but you must feel like a zoo animal.'

'A lady, my governess told me, is always on display. I don't mind.'

'You are sure?'

'If I had minded, I would have told you. I am here, as I am sure that you know, because I wish to be. No one makes me do anything.'

'No, they don't, do they? And how many have been broken into bits trying?'

'A few,' Phryne smiled. 'Now, tell me about this street. And what is the See Yup society? It seems to own a lot of buildings.'

'They are a … well, sort of like a trade union, no, a brotherhood … there isn't a proper word. The people who came to dig for gold needed to band together. In the beginning, the Chinese lived in Spencer Street, much exploited and in dreadful conditions – rats and so on. So they gathered together, all the people from the four provinces, in order to protect each other and to fit into Australian society, because societies are like any other group of animals – if you do not adapt, you are destroyed. The aim then was to make a lot of money and go home to China. See Yup was founded to make sure that nothing awful happened to the members – to protect them. There was a joining fee and it provided medical care and housing and funeral expenses. They have rules and they enforce them. It is … ah, yes. A Benevolent Society. That even sounds Chinese. "All people who come to dig for gold must love and help each other." "The gods alone are liberal, and confer happiness and protection to men. Is this not excellent? Is this not noble?"' he was evidently quoting. 'A Chinese, unless he is the sole survivor of a

241

disaster, is never without relatives, Phryne. Even if the entire immediate family is lost, as used to happen under some of the more touchy emperors, there are always other branches of say, the Li family, which is the most numerous in China. Or the Lin, for that matter. Kung Fu Tse said, "The family is the foundation of the Empire," and it was true. If all is well with the Emperor, then all is well under Heaven – but if the family is disordered, then the corruption spreads upwards.'

'What are you trying to tell me?' The waiter brought a platter of something that looked fried, and ostentatiously laid down a large polished silver spoon before Phryne. 'Tell him I can use chopsticks,' she said, and Lin Chung snapped something which produced a pair of new wooden chopsticks with remarkable speed.

'Where did you learn such an arcane skill?' he asked as she clicked them together, hoping that the art had not deserted her.

'Shanghai. You were saying about the family?'

'Have a taste,' Lin Chung urged. 'This is *geung-chung haai*, crab with ginger.'

Phryne picked up a morsel of crab and conveyed it to her mouth without dropping it. She caught the eye of a goggling child and smiled at it, and its mother immediately cuffed it lightly and turned its chair around.

'Very nice crab.' She was beginning to get the hang of Chinese conversation, which required that direct questions must not be asked. Observations, however, could be offered. 'Mine is not a close-knit family. I left most of it in England and I do not expect to see any of them for a long

242

time, which is fine by me. I have some relatives here, but I don't see them often.' Lin Chung looked vaguely shocked. 'I believe that my father hoped that I would marry into the aristocracy, but I did not like what I found there.'

'Indeed one cannot direct one's heart,' said Lin Chung, emptying his teacup and allowing the waiter to fill it again.

'And sometimes it wanders into strange places,' she agreed. The waiter heaped steamed rice into a small bowl for her, and produced an array of dishes. 'Salt-and-pepper squid, chicken with lemon and Cantonese mushrooms and vegetables,' said Lin Chung, waiting for her to make a choice. Phryne took some mushrooms.

She could not identify any of the vegetables in the leafy mixture, and she considered it carefully as she ate. Nuts, perhaps? Was that a spinachy taste along with a bland watery crunch? Fascinating.

A rhythmic sound like the scrape of a wire brush on a drum attracted her interest. The young men in the corner were playing some sort of game. It involved laying a certain number of beans on the table, then shaking and tossing a handful of sticks.

'What are they playing?'

'Fan Tan. It is an odds-and-evens game. One bets on the number which turns up.'

'Yes, somehow I didn't think they were playing spillikins. Isn't that illegal? Betting, I mean?'

'Who can say that they are betting? There are only beans on the table, not money.' Lin Chung deliberately adopted an inscrutable expression and held out both hands. 'So solly, Mist' P'leece-man. No understan'.'

'So solly indeed. You disconcert me when you do that,' complained Phryne.

'Disguise, Silver Lady. Concealment. Protective colouration. If a Chinese wants to live in a foreign country he has to be twice as clever as the inhabitants and make perfectly sure that they never suspect it.'

'Not a new idea,' said Phryne, helping herself to squid. 'Women have been doing that for a thousand years.'

Lin Chung laughed.

For the second time in the evening the café fell silent. Even the brush of the Fan Tan sticks ceased.

In walked the girl Phryne knew as Annie, Hu San-niang. She was radiant with joy. Her hair was loose and brushed until it shone and she was dressed in a red satin tunic over black trousers. Behind her came an old woman and a tall young man.

They sat down at a table next to Lin Chung and Phryne. No one spoke. The air slowly thickened. Lin was looking across the room at the family party, where an old man was slowly getting to his feet, assisted by two men.

Phryne wondered if she would have to produce her little gun. The air of menace increased until the atmosphere was close to inflammable. Every step the old man made was audible. Women grabbed children and drew back against the walls.

'What's happening?' whispered Phryne, and Lin Chung put a finger to his lips.

'Later,' he said, so quietly that she had to lean

close to hear him.

Thump, thump, came the ancient's feet. San-niang's face was blank but she bit her lip. The young man reached out and took her hand.

Then the old man spoke. His voice seemed flat but Phryne could not read the nuances in the toned speech. She watched Annie.

The girl flinched, then spoke up, retaining her hold on the young man's hand. The old man spoke again, beckoning her to come. She shook her head so that the black hair sprayed across her face and stayed where she was.

The old woman walked forward and said some-thing to the old man, who replied quickly. The old woman was not cowed. She stood back on her heels and scolded, her voice high and angry, gesturing at the young man. Then she looked at Lin Chung, who said something and made a pushing gesture with both hands.

Phryne was fascinated. The café held its breath.

In a moment, it seemed, consensus was reached and everyone returned to their chairs and began to eat again. The Fan Tan players resumed their game. The old woman, accompanied by Annie and her lover, walked across the room to the family, where more chairs were arranged to accommodate them. Lin Chung was still tense. His eyes were fixed on the group. But when the old woman and the old man raised cups and said something in unison, he relaxed and groped for his cup of tea. Phryne refilled his cup and said, 'What hap-pened?'

'Mr Li told me that it was all solved. This must be what he meant. Annie has left my grandmother's care and gone to join the Li family. It is their eldest son who is holding her by the hand in shameless defiance of all custom, may he live forever, bless him. That is the Hu family, and now Annie will go back to them to prepare for her marriage and I have repudiated all claim on her. I am free.'

He smiled across the room at Annie who smiled in return and left her seat to join them.

'It's all fixed!' she announced in English, sounding like a schoolgirl announcing that she had passed algebra at last. 'Hello, Miss Fisher. I'm sorry I snapped at you that night, but they were going to exchange Grandmother for me and I really do love Tommy. Oh, Lin, I'm so happy. Now you don't have to marry me and I don't have to marry you and I've got Tommy Li and Grandfather has forgiven me and you've got Miss Fisher.'

Lin Chung coughed. 'Oh, sorry, Miss Fisher, I didn't mean that,' Annie rattled on. 'I mean, I ... er ... anyway, it's all worked out for the best.'

'So it has and I hope you'll be very happy,' said Phryne warmly, reflecting that she had said that a lot lately. Was everyone in the world convinced that they had found their perfect mate?

And then again, she might have found hers. Not forever – Phryne resisted forevers. But for a while, certainly for a while, until his family decided that he must marry a girl of the right class and background – until then, she had found a very delightful man.

The delightful man bestowed a few phrases in Cantonese on Annie which sent her back to her own family with the speed of the fairly rebuked.

'Phryne, that thoughtless girl...' His brow creased in a frown. 'I regret the implication...'

'I think it's a perfectly good implication,' said Phryne, pinching up some delectable lemon chicken. 'You said yourself that I am a courtesan, my dear. I think we can live and make love with mutual respect and joy – don't you? I have no desire to marry and I can please myself. What do you think?'

'I think ... I think that you are right,' he said carefully. 'I will accept your bargain, Silver Lady, and spend with you all the nights of spring.'

'Wrong season,' she commented, resisting an urge to melt.

'All nights with you are nights of spring,' he responded.

Against custom, he put out his hand and she grasped it.

'Now, tell me all about calling up spirits,' she said, reining in her baser emotions. She was positive that if hand-holding was seen as shameless, then the kind of thing she had in mind would be a complete social outrage.

'On stage?' he asked 'Oh. Well, yes. All you need is a competent painter, a sheet of glass, and a light.'

He talked steadily through the remains of the food and the almond soup which concluded the meal and Phryne listened carefully.

They left the restaurant and knocked at the door of a small shop. There a Mr Koh, dressed in pyjamas and slippers, listened to Lin's request and showed them into the shop, flicking on the light.

'These are glass sleeves which fit over a light bulb,' said Lin Chung. 'You put the scent in them and when the globe warms, the perfume is diffused. It might be a good idea to buy one, since we have got Mr Koh out of bed.' Phryne purchased three of the delicate sleeves and let Mr Koh return to the virtuously early couch of those who get up at five o'clock in the morning to go down to the docks.

They then had a short consultation with the herbalist Mr Li, to whom Phryne offered her congratulations on the engagement of his grandson. She purchased from him a small phial of dark oil, and left the shop carrying it gingerly, as though it might explode.

'Lin, I have to go back to the theatre. Can you put on some working clothes and come with me?' she asked, pausing outside the Chinese mission. 'I think I know how the ghost is being produced, but I have to check.'

'Certainly,' he agreed. 'Come in, Silver Lady,' he invited, opening the warehouse door. 'I must in any case tell Grandmother what has happened about San-niang. If she has not already heard, which I expect she has.'

He brought her through the warehouse, replete with fascinating scents, and into a reception room. It was walled with polished wood on which hung scroll pictures. Phryne was left alone while Lin went to find his grandmother, and she inspected the pictures and a delicate statue of the Goddess of Mercy, Kuang Yin. The hands and face and feet were made of the palest porcelain, barely tinted, but the robe was a highly coloured and textured gilt slip, draped around the figure.

She was contemplating a painting of a branch just breaking into blossom with bright red flowers against a black stem on a white background when she heard a stir at the door as the old lady of the Lin family appeared.

'Miss Fisher,' she said in a voice as dry as autumn leaves, 'I believe that you have some involvement with my grandson.' She spoke excellent English, with a strong, lilting accent. It was disconcerting, as though the emphases were all on the wrong syllables.

'I have,' said Phryne steadily. The gaze of the dark eyes was as hypnotic as a snake's, though not inimical.

'He has spoken about you. I have listened. I believe that you will do him no harm,' pronounced Grandmother Lin. 'I am pleased with you.'

Phryne did not know what to say. She waited.

'Do you like that painting? It is an allegory. New flowers spring out of dead wood; blossoms are opposed to snow. A tree, however, cannot do other than produce flowers and leaf in season. A plum tree cannot produce quinces; neither can a melon vine grow cherries. Each tree is required to reproduce its own kind when the time is right.'

'I understand,' said Phryne. She was being warned against trying to take Lin Chung away from his heritage and his destiny as the eldest son of the Lin family. Since she had no intention of doing that, she could reply with a good conscience. 'I wouldn't try to convince any peach tree to produce oranges.'

'In that case, you will have no more watchers,'

249

said Mrs Lin, and drifted away.

Lin Chung, dressed in workman's trousers and a khaki shirt, escorted a slightly shocked Phryne back into the street some ten minutes later.

Phryne unlocked the stage door and took her accomplice inside. The lights were off. It was as dark as the inside of a coal mine.

'Your grandmother...' said Phryne.

'What did she say to you?' demanded Lin Chung quickly.

'I think those men were sent by her, to make sure I didn't seduce you away from your destiny,' she whispered. He was reassured by the undercurrent of laughter in her voice.

'It's possible. She is a woman of strong purpose. Did she agree to...'

'Our liaison? Yes. I am approved. Now, I need the fuse box.' He heard her collide with something hard. 'Damn! That's the stage doorkeeper's little coop. The switches should be here.' A light clicked on. 'Yes, and here are the working spots. Good.'

'Won't someone wonder why the lights are on in a theatre at this time of night?' asked Lin, following her determined back up the steps.

'No, it's common to work all night. Now,' she said, stopping under the lighting gantry, 'climb, and see if you can find what we're searching for while I have a look at these globes.'

Phryne walked under the electric lights which lined the corridor leading to the stage.

'This is where everyone has seen her,' she mused. 'They were about here when ... aha.'

250

She fetched a chair, climbed up, sniffed at the cheap tin shade and turned towards the stage as she heard a rustle. Then she froze in pure superstitious horror. Ice-water gushed into her veins.

There in the entrance was a woman in Rose Maybud's costume, her sunbonnet thrown back, her black hair flowing down over her shoulders. Phryne could see through her, yet she was undeniably real. Phryne could not move.

Then she gathered her courage, leapt down, and ran towards the ghost.

Someone caught her arm and swung her around.

'Care, take care, Phryne! She's glass and glass is fragile,' came Lin Chung's voice. 'Convincing, isn't it?'

'You could have warned me!' gasped Phryne. 'How is it done?'

'It's a glass slide, just a big piece of glass in a frame the same size as the door. The image is painted on the glass with the dye they use for gels. You can't see her unless there is a light at the right angle. I found this one lashed and knew it must be the one – it doesn't point at the stage. In ordinary light the phantom is invisible. When not in use the slide is hauled up to lie flat against the wall. No one would notice it among all the other things hanging up there.'

'Is there another one?' asked Phryne, still amazed at the effectiveness of the illusion.

'No, why?'

'Still doesn't dispose of the ghost,' she said, a little breathless. 'Leila saw her in another costume.'

251

'That cannot be explained. This is the only glass slide here,' said Lin Chung definitely. 'Such good craftsmanship! It's nearly soundless.' He hauled on the line and the ghost rose and vanished. Lin Chung secured the rope to a bracket on the wall.

'Well, Missee,' he bowed, 'there is your ghost.'

'Yes. Now we have to search again. You take that side, I'll take this.'

In ten minutes, Phryne had found a glass sleeve, identical to those which she had just purchased, in a box containing bits of wire and canvas and repairing equipment. She shook it and a heavy scent of hyacinths was apparent.

'That light is on a separate switch,' observed Lin Chung. 'Your magician could turn on that one by itself when he wanted to produce the scent. He could probably have afforded to leave the perfume sleeve in place. No one ever looks up, and who has time to investigate a globe under those tin reflectors? Have we finished?'

'Yes,' said Phryne, 'I've discovered how, and I think I know who, but I can't for the life of me imagine why.'

'Come home with me,' suggested Lin Chung, 'and we will try and think of some answers.'

CHAPTER FOURTEEN

He can raise you hosts
Of ghosts
And that without reflectors.

Gilbert and Sullivan
The Sorcerer

Phryne woke in a silken bed and yawned in pure luxury. The room was hung with silk, the sheets were finest linen and the wadded quilt was of just the sky blue she had envisaged for her parlour. Scroll paintings of erotic scenes decorated the walls. She had enacted several of them with her highly skilled lover, and looked forward to trying the rest in due course. Phryne had always believed in education. The young man sleeping beside her sighed and opened his eyes.

'Silver Lady,' he said softly.

'Lin Chung,' she answered. 'I have to get up.'

'Will there be a day when you don't?' he asked resignedly, watching her pull on a gown made for an empress and go into his bathroom. 'The Taoists would say that you are meddling.'

'Meddling?'

'Yes. "Yield and overcome."'

'I don't understand.'

'No, I suppose you don't. It's not a philosophy that would ever appeal to the West.'

'Try me,' she demanded, standing up out of the bath and distracting his mind from religion completely.

'"Yield and overcome, bend and be straight, empty and be full, have little and gain." I am not explaining this at all, am I? The Taoists told a ruler never to act until he absolutely had to, and then he would be successful. There was a state in China ruled by such a Taoist, and he was so successful that he was asked to explain how he did it. "I leave people alone," he said.'

'Interesting but not helpful. If I left the affair at the Maj alone, then a death would go unavenged and the trickster would continue.'

She put on clean underwear from the little overnight bag she always carried in the Hispano-Suiza. Lin Chung dragged his eyes away from the progress of her stocking up her leg and said, 'Yes, that is true. You are a follower of Confucius, Moon Lady. "A crime is a rent in the social order, which must be stitched." Do you live at this speed all the time?'

'No, after I have finished this case I am taking a holiday.'

'Where?' he restrained his hands, which reached for her automatically, as though her flesh was magnetic.

'Nowhere. I mean, here. I don't need to travel to find anything I want at the moment,' she said. 'Put on some clothes. You're coming too. You have to work the ghost.'

Lin Chung stretched, assumed some unremarkable clothing, and conducted her into the courtyard.

'Chinese or Western breakfast?'

Phryne sat down on a blackwood chair and stared. This was unexpected. The warehouse, which had looked very solid from the street, was actually hollow. In the middle was a garden, exquisitely planted with vines and bamboo. Small gravelled paths wandered through the thickets. It was as though the verandah of the standard Australian house had been turned inside out. She could hear the bamboo rustling. The noise of the street was damped by the building. Melbourne sparrows, unable to believe their luck, took splashing, noisy baths in the goldfish pool. 'Chinese,' she said firmly. This dreamlike, scroll-painting picture was no place to demand eggs and bacon. Lin Chung gave an order to someone.

'I got used to – I even liked – the English breakfast,' he said, sitting down beside her. 'But I still prefer this.'

Phryne accepted a delicate porcelain bowl of what looked very like library paste and took up her spoon.

'What is this?' she asked, sipping at a smooth, bland soup.

'Rice gruel – the French call it congee. It tastes better than porridge, I think.' An attendant girl poured out some tea for her. It was a bracing brew with an undertaste of metal. 'And this is what you gave me yesterday – was it only yesterday, Moon Lady? Iron Goddess tea. Later in the day we might try chrysanthemum. Tea is a cult in China.'

'I'm not even going to ask what you think of Western tea with milk and sugar.'

'To such a dreadful brew milk and sugar must

255

be added; they mitigate the taste,' he said politely.

Phryne was languid with pleasure and could think of nothing she wanted to do more than to sit in this magical garden and listen to the grass growing; but there was a mystery to be solved and she had to get to the theatre for morning rehearsal. So she nibbled a flat cake which was far too sweet, drank her tea, and gathered her resources.

Phryne marched into the Maj, gathering the policemen, Lin, Marie-Claire, Herbert, Leila and Sir Bernard in her wake and shutting the door on them in Bernard's office. She surveyed them. Jack Robinson looked worried, as he always did. The sergeant and the constable preserved the customary blandness of stuffed fish. Leila was blooming and Sir Bernard looked more rosy and pleased than any manager with an unsolved ghost on his hands should look. Herbert was bubbling over with news about his new home and Lin Chung was silent and alert.

'We have to lay a trap,' she said. 'And I don't know who we'll catch, except for the trickster and the person who murdered your mother, Leila. I think I know who it is. And I think I know who's been helping the trickster. But I haven't any proof at all. I need your help and everything I say has to be absolutely confidential. Will you do as I say and not ask any questions?'

They nodded.

'Jack, post your officers at both exits. Lin, can you operate the ghost?' He assented quietly. 'Marie-Claire, Leila, we have to go to your dressing rooms. Bernie, I want a general call of the

256

whole company, including all the auxiliary staff, on stage in half an hour. Tinker, you keep the stage door and make sure old Tom is up on stage with the rest. Can you manage that?'

The boy's confidence had gone up with a rush, removed from the threat of violence and now firmly attached to the theatre. He said 'My dad signed – I belong here now. Don't I, Sir B? So I can do it. He'll be there, Boss.'

'What am I going to say to the company?' asked Sir Bernard.

'I don't know – confirm the roles and pay for New Zealand,' snapped Phryne. 'Make sure that the dressers and Mrs Pomeroy and all her girls are there too, Bernie. I don't want to waste all this effort and we'll only get one chance.'

'Phryne darling, can't you give me a hint about what is going to happen?' begged Sir Bernard. 'Just a teeny weeny idea?'

'Not so much as an ickle pretty one. Off you go. Leila, come with me.'

Lin Chung, with a new respect for the sort of organising ability he had thought confined to Chinese grandmothers, climbed up the lighting gantry, which was unoccupied, and waited for his cue.

Phryne, having coached Leila through her role with some difficulty – it was dawning on her that Leila was not very bright – left her applying grease-paint and went to lurk at the stage entrance. Sir Bernard had summoned the whole cast and crew on stage, facing stage left in a large semi-circle. Phryne looked at them.

The chorus gathered together around André

Dupont. Melly, standing next to him, seemed to be showing them a new ring. Violet Wiltshire and Mollie Webb were talking about knitting, from what Phryne overheard as she stealthily climbed on a chair and fitted a glass sleeve over a different light. Leila, in Rose Maybud's sun-defying bonnet, stood next to Sir Bernard with her head bowed, her black hair falling around her face. Phryne saw Gwilym and Selwyn attempt to edge near her, to be foiled by Sir Bernard. He really was doing frightfully well.

'Now New Zealand is a long way away but it is Australia's nearest neighbour,' he announced. 'There's no point in taking such a long voyage unless you mean to do your best, each and every one of you. Anyone who hasn't a wholehearted devotion to the craft is not welcome. I mean, we are not going to have any more nonsense. I'm not naming names but I've had enough of these disruptive flirtations. You're all behaving like schoolchildren. I want a professional attitude. Do you understand?'

The company shifted from foot to foot and murmured that it understood.

'Now, I want to read the company list. Please listen very carefully.'

Tom Deeping growled to Mr Brawn, the stage carpenter, 'Why do they want us up here? This ain't our business.'

'Dunno,' said Mr Brawn. 'You know Management. Love the sound of their own voice.'

'Can you smell something?' asked Tom Deeping, coughing. 'A sort of sweet smell?'

'I can smell it,' said Mrs Pomeroy. 'Flowers.

258

Hyacinths, isn't it?'

'Hyacinths,' said Kitty Collins, drawing closer to her sister for the first time in years. 'Can you smell it, Jill?'

Then the lights went out.

The company blinked until they began to see again in the faint pale sunlight coming through the windows. Then Mollie Webb screamed, 'Look!'

'It's her!' cried Jessie. 'Dorothea!'

'Yes,' said Louis. 'See? That's how I saw her. Rose Maybud. Can you see her, Monsieur Dupont? That's just how she looked, eh Col?'

'Just like that,' said the bass dubiously.

'It's a trick,' said Phryne, leaping down from her perch. 'She's a drawing.' Phryne approached the slide and tapped it. 'Painted glass. You can only see her when she has a light behind her.'

Someone in the chorus, lost to all decent feeling, chanted from *Trial By Jury*, '"She may very well pass for forty-three in the dusk with the light behind her,"' and there was a general, if shaky, laugh.

'If she's a trick,' said Sir Bernard, 'who had the infernal nerve to play it?'

Phryne seemed to be waiting for something. There was a pounding of feet, then a crash and a wail.

'Bring him up, Constable,' she said to the auditorium, and the huge policeman clumped up the aisle and on to the stage, carrying a struggling figure in overalls.

'Told you,' he said to Jack Robinson. 'Told you, sir,' he repeated, as he stood Leonard Brawn the stage carpenter on his feet.

'Why?' asked Sir Bernard.

'You never noticed us,' snarled the carpenter, eyes alight with fury. 'Never even noticed us. Just technicals, you said. Just slaves. There to do all the dirty work and never praised when we've worked miracles, there to complain about if some damn-fool idea doesn't work. But I showed you.' He bared his teeth. 'I showed you all right. You were wetting your drawers with terror, all of you, from the high and mighty Management all the way down, turning on each other and blaming each other. I've been laughing at you all week. Took a clever one to catch me,' he snarled at Phryne, and reached out clawing hands. 'Took a private detective and a Chink to catch me. Nearly got you, though, Miss Fisher. I saw you when that weight fell, you was right underneath. I never meant it to get poor Prompt, she wasn't no better than us, with the stage manager on her back all the time. I'm sorry about Prompt,' said Mr Brawn, 'I never meant to kill Prompt. But you – all of you – I scared you all right!'

The company had drawn together under the lash of the carpenter's hatred. He was screaming now, spittle flecking his lips, and they turned their eyes away from him.

'Well, is that the end of this charade?' demanded Selwyn Alexander, supporting his half-fainting dresser Bradford. 'Can we go home now?'

'Detective Inspector, we will have to get a lawyer, a doctor – surely the poor fellow is insane,' said Sir Bernard. 'Can we arrange something for him?'

'Yes, a loony-doctor is a good idea. Can't hang

a madman. Take him out, Constable. Sergeant, read him the usual warning. Well, that's the end of that,' said Jack Robinson, dusting his hands.

Then he sniffed. The smell of hyacinths again, heavy, almost rotting. 'Lilies when they fester smell far worse than weeds' – the words of Shakespeare came unbidden to his mind. Valuable fellow, Shakespeare. Words for everything.

It suddenly seemed to have become cold. An icy wind scoured the stage. The chorus, who had been warming into a four-part harmony version of 'Around Her Neck, She Wears A Yellow Ribbon,' had just got to the bit which explains that 'she wears it for a singer who is far far away' when the voices died.

On the breath of the cold wind, a bride came, her draperies fluttering, her veil blowing. She was so like Leila Esperance that the resemblance was uncanny. The smell of hyacinths grew chokingly strong, mixed with an exhalation of the grave. The chorus squealed and backed away as she came towards them, walking without a sound, her face as white as death, her black eyes as sharp as diamond-pointed gramophone needles.

Straight towards Tom Deeping she walked, where he huddled with Alexander almost in the wings.

'You,' she said with dreadful coldness. 'You killed me. I didn't want to die. I had a child and a lover and everything to live for and you poisoned me, you man!'

Leila turned her bonneted head into Sir Bernard's chest and whimpered.

Cold malignancy seemed to ooze from the

261

bride; her voice was clear and the extended hand and arm as fixed as wood. She seemed to have unearthly patience, willing to wait for an answer until time wore out. She advanced another step and Tom Deeping dropped to his knees.

'Not me,' he pleaded. 'Not me, Dot! Not old Tom. I knew you when you was a baby. I never touched a hair of your head, Dot. You shouldn't never got wrapped up in them nobby folk, Dot. That's what done for yer.'

The ghost stopped, seeming to be considering what he was saying. Then she moved again, one more soundless step in her miasma of rotting flowers.

'Yes,' someone screamed. 'Yes, it was me. I did it. I put the stuff in that madeira you drank. You were going to leave me. You were going to marry Bernard and leave me. I couldn't bear that any-one else should have you.' The ghost stood as still as a spear of ice, shining in her draperies, and the voice went on, 'I've been a broken man since you died. I never amounted to anything without you. So I'm ready. Take me with you, Dorothea, I've always loved you. When you died you tore out my heart. Take me with you,' sobbed Bradford, tear-ing loose Selwyn Alexander's grip. 'I love you,' he sobbed, and fell down at the ghost's feet.

The ghost shrank away from his touch and ran to Sir Bernard, who put aside Leila and em-braced her.

'There, there,' he soothed automatically. The sun-bonneted girl pulled off her headgear and wig and revealed herself to be Marie-Claire.

'You bastard,' said Tom Deeping, levering himself to his feet and kicking the recumbent dresser in the ribs. 'I thought it was you.'

'I think,' said Phryne, 'that we ought to put some lights on and have some drinks sent in and then we shall have lots of explanations. But first, Leila, come with me.' She detached the actress from Sir Bernard and led her through the stunned company. 'Stand there. Lin, put on the other light. This is what you saw when you saw the ghost, Leila,' said Phryne gently. 'The bride at the end of the corridor.'

The different angle of the light turned the surface of the Rose Maybud slide into a mirror.

Leila gazed at the apparition and laughed shakily, 'I saw myself. She was never here at all.'

'That's right,' Phryne agreed. 'She was never here at all.'

Jack Robinson had placed his captive in a large chair on stage. Phryne had sent out for a suitable array of drinks from the nearest pub, which also supplied glasses. Rehearsal had been cancelled and the company had resumed their ordinary clothes and were gathered together, talking fast.

Phryne made sure that everyone had a drink and a place to sit and Sir Bernard clapped his hands.

'Miss Fisher will now tell us how this was contrived.'

'Let me introduce you to Miss Mobbs.' The elderly lady was helped onto the stage by Louis and Colin from the chorus. She marched to the chair and snapped at the quivering occupant, 'Charles Sheffield. What are you calling yourself now?'

'Bradford!' said Selwyn Alexander. 'He's Shef-field?'

'Both industrial cities,' said Miss Mobbs. 'Never did have any imagination. Is that all you want of me?' she asked Phryne.

'Yes, thank you. Would you like to stay?'

'No. Not in the same place as this ... wretch. You may come and take me to the trial, however. I regret that they have abolished public hang-ings.' Miss Mobbs was escorted offstage right, and stopped when she encountered Leila.

'Oh, yes,' she crooned, putting out an arthritic hand to the milk-and-roses cheek. 'Oh, my pretty, my pretty! Dorothea's child, and the image of her! Will you come and see me?' she asked, and Leila surprised Phryne by patting the old hand and say-ing, 'Yes, of course. I want you to tell me all about my mother.'

Louis and Colin took Miss Mobbs carefully out of the theatre and put her into the taxi which Phryne had hired for her.

'Charles Sheffield, alias Charles Bradford,' said Jack Robinson, 'I'm arresting you for murdering Dorothea Curtis. You do not have to say anything, but anything you do say will be taken down and may be used in court. Do you understand?'

'Yes.' The dresser's voice was deep with despair. 'I did it. She was going to marry Bernard and I couldn't bear it. I knew I was nothing without her. Take me away and hang me.'

'It's a bit more complicated than that, sir,' said Robinson. 'But we'll see if we can oblige you. Take him away now, Constable. Miss Fisher, you've done me a bad turn,' he added in a lower tone.

'Me? I've caught you a murderer!' Phryne was feeling rather pleased with herself. 'Thirty-one years too late, I admit, but still...'

'You've verified Big Billy's judgement. He said it was the stage carpenter. Now I'm stuck with him.'

'Into each life some rain must fall, Jack dear,' said Phryne unsympathetically.

'Yes,' said Jack Robinson heavily, and left the Maj for, he fervently hoped, the last time.

'How did you know about the ghost?' clamoured several voices.

'It couldn't have been any one of you, acting alone. My assistant made a timetable which proved that impossible. Therefore it was either a conspiracy, a real ghost or a trick. I couldn't see any natural conspiracy amongst you and everyone knows that there are no ghosts,' Phryne said boldly, suppressing the memory of the medium. 'I didn't work it out until my friend, who trained in stage magic in China, explained how to produce spirits. As to who did it, the stage carpenter was the only one who was skilled enough; I bet none of you have ever handled stage machinery.' The murmurs increased.

'Of course not, we're actors, not technicals,' said Cameron Armour. 'If I'd wanted to be a trades-man, I wouldn't have done all that voice training.' Phryne began to understand Mr Brawn's rage and scorn.

'It could have been the electrician but he wasn't always here when she was seen, and he wasn't here when the weight dropped on Prompt.'

'Poor Prompt,' came a whisper.

'Prompt is the one I was angriest about,' said Phryne, 'because she was a total innocent. If it had hit either Mr Evans or me it would not have been so bad – at least one of us might have deserved it. But not Miss Thomas. So. Where was I? How did I produce the ghost? I told Leila that the target of all this activity was Selwyn Alexander and in the old murder of Dorothea there were only two possibles – Tom Deeping or Sir Bernard. I never even thought of Bradford – Sheffield. I lost sleep worrying how Selwyn Alexander could possibly be involved. So I bought some glass sleeves for perfume and added a Chinese herb which smells like nothing on earth and got Herbert to open both doors so that there was a gust of wind. I dressed Marie-Claire as Leila so you wouldn't miss her and Leila played the ghost.'

'Yes. It felt really odd, though. I seemed to be drawn to Mr Alexander. In those padded slippers I couldn't feel my feet, it was like I was floating. And that's the way I had to go.'

'They weren't your lines, either,' said Phryne, and the beautiful Miss Esperance wrinkled her marble brow.

'No, I don't know where they came from. Normally I can't ad lib for toffee.'

'But I don't know who pinched the bag and planted all those things on Mr Alexander,' Phryne confessed.

'Has that cop gone?' asked Tom Deeping from his seat on the stage. Phryne said, 'Yes, he's gone.'

'Well, it was me. I recognised the bastard, I mean that bastard Sheffield. Not right away, see, but after a few weeks. I knew him from the old days. I saw his back. You can't mistake a back. I liked Dot – Miss Curtis. She was a bit of all right. Hard as nails but straight. I never thought she'd kill herself. So I planted things on him and I put that mad technical up to producing a ghost. He was going to do something,' he said defensively, 'so he might as well have done that.'

Phryne wrested his bottle from his yellow fingers and said crisply, 'Not another drop passes your lips until you tell us the whole story.'

'And then I'll be out on my neck,' muttered the old man with a glance at Sir Bernard.

'That's as may be,' said the Management. 'Say your piece, Tom.'

'The carpenter, he says to me, "I'm going to play a trick on these head-in-the-air actors, I'm going to give 'em a good scare. They never notice us, they never appreciate us" – he was a bloke with one of them things ... you know, a mono-mania about not being appreciated. So I says, rather than light fires all over like he wanted to do, using flash-powder, I says, "Why not do a ghost? You can scare 'em out of their wits and have a good chuckle about it, you like a good chuckle, don't you, and I'll help you." So he gives me the nod, and I nick the bag and plant it on Mr Alexander, meaning to point to that bastard Shef-field. I was sure he done my Dorothea. Trouble is, no one notices dressers, either. Then it got all mixed up with that business of Walter and his fancy man Hans and I couldn't see no way to make Sheffield crack and confess but to keep on, so then we kept on. Gimme back me bottle.'

'Not yet,' said Phryne sternly.

'Them glass things were my idea – I seen 'em in the shop in Little Bourke Street. Ladies used to use 'em in the old days – Dorothea had one, so that she'd always have the scent of hyacinths about her. Then the carpenter, he went loopy – well, he was already loopy, he went loopier. He tried to kill you, Miss. I couldn't have that. So I did what I always do when I can't decide what to do.'

'What's that?' asked Phryne.

'I crawled into a bottle and I didn't come out until I saw Dorothea's ghost floating towards me and I thought my last hour had come, strike me dead if I didn't. So that's it,' said Tom Deeping, holding out his hand. For a moment, as the battered face creased into a smile, Phryne saw the ghost of the handsome young man he must once have been. Then he applied his lips to the bottle and the glimpse was gone.

'What are you going to do to him, Bernie?'

'Old Tom? Nothing, Phryne darling. What would the Maj be without old Tom?'

'What indeed?' said Phryne blankly, suddenly possessed by an urge to escape from 'this wooden O', as suffocating as Shakespeare's own Globe theatre. 'Are there any questions?' she asked and the company stared at her. Clearly they considered it all settled.

'Then I'll thank you for your attention and I'll take my leave,' she said.

She turned as she and Lin Chung reached the auditorium door to look at them all for the last time. Mollie and Doctor Fielding. Cameron Armour and Miss Gault. Leila and Sir Bernard.

She stopped at the door as they all started to sing a duet from *Ruddigore* for her.

'The battle's roar is over,' sang the men, 'O my love!'

'Embrace thy tender lover, O my love!' sang Gwilym Evans, with his arms round two of the chorus.

'From tempest's welter, from war's alarms,' sang Selwyn Alexander to Miss Wiltshire.

Cameron Armour sang to Miss Gault, 'O Give me shelter within those arms!'

'Thy smile alluring,' sang Sir Bernard to his daughter, 'All heartache curing, Gives peace enduring, O my love!'

'If heart both true and tender,' sang Mollie Webb to Dr Fielding, 'O my love! A life-love can engender, O my love!'

'A truce to tears and sighing and tears of brine,' sang Herbert, and Tom Deeping, unconscious of irony, sung 'For joy undying shall aye be mine.'

'And thou and I love,' they sang in unison, 'shall live and die, love, without a sigh, love – my own, my love!'

Then they romped into a chorus from *Iolanthe*, with the world's most rollicking tune, but the words were clichés.

Nothing ventured, nothing win
Blood is thick but water's thin
In for a penny in for a pound
It's love that makes the world go round!

Phryne decided that actors were very, very strange. Agony and terror washed over them and left no trace – not of dead Walter Copland or Hans or poor Miss Thomas, not of the carpenter's rage or Tom Deeping's revenge. The voices carrolled merrily on and Phryne left the theatre positively ill with happy endings. She put the key on the stage doorkeeper's table and closed the door, softly, behind her. All the mysteries were solved and she felt somewhat tired and let down, like champagne left too long in the glass.

Waiting at the door as she opened it was a tall woman with glassy blonde hair and bright blue eyes. Phryne and Miss Diana Ffoulkes stopped short, nose to nose.

'Miss Fisher,' gasped Miss Ffoulkes. 'Is ... Gwil on stage?'

'Yes,' said Phryne, grinning 'He's there. Catch him while you can, Miss Ffoulkes.'

'Oh, I shall,' agreed the flapper. She squeezed past Phryne, who received a musky blast of 'Love's Dream' full in the mouth and sneezed. With the grace of a stalking lioness intent on prey, Miss Diana Ffoulkes entered the theatre.

So there went Gwilym Evans, Phryne thought with a touch of regret. But there was someone beside her, moving as unobtrusively as a cat. He was a mystery which might take years to solve.

In the dark beyond the door, in flat defiance of all custom, she turned into Lin Chung's arms and kissed his silky mouth.

CHAPTER FIFTEEN

When day is fading
With serenading
And such frivolity
Of tender quality—
With scented showers
Of fairest flowers
The happy hours
Will gaily fly!

Gilbert and Sullivan
Princess Ida

A week later, attired in dark blue and holding a bunch of flowers, Phryne wandered away from the combined funerals for Prompt and Walter Copland. The Company had departed for New Zealand, and there was only a small gathering at the graveside. It was not usual for ladies to attend the actual burial, anyway, and Phryne considered that occasionally conventions had their uses.

The Copland ladies had seemed relatively calm at the service, Phryne thought, walking away through the city of the dead. Mrs and Miss Copland had been relieved, they said, by the absence of the Company, bitterly resenting the woman who might have seduced their Walter away from them.

Phryne was pleased that they had not been at the

cemetery to peer down into the grave. There had been another coffin already there, an undecorated affair of deal. It had struck Phryne as only fair that his last wish should be granted and his long devotion, however misplaced, should be rewarded. She had seen to and paid for the arrangements. Hans had been buried with his lover. Walter Copland was not going alone to the grave.

Lin Chung seemed uneasy.

'You don't approve?' she asked, and he said carefully, 'It is not my place to approve or disapprove, Phryne, and I am not in a position to cavil – the Ming Emperors had hills levelled and valleys dug to provide a place for their dead to rest in glory. But, yes, you are right, all this soaring stone makes me uncomfortable. Where are we going?'

'Just one more grave, and I believe that it is over there,' she said, leading the way over damp grass paths towards a towering bluestone pillar on which a white wreath was hung. The inscription was 'John King'.

'Sole survivor of the Burke and Wills fiasco,' commented Phryne. 'And that angel with a sword is Michael Dawson, the iron founder. The broken column is Thomas Fulton – he fell into a mine shaft in Bendigo. Then there are lots of clergymen and then there is that Celtic cross, that's John Templeton, and here is poor Derrimut.'

'Over there is the Chinese cemetery,' said Lin Chung. 'That is the oven to burn offerings. My family are buried here.' She felt him shiver lightly. 'I do not like this place, Phryne.'

'"But at my back I always hear Time's winged

272

chariot hurrying near,"' she quoted, mockingly.

"'And yonder all before us lie, Deserts of vast eternity,'" he agreed. 'I know that it is not proper to leave a lady to walk unaccompanied through a cemetery, Phryne, but I am leaving you here unless you find what you are looking for fairly soon. I have nothing against my ancestors, illustrious as they were, but I do not want to be reminded that I shall have to meet them one day. They will not approve of me, I am sure.'

'It's all right. Here she is.'

The marble monument was large and imposing. A sorrowing angel leaned on a broken column – the symbol of a life cut short. An open marble book with a five-bar stave carved in it stood just at Phryne's eye-level.

She could not resist. She peered closely and deciphered the notes from the book.

'I know that my Redeemer liveth,' she read, and laid her bunch of flowers down on the grave of Dorothea Curtis.

Sitting back on her heels, she considered Dorothea's life, and her death. Lin Chung waited silently. Phryne stood up and took a step back and Lin Chung bowed.

'Phryne, can you smell something? A sweet scent,' he said, as she pulled on her gloves. Phryne sniffed.

'Yes. And there are none of them in that bouquet, either. It was everlastings and gum tips.' She laid her hand on his arm and smiled up at him, her green eyes warm with appreciation. 'She's pleased with us, I think.' She drew him away into Tenth Avenue and the exit from the cemetery.

'Yes, now I recognise it, but it's fading already,' he said, turning his back on Dorothea Curtis. 'The scent of...'

'Hyacinths,' said Phryne Fisher.

The publishers hope that this book has given you enjoyable reading. Large Print Books are especially designed to be as easy to see and hold as possible. If you wish a complete list of our books please ask at your local library or write directly to:

Magna Large Print Books
Magna House, Long Preston,
Skipton, North Yorkshire.
BD23 4ND

This Large Print Book for the partially sighted, who cannot read normal print, is published under the auspices of

THE ULVERSCROFT FOUNDATION